Joshua's Closet

Melody Porter

ISBN: 0615576680
ISBN-13: 978-0615576688

CHAPTER 1

"Where is he? We were supposed to meet here at two. I hate when people are late. If I could afford for my GPA to drop, I would leave," Ryan mumbled to himself as he looked around the student hall in agitation. "If he isn't here in ten minutes I am gone." All he saw were young women in tight skirts flipping their hair and smiling at anything with testosterone. *Wish I had the time, but I've got too much to do today.*

One young woman, however, stuck out. She was sitting in the corner with her legs up in a chair reading a book on early Egyptian artifacts. Even with the Charm's Pop in her mouth, she looked intellectual. Her hair was natural ringlets of tight curls that fell on her shoulders. The oversized sweatshirt and baggy sweatpants gave the appearance she was hiding herself and didn't want to be noticed. Ryan felt that if he asked her about Ronnie Somers she wouldn't think he was flirting with her.

He walked over to her with his hands in the pockets of his hoodie; they had a game today and he didn't want to be late getting to the field. He loved playing baseball, but played now only for the scholarship. Something about having to play for a reason took the joy out of it.

Ryan was tall in stature with strong lean muscles etched like a stone statue. He decided to ask the young woman sitting in the chair if she had seen the tutor he was looking to meet in the hall.

"Excuse me," he spoke to her, but received no response immediately. "Excuse me," he spoke a little louder this time, but

1

noticed she was wearing ear buds and was listening to music. He lightly touched her on the shoulder. "Excuse me."

Surprised that someone had interrupted her, she looked up from her book. He finally saw her face. It was a pretty one, oval in shape with high cheekbones, and eyes dark as night that pierced into his soul. Her skin was pure with no makeup and was the color of cocoa.

She looked at him, questioning his actions. If she didn't like his answer she would let him know immediately.

Ryan felt afraid but wasn't sure why, and tried to gather his thoughts. "I'm sorry to interrupt your reading, but I was wondering if you know a Ronnie Somers?"

Annoyed she sighed before asking, "Who wants to know?" Realizing she might have a less than friendly face, she tried to soften her expression while she took out the ear buds.

He began to explain his inquiry. "I am supposed to meet him here at two, and he hasn't shown up. Do you know him?"

"Yes, but Roni is not a he. I am Roni." Shaking her head, she asked, "Are you my student?"

Feeling like an idiot, he said, "It looks that way. Hi, I'm Ryan Grant," and extended his hand.

For a brief moment, he saw a slight smile on her face. Looking up she told him, "Professor Lincoln thinks it is hilarious for students to walk in and find out Roni is a female." She accepted his hand. "Nice to meet you. What is your schedule like tomorrow? I have one morning class and one after three."

"Well, I have African American Studies after three so I probably need to study before then. Will one o'clock be okay?"

"Sure, meet you here?" she asked.

"Yeah, now that I know who you are, I won't be standing around looking stupid."

"Now you know I am just a tutor," she teased.

Thinking of what he had just said, he smiled. "Sorry about the mistake, please don't hold that against me."

"Don't worry, it happens every time," she told him while putting the book in her backpack. He noticed her eyes again, deep and dark. Very strong eyes that were not easily intimidated. He could tell because she didn't look away when she spoke to you. She knew her strengths and didn't have to play the games he saw so many young women playing on campus.

Roni walked to the door of the student hall as he followed her and then reached for the door. Used to opening her own doors, she tried not to show her uneasiness at Ryan's gesture. As she passed him, she noticed his green eyes. Only two percent of the world population has green eyes she remembered reading somewhere. Deep green eyes that seemed shy and frightened if pressed.

The cleft in his chin made the light stubble of a beard apparent in the sunlight. His hair was very dark at the roots, but was bleached slightly by the sun giving it a brown highlight. The loose curls gave him the appearance of a Greek God statue, identifying him as an athlete. He caught her stare, but only briefly was able to look into her eyes before having to look away.

Walking through the door, she turned to look back at him. "Don't forget to bring your book tomorrow."

"Yes, ma'am," he answered with the smile of a child who had just gotten her approval.

Roni knew she seemed frightening to those unfamiliar with her, but she was always on guard. Her mother died when she was entering high school, leaving her to face all the things most girls had their mothers around to help them through: first crush, dating, first kiss, and first heartbreak. Knowing she would be alone with these teen dilemmas, she decided to apply herself more academically.

Although her father tried hard to be strong for her and Lawrence, losing the love of his life was devastating. He saw her image every time he looked at Roni. She knew her father loved her, but the pain was too great for him to be around her. Therefore, she helped Lawrence with his homework and took care of things around the house while Larry worked.

Larry was a contractor, building and remodeling homes all over New York. Their brownstone was one of his projects in his spare time. He had met Bernice, an artist, while remolding the gallery where she worked.

Bernice left South Carolina to attend the New York Academy of Art for her graduate degree. Although Bernice's family did not want her to leave, she wanted to create things and sculpting was her passion. When her children were born she created images of them on pieces of wood she found when she visited her birthplace of Rock Hill.

She spent hours walking in the woods behind the family home looking for the right piece of wood to speak to her. Bernice had always said, "Every living thing will speak to you, if you are willing to listen." Sometimes it was as if her mother was whispering words of advice to Roni when she was lonely.

Roni understood her father's pain; it felt as if she had cut her finger on the edge of a piece of paper. Small and unseen to most, but it hurt worse than a gaping hole when she least expected it.

Ryan waited as she walked around the corner of the building before he began his sprint to the gym. It was close to game time and he needed to hurry before his team took the field.

He had played baseball since he was a little kid when he hadn't even been big enough to keep his batting helmet on his head, but had run the bases as if he were a pro. As Ryan got older, his catching skills and quickness groomed him for the position of shortstop, which was his favorite position because it was always busy. In the outfield if the game was slow, a person could get lost in their surroundings, but as shortstop, you had to keep your eyes on the ball.

"Ryan, you just made it," Coach Rey teased him. The coach knew if anyone was going to be on time it would be Ryan. The first to show up and the last to leave, he wished Ryan would be more serious about pro ball. "That kid would make it to the majors easily," Coach Rey would say. Unfortunately, Ryan wasn't interested in pro ball; he desired to finish college and become an architect.

Growing up in a family of mechanics, Ryan had chosen a different path. He had learned from hanging around the garage with his grandfather and father that being a mechanic was not something he wanted to do for a living.

During the summers and after school he assisted with oil changes, wheel balancing, and rebuilding motors, which was fun but not his dream. Although it was an honest living and provided well for their family, he wanted something different out of life. Besides, his cousin Jake was there with his father now and he loved working in the garage.

Walking over to his locker, Ryan turned the dial on the combination to 4-25-42 and opened his locker. He sat on the bench reaching for his socks and began to put them on. *Why would anyone name a girl Roni? Strange, but I still feel like an idiot for looking for a guy.* Ryan began to analyze the events from earlier as he dressed for the game. *How was I to know he was a girl? I mean she was a girl. Even in my own mind, I can't get it straight. She is graduating this year; I wonder why I haven't seen her before. Well this is a big campus, but we must have had a class somewhere together,* he thought while tying up his cleats before grabbing his glove to walk out of the locker room with his teammates to take the field.

Ryan made conversation with his teammates, not really listening to what was being said as they sat in the dugout. His mind kept taking him back to meeting Roni. Even though he saw her when he first walked in, he didn't really notice her. Why had he not noticed her? Was it because she wasn't talking to anyone or because she wasn't wearing a short skirt and flirting with all the men in the room? Strange that she wasn't flirting with anyone. After all, she wasn't the only black female there. What made him ask her about Roni Somers?

Once she looked up, he had to admit she was beautiful even with the attitude. It wasn't the fact she was a woman that made him stumble for words; it was her, just her. It could have been any other woman in the room and he wouldn't have been so stunned. *I have got to get her out of my head, I have a game to play,* Ryan reminded himself.

"Grant," Coach Rey yelled for the third time, "are you sleeping over there?" A roar of laughter came from his teammates; Ryan just smiled bashfully and climbed out of the dugout and onto the field.

He jogged out to his position, looking back into the stands and wondered if Roni had come to the game, but there was no sign of her. *What am I thinking, why would she be here? She doesn't look like the sports kind of woman,* he thought to himself. *It might be to my advantage for her not to be, because I would be trying to look at her instead of watching the ball. After all, she seemed more like a ballerina type of woman, never getting her hands dirty, and probably thought men that spit were nasty. No, she wouldn't be at a baseball game; they spit all the time. Yeah, she would prefer to be at some poetry reading, an art exhibit, or wine tasting event. That's it; she is a wine tasting kind of woman.*

Why did that matter to him? He didn't care what she did as long as she helped him get a better grade in African American Studies. Although he knew the reason for their meeting, his mind kept taking him back to Roni's beauty. She looked like an Egyptian queen with those dark eyes and brown skin. The kind of woman that when she walked into a room you knew she was in charge.

"What is my problem? I act as if I have never seen a beautiful woman before. She isn't the first nor will she be the last. Okay, Ryan, get your head in the game," he tried to discipline himself.

Trying to settle into the position of shortstop, he adjusted the brim of his cap determined to get through the game uninjured. Ryan knew he was in for a very long game.

* * * *

"What era are you studying now?" Roni asked without looking up from the book as she turned the pages slowly.

The Cougars game was last night and Ryan hadn't even cracked open his book before their study session. He opened up his schedule and saw they were now on the period after the Civil War. "We are starting the reconstruction after the Civil War," he nervously told her. How could he have been so stupid, not being prepared for this session? After all, he thought about it all night. Feeling her eyes on him, he was afraid to look up and stare into them.

Roni saw he was very nervous, but she couldn't understand why. Sensing this, she touched his arm and smiled, causing him to look at her. For a brief moment, she was lost for words. His eyes were captivating. To break the trance she looked back at the book, fumbling with her own words. "Strange time in history for former slaves. They were released from their chains but not really free. Some went North; others became share croppers putting themselves in a different kind of slavery."

"Different kind of slavery?" he asked.

"Yes, they were still pretty much living on the land of the slave owners and worked for a portion of the crops. Many were cheated or forced off the land after the crops were harvested when the landowners didn't want to give them a share. The former masters would accuse them of stealing, or if they questioned their share would run them off the property. They would then have to find a new place for their families to live and a place for them to work."

She adjusted in her chair before finishing. "There were improvements in some areas of the South like Louisiana. The streetcars were desegregated in 1867; experiments with integrating public schools in 1869; and legalization of interracial marriages between 1868 and 1896. They also elected a total of thirty-two black state senators and ninety-five state representatives, and had integrated juries, public boards, and police departments."

"Wow, how do you remember all that?"

"I'm reading it from this chapter in your book," she giggled looking at him.

Ryan felt like he was two inches tall and put his head on the table. "Just shoot me now and put me out of my misery." Feeling her hand on his back patting him lightly made his body tingle at her touch.

"It's okay, loosen up, don't be so tense," she said, hoping she was making him feel a little more at ease. She had to ask herself, *Am I that intimidating?*

Raising his head slowly, he hoped she was still smiling so he could see that glow about her. When she smiled her eyes danced to their own music, and her nose would wrinkle just a little as her lips curled to form the fullness of a smile. In his mind, she turned her head in slow motion to look back at the book. His eyes didn't want to lose one frame of her face from memory.

"Now, during this time period the 'black codes' were established to limit black opportunities. Taxes were placed on free blacks who tried to pursue nonagricultural professions and restricted their ability to succeed. They weren't allowed to rent land, buy guns, and in some cases, their children were taken and put into apprenticeships of former slave masters. During this time the KKK was established to terrorize blacks into submission."

"Hi, Ryan!" the voice of a young woman interrupted them as she walked toward their table. "Great game yesterday." She stood beside his chair leaning on the table making sure he saw her breasts.

"Ah, thanks," he clumsily replied then looked toward Roni. She was reading the chapter for more information, seeming to ignore his conversation.

Noticing she didn't have his complete attention, the young woman wrapped his hair around her finger. "What are you doing this evening?" she asked.

"Right now, I am in the middle of a study session."

"Will you be available later?" she asked leaning closer to him.

"Don't think so, have a crap load of stuff to do."

Looking at Roni, she competed for his attention. "I might need some tutoring tonight."

"What subject?" Ryan looked at Roni, asking her, "What subjects do you tutor?"

Roni looked up from the book. "African American Studies and Art History, but I don't think she needs me." Without emotion, she went back to reading the book.

"I don't tutor anything so you might want to check the board for the subject you need," Ryan suggested.

Releasing his hair the young woman straightened herself. "I guess I will check the board."

Without looking up, Roni teased, "You know, you were wrong for that."

"What? She is husband hunting and probably knows more about my GPA than I do. Besides I am not the only one she is after."

"Oh, really now," Roni looked at him sternly. "So you're not her only option?"

"What are you trying to say? I'm not a good catch?" he questioned with his eyes fixated on her.

When he looked at her, she saw his beautiful green eyes staring back. Powerless looking into his eyes, she turned away from his stare. "I just thought you were the big man on campus." Unable to contain her laughter she laid her head on the table. "I'm sorry. I couldn't resist teasing you a little." Roni leaned back into the chair as she looked at him with her laughing eyes.

Finally he saw the real Roni. She had a sense of humor and seemed easy to talk to. "Okay, you got me. It's just that we are here studying and she didn't respect that. Sorry if I seem so tense, but I am worried about this class."

"Don't worry; history is easy when you connect it with the people. Most of the time we see history as dates and events instead of a peek into the hearts and minds of the people; in time you will start to understand the people too. Besides you've got me to help you with your next test." Roni picked up her cell phone to turn off the alarm. "Time is up!" Like a robot, she began to gather her things.

Not wanting their time to end, he asked, "Going to lunch?" *Now that was a stupid question*, he thought to himself, but tried not to let that show on his face.

She looked over her shoulder. "As a matter of fact, yes. Are you?"

Shocked she didn't just smack him down, he said "Yeah! You go on campus?"

She nodded. "You can pick my brain, and I won't charge you for the time." Slinging her book bag over her shoulder, she waited for him to finish putting his stuff away. After he tightened the straps and slung his bag over his shoulder, they walked to the door of the student hall.

On their stroll to "G" Hall for lunch, he wanted to engage Roni in conversation but didn't know how to start.

Sensing the awkwardness of the stroll, Roni asked, "Where are you from?"

"Born and raised in Virginia, you?"

"Harlem, New York."

"Harlem?" he repeated before he thought about how it sounded. "I didn't mean that the way it came out," he apologized.

Roni stopped in her tracks. "What's wrong with Harlem?"

"Nothing, never been there. Just thought it was a rough area and you don't seem like you come from that environment."

"What environment?" she inquired of his comment.

"Look, when you say Harlem things like crime, street gangs, and total chaos come to mind. Like I said, I don't know anything about Harlem and I am sorry if I offended you." Ryan looked into her face to sense how bad he had insulted her.

"Sorry, I can be a little sensitive sometimes." Roni began to walk with him again. "Harlem is not what you see on TV or in the Blaxploitation movies from the seventies. Like most towns or cities, Harlem has its pluses and minuses. My father does construction and my mom was an artist so we live in Central Harlem. Contrary to common belief, life in the city isn't a hip-hop video. I'm sure in the town you are from there is crime."

Ryan had to admit Roni was right; he had prejudged Harlem by media images that only showed the negative. Just because the majority of the people were African American didn't make it a bad or dangerous place. The people that lived there wanted the same things as everyone else. He began to realize people weren't as different as he had thought.

"G" Hall contained the campus dining room and was the place you were most likely to get food poisoning. Roni reminded herself, *He wants to have lunch, so it won't kill me or at least I hope not.*

Looking at the array of things on the daily menu, she decided on the lasagna and garlic bread with a side salad. Walking behind her, Ryan got the same thing without the salad, exchanging it for a piece of cake for dessert. Watching closely when they arrived at the cashier, Ryan told the student at the register, "I got it."

"You don't have to do that," Roni told him but was flattered at the gesture.

"I invited you, remember," he flashed a boyish smile as he paid the cashier.

Feeling this was an argument she wasn't going to win, Roni just smiled, shaking her head as a sign of surrender. She then looked for an empty table. Seeing one in the middle of the dining hall she asked Ryan, "Will that one be okay?"

"Hey, Ryan, over here," came a voice from across the room. Ryan looked back where some of his teammates were eating with a group of young women, one of whom he had just seen earlier.

"Thanks, but Roni and I are eating together." He glanced down at her and smiled. Again, the voice louder this time, "You can bring her," with some childish amusement that followed. Ryan just ignored them, looking back at Roni. "Some people never grow up."

Roni pretended not to hear and proceeded to the table. After getting herself situated, she waited for Ryan to get comfortable in his seat. Not wanting Ryan to feel bad by the silliness of his teammates, Roni decided to make light conversation. "How long have you been playing baseball?" she asked while eating her salad.

Ryan was still embarrassed because of that stupid comment, forgetting that if it had been someone else, he probably wouldn't have thought anything of it. Roni was not a pet or an object but a person. Now that he was studying African American history, it had opened his eyes to the reality that life was not always fair to people of different races. Developing this friendship with Roni had brought forth feelings he had never noticed before.

Looking into her face, he saw the small patch of freckles on the bridge of her nose. They looked like someone had dipped their fingers into paint then splattered them on her face, each one landing in the perfect spot, enhancing her cheekbones and showing their strong structure.

Not receiving an answer, Roni looked over at him. Ryan tried to get his thoughts together to remember the question she had asked. Reaching for the peppershaker on the table, he said, "Since I was big enough to hold a bat around three or four with tee ball," not looking up because he couldn't look at her without getting lost in thought.

"Tee ball?" she asked although she knew the answer having played it herself, but wanted to keep him talking.

"It's like baseball without the pitcher. At that age most of us couldn't hit the side of the barn, much less swing a bat to hit a ball." They both laughed quietly at the comment. Ryan wanted to keep her smiling as he watched her wrinkle her nose as she laughed. "I remember being at bat once swinging so hard I hit myself in the head with the bat. Do you think I could still have brain damage from that?" he joked.

Roni began to laugh at his poking fun at himself. "No, I don't think so," she settled back to herself. "So that was the beginning of your career in baseball?"

"Yeah, I guess, but it isn't as much fun as it used to be when I was a kid. It really makes a difference when you do something for fun and then having to do it for an education. When I was growing up, I would play all day never getting tired. Now I sometimes dread going to practice. Playing the game is like going to a job you hate, but know you need the paycheck."

"What position do you play?" she asked looking into his eyes as they stared back at her. They were such an odd color of green, more of a deep emerald with golden flecks that seemed to dance around the pupils. She wanted to look away, but couldn't.

"Shortstop," he said with excitement now. "In the past I have played all over the field, but shortstop was always my favorite position."

"Why shortstop?" she inquired of his choice.

"I guess because you have to keep your head in the game. In that position, most hitters are right-handed and when they hit, it generally goes between second and third base. Being left-handed, I catch with my right hand keeping most grounders from getting to the outfield. When the other players move around the diamond, I have to move in to cover their area for double plays." Embarrassed by his excitement, Ryan apologized, "I'm sorry, I don't want to bore you with talk about baseball."

"You're not boring me; you should see the thrill in your eyes when you talk about playing that position. Admit it you really love the game. Come on, it's okay to love it," she lightly nudged his upper arm. *Nice arm*, she thought to herself. Lean muscles, not bulky, almost like one of those dancers in that play the Lion King she remembered seeing when she was younger.

Wanting to know more about the seemingly mysterious woman sitting with him he asked, "What is your major?"

She sighed, because Roni hated talking about herself. "I did my Bachelors in Fine Arts, but I am now working on my graduate degree and am geared more toward ancient Egyptian artifacts." Feeling the excitement, she continued, "It is awesome looking at those pieces created thousands of years ago with limited tools but so precise in creation. Think of the pyramids, the way they were built was phenomenal." She saw him laughing at her because she had gotten so into the conversation her hands were moving as she talked about her major. She wasn't sure why, but she felt comfortable letting herself go in front of Ryan.

"Hi, Roni!" she heard a voice with a Middle Eastern accent. "Is this seat taken?"

She looked at Ryan to see if he objected. He didn't but he hated having to share her. "No, join us. Ryan, this is Ansari. Ansari, Ryan," she introduced the two men.

Both men acknowledged each other; Ryan tried to put on a pleasant face as Ansari took his seat. Feeling the tension, Roni started the conversation moving again. "Ansari is majoring in engineering." Although she was really enjoying chatting with Ryan, Ansari had been a longtime friend and she wouldn't insult him.

His first year had been tough enough for him when they both arrived on campus as freshmen. With his small frame, he was targeted and his being from the Middle East by way of Chicago didn't help. With the terrorists attacking on American soil, anyone that looked like him was fair game for bullies.

His black curly hair was longer on the top, shorter on the sides, and shined like glass. Ansari's complexion was darker than Roni's and flawless. His features were almost fairy-like, giving him a youthful appearance. The two had met at orientation when some older students bumped into him causing him to drop his books. Roni rushed over to help pick them up, starting their friendship.

Ansari knew it would be hard attending a Southern university, but never dreamed he would have to deal with such hatred. Roni was one of the few students that saw him as a friend when all the others, even those of Middle Eastern decent, wouldn't speak to him.

They wanted to be like the traditional American student and had lost who they were to achieve that, which puzzled Ansari. Just because he was Arab and celebrated his heritage didn't make him a foreigner. He was a second generation American.

"Are you majoring in engineering, Ryan?" Ansari asked as he ate his lunch.

"No, architecture. Did I have a class with you a couple of years ago?" Ryan seemed to recognize him. "Did you have Dr. Vishal?"

"Don't say that man's name. I still have nightmares about him." Speaking in a fake Indian accent, pulling his chin into his chest, Ansari mimicked Dr. Vishal. "Mr. Amin," he said, shaking his head as if he had a nervous twitch, "I am sure you know the answer to this formula." They all burst into laughter and everyone in the dining hall was curious as to what was so funny.

It took Ryan back to a class that had almost made him run home to his mother. Dr. Vishal seemed to pick on them even though they sat in different parts of the classroom. They had both tried to move, only to be found by his evil eyes.

Dr. Vishal was a tall man without expression of any kind. No smile, with dead eyes that stared sternly at you, making you stammer your words. You knew he received joy from intimidating you, but it never showed on his face. His towering structure only made him more threatening, but in reality, he only wanted the best from his students and challenged those he knew would go far. If it had not been for Dr. Vishal, they both wouldn't have excelled in their chosen majors, because you had to think three steps ahead of him.

"I had forgotten about him," Roni sighed at the forgotten memory. "I remember Ansari coming to study sessions and he would be literally pulling his hair out."

"See," he pulled his hair back, "that bald spot belongs to Dr. Vishal." Again, they erupted with laughter and spent the next hour just laughing and sharing class horror stories.

Roni looked at her watch. "Oh, look at the time. I have got to get out of here." She began to gather her things and so did Ryan and Ansari as they prepared to leave.

"Good seeing you again, Ryan." Ansari leaned over and kissed Roni on the cheek lightly. "Are we on for Friday?"

"Yeah, around seven thirty okay?"

"Great, see you then." Like the whirlwind he came in on, he whisked away just as quickly.

Ryan's heart sank when he saw him kiss her. How could he have been so stupid? They were dating. Looking a little nervous, he mentioned to Roni, "I didn't know you and Ansari were dating."

Looking puzzled Roni asked, "Dating? Oh, no, we are just very close friends and I can't say I ever looked at him that way or he, me. What made you think that?"

"Well, he kissed you goodbye and you have plans on Friday. I just assumed the two of you were a couple, sorry."

"Friday night is our group bonding time. We just hang out, eat pizza, talk about the week, and make each other laugh. Nothing major, just time we relax from classes."

Ryan was curious about her comment "we" and it showed on his face. Roni sensed this and continued, "Just a small group of students from different countries and cultures. We all met our freshmen year and have been there for each other like a family."

"Oh, okay."

Put into a peculiar situation, Roni felt she should invite Ryan to the gathering. He would be the only one there not a person of color or different culture which might be a little awkward, although she and the others often joked about it being the rainbow club. "Would you like to come?" she asked.

"Yeah, sounds like fun." He could barely keep his composure because he was hoping she would invite him. "Only on one condition," he paused, "if you come see me play tomorrow."

"Are you serious?" she smiled broadly up at him.

"Yeah, come watch me play. It might rekindle my love of the game."

With a smile she sighed, "Oh, okay," dragging the words from her tongue, trying to hide her feelings of excitement that he had invited her.

"Now, you can pretend to be a little more excited when you say that."

She smiled with that little wrinkle of her nose. "I would love to come to your game tomorrow. What time?"

"Three o'clock and don't be late," Ryan told her as he turned to leave. Walking out, he noticed his teammates staring at him inquiringly. At that moment, he didn't care, because Roni was coming to his game and that's all that mattered.

CHAPTER 2

Ryan kept looking into the stands, but there was no sign of Roni. He was starting to get nervous wondering why she had lied to him. Then he reminded himself it wasn't even three o'clock and the game hadn't started yet, reasoning that she was probably on her way.

Closing his eyes and feeling the heat of the sun on his face, Ryan climbed out of the dugout to warm up before the game. He threw first to second base and then third, feeling a little down that she hadn't arrived. His heart felt heavy, because he wanted so badly for her to come watch him play.

Warm-ups were almost finished, but still no Roni. Something must have happened or she would've been there. Although he had only known her for a short period of time she had always been true to her word. Definitely, something had happened to prevent her from coming, because she would have phoned him to cancel if she didn't intend to be there. *Come on, Ryan, get your head in the game*, he scolded himself.

I hate being late for anything even a baseball game, Roni chastised herself as she walked almost at the pace of a jog to the baseball field. It was now three thirty and she was only halfway there. She hoped he hadn't noticed her not being there, but knowing Ryan he had probably already looked up into the stands many times for her. After the game, she would apologize for the delay and maybe go out for something to eat with Ryan.

Roni hated to admit Ryan was very nice and she enjoyed being with him. He was funny, charming, smart, and definitely easy on the eyes. Oh okay, handsome was the word she had tried hard to avoid. Without a doubt, he was a very handsome man with that natural tan that made him look normal, not an orange color you see so much from those who use tanning beds. His dark hair with loose wavy curls fell around his face to frame a strong jawline. The sexy little cleft in his chin showed the signs of the five o'clock shadow before the rest of his face. It was funny how she noticed so many little things about him.

She would miss that little quirky smile of his when they graduated because they both were returning to their home states. Sure, they would keep in touch for a while but eventually go back to life as usual only to see each other in about ten years or so at some alumni event. Bored stiff, they would make small talk and promise to keep in touch this time, but would soon fall back into the same old routine of classmates.

Finally arriving at the field, she looked for a place in the stands close to his position ensuring that he saw her. Finding a set of bleachers near third base, Roni eased in sitting midway.

Roni's meeting with Professor Lincoln had run later than expected. Well, it wouldn't have if Karrie hadn't tried to show how smart she was by asking stupid questions. *Why do some people do that? Just ask crazy questions that only meant something to them*, Roni asked herself.

After about ten minutes of debate with Professor Lincoln, he just asked Karrie to make an appointment, because she was the only one seeking the information. Roni couldn't even remember what the discussion was about but was showing signs of distress at the length of the meeting. Generally, debate on an issue was exciting for her, but today was not the day. She had made a promise and was going to keep it.

Over the speakers, she heard the voice of the commentator, "That was strike three and the Cougars will take the field."

The Cougars were down by one but it was only the second inning and they had time to catch up. *Good*, she thought, *I didn't miss much*, although the game seemed to be moving rather quickly.

Squirming in her seat, Roni had forgotten that aluminum bleachers were hot after having the sun beat down on them all day. As she sat in the warm sun, the sweat glistened on her skin from the heat and her sprinting to get to the game. Feeling the beginnings of a cool breeze, Roni lifted her hair off her neck to catch it. She hadn't taken time to do anything with it, but really wanted to look special today.

Usually she didn't care what people thought about her hair, but for some reason she cared that Ryan liked it. He had never made any negative comments about it or any positive ones. Like most men, maybe he didn't care what it looked like as long as it wasn't on her face. Roni smiled at that thought.

Feeling down that she hadn't arrived, Ryan decided to take one last glance into the stands and like a dream, there she was. Pulling her hair up in the back, she looked like a model posing for the camera. She was so beautiful, even in a tank top and shorts she was elegant. Her brown skin glowed in the sunlight, making it extremely hard for him to take his eyes off her as she posed.

Ryan knew the poses were involuntary but enjoyed watching her as the cool breeze flowed over her body, making her clothes cling to her slightly. Her hair blew across her face as she released it to fall. She lifted her delicate hand up to her face as she moved her hair back before sliding it down to the bleacher as she crossed her perfectly toned legs. She might have been a dancer or a runner in high school, Ryan thought as their eyes met.

Roni smiled shyly because she knew he had been watching her. For how long she wasn't sure.

Slowly Ryan moved to his position on the field, tipping his hat in her direction to let her know he saw her. It was wonderful having her there but such a distraction for him.

As he turned to face the pitcher, he heard a voice from the stands too familiar and annoying to his ears. "Hi, Ryan," she shouted, leaning over the rail in the stands making sure Roni saw her as she tossed her hair back from her face.

Not looking in the direction of the voice, Ryan settled into his position as shortstop. Playing the game was exciting for him, now that Roni was watching. He couldn't look at her but as long she was there Ryan was satisfied.

The game went quickly with Ryan assisting in two double plays, winning the game 7 to 4. After congratulating each other, the teams began to drift into the dugout and on to the showers. Ryan was grateful for the win, because he would have hated to lose with Roni there.

Ryan couldn't go straight to the showers without speaking to Roni. He wanted her to know he appreciated her coming. As he walked across the field to the stands, he saw her. *Oh, damn, here she comes. Why does she keep coming onto me?* he questioned the actions of the young woman approaching him.

"Great game!" she screamed trying to hug him.

"Ah, thanks! Excuse me," he brushed past her to catch Roni before she could leave the stands. Ryan ran to catch her as he shouted her name, "Roni!"

A little unsure Roni started toward the field. After seeing how he had swept past the young woman, she hesitated before proceeding. "Great game," she congratulated him with a beaming smile.

"Thanks." Ryan hadn't thought past that, then he asked, "Where are you going?"

"No plans, why?" she asked hoping Ryan was inviting her to hang out with him.

Suddenly, the sexy voice of a Caribbean man came into the conversation. "Ryan, you know Roni?" It was Felipe, the Cougars' third baseman.

Ryan, a little shocked, asked, "You know Roni?"

"Yeah, Felipe and I met a couple of years ago. He was dating my roommate," she told him feeling the need to explain their relationship.

"That relationship didn't last but we all remained friends," Felipe declared seeing the concern in Ryan's eyes that he and Roni were together. "Roni, has Ryan invited you to the Doug Out with us tonight?" Felipe asked to help his teammate.

"You didn't give me a chance to before you interrupted me," he lightly shoved Felipe. "I was just about to. Roni, want to come celebrate with us at the Doug Out tonight?" He was very grateful to Felipe for making that suggestion.

"Sure, sounds like fun, but I need to change and I think you two need a shower."

Ryan raised his arm pretending to sniff. "Are you trying to say I stink?"

Holding her nose, Roni shook her head no, as she playfully smiled.

"We are a little ripe and need to shower, come on, Ryan. Meet you there in an hour, okay?"

Ryan pretended he wanted a hug and started toward Roni. "No hug?"

"Go find some water," she laughed, "I will meet you there. Oh, Felipe, will it be okay for the rest of the crew to come?"

Felipe shouted back as he and Ryan ran for the showers, "Sure bring them all, even that devil woman."

"Who is the crew?" Ryan asked as they sprinted across the field to the dugout.

"Don't worry, just the group that hangs out together on Friday night. You'll like them," Felipe assured him.

"The last two to hit the showers, huh?" Coach Rey mocked as they both walked in undressing quickly. They both grabbed towels and soap retreating to the showers.

Felipe had known Ryan since coming there as a freshman when Ryan was a sophomore. They had always shared general conversation and laughs during practice. The two of them generally sat near each other on bus trips to discuss game strategy and what errors they had made during a game. Until now, they hadn't spent time outside of baseball to get to know each other.

A tall Dominican man, Felipe had very dark skin like that of an African warrior painting. Like Ryan, he had those athletic lean muscles chiseled into his frame. His eyes were very dark and penetrating at times when he looked at you. With his striking good looks, Felipe was no stranger to beautiful women. When he smiled, women swooned and gravitated toward him.

Why hadn't he tried to go out with Roni? Ryan was dying to know. He had to have at least tried once or twice. How could he allow such a beautiful woman to pass him without being tempted?

During his shower, Ryan wanted to ask but didn't know how to begin the question. What was wrong with her? Was she a lesbian or something? Felipe was good-looking for a man and seemed to be popular on campus. Well, maybe she didn't like that kind of guy, Ryan tried to reason with himself under the warm water.

As he got out of the shower, he reached for his towel and wrapped it around his waist. Tucking it in snugly, he sat on the bench next to Felipe's locker. Putting on his deodorant, he decided to ask him, "Hey Felipe, why haven't you ever dated Roni?"

"Roni and me, oh never," he laughed wildly at the suggestion as they dressed. "No, Ryan, I dated her roommate and became friends with her. She is taboo for me; you don't go out with a woman then date her friend. Man, a black woman will kill you for that."

Feeling a little embarrassed Ryan laughed at the thought of him thinking she was a lesbian. "When are you going to ask her out, Ryan?" Felipe matter-of-factly asked, looking up as he tied his shoes.

Not knowing how to respond he looked back at Felipe blankly. "Ah, we are just getting to know each other."

"Oh, come on man, we both know you have wood for the girl," Felipe teased Ryan.

Ryan had to smile, because he was very attracted to her and not just physically. Trying to change the subject, he slapped Felipe on the back of the head. "Bring your slow ass on; if you moved faster I wouldn't have to do all the work on the field."

Felipe ran past Ryan for the door, turning back to shout, "Ryan got wood for the girl!" Felipe's laughter was heard in the corridor as Ryan chased him out of the locker room down the hall.

Ryan and Felipe were the first to arrive at the Doug Out, finding an empty table that was big enough to accommodate everyone. Not many people were there because the game didn't start for another hour, which gave them choice seats near the TV. The two men sat down and ordered beers waiting for the others to arrive.

Felipe gave Ryan a devilish grin. Which led him to believe that Felipe was about to do something crazy. Before he could speak, the door opened and in came Ansari with Roni, Abe, and Effie. He heard their laughter as they walked to the table.

Ryan and Felipe stood up in respect of the women coming to the table, but Felipe had other plans for standing.

Leaning over to Ryan, Felipe whispered, "Here she comes, the bride of Satan." Ryan didn't know what to think or how to react to the comment, only looked at Felipe. Was he talking about Roni or the woman with her? Felipe moved from the table. "Come here you devil woman," he said as he approached Effie.

"Who are you calling devil woman, you four-toed demon?" Effie spat back at him.

"Oh, shut up and give a hug," he grabbed Effie and started to kiss her face.

Effie was really enjoying the attention. "Stop acting with your silly self." Her accent seemed to be from Jamaica and so was her voluptuous body.

Felipe moved from the seat next to Ryan and sat next to Effie and Ansari, leaving a seat vacant.

"Do I need to separate the two of you?" Roni teased as she sat next to Ryan. She was so sexy with her orange spaghetti strap top over cropped pants that fit low around the waist. Just low enough to show the little chill bumps on her stomach near her navel with a silver belly ring of a turtle. He smelled the scent of fresh lilacs as she sat down. Her hair was pulled back from her face in a low ponytail held with a large wooden barrette. Some of her hair had fallen near her right eye giving her a carefree look. Ryan wasn't sure if it was intentional, but he loved it.

"Let me introduce you to my partners in crime. Ansari you know, but this is Effie, my old roommate, and Abe, Ansari's roommate."

"Devil woman I tell you," spouted Felipe.

Abe was another small-framed young man wearing a kippah signifying he was Jewish. Ryan thought that was a strange combination, an Arab and a Jew in the same room, but they seemed to be great friends. With his olive skin and light brown hair and eyes, Abe was nice looking but forgettable in a crowd. You could see he was very shy unlike Ansari.

Ryan acknowledged them at the table, while Felipe put on his charm as if he were flirting with Effie. All in fun, Ansari grabbed Effie to join the teasing. "You had your chance and you couldn't handle the woman." They all laughed at their pretend fight over Effie.

"Abe, what is your major?" Ryan asked to get to know him.

"Chemistry with a geology minor," he smiled but immediately lowered his head shyly.

Ansari injected, "Abe and I are brothers from another mother." That even made Abe laugh aloud. "We are both descendants of Abraham," he continued, "him from Sarah, me from Hagar, two religions from the loins of one man."

Why did he have to mention loins? Ryan thought to himself. He was trying not to show his attraction for the woman sitting next to him. In her laughter, she bumped into him making his body ache from the thought of her naked skin.

Without thinking, Ryan extended his arm over the back of her chair as he stared at her. He noticed that Felipe was watching him with that devilish smirk of his as if to say mission accomplished.

Ryan's eyes widened with embarrassment. That only made it more fun for Felipe to watch him squirm because he knew Ryan's secret.

"What'll you have?" the waitress asked as she brought the beers for Ryan and Felipe. Hoping they would say no, she asked, "Will this be separate tickets?"

In unison they all said, "Just one," then laughed that they all thought alike.

Roni looked over at Ryan. "I hope you don't mind, but we just get one ticket and split the cost."

Looking at her, he was lost in her deep brown eyes. "Sure, sounds great," he finally managed to get out as he saw Felipe making faces at him. Without thinking, he shot him the bird, which only made it hilarious to Felipe.

As usual, Roni took charge looking at the menu and asking the group, "Okay, what are we getting tonight?"

"Hot wings with blue cheese dressing," Effie requested.

Cheesy fries for Ansari, fried mushrooms for Felipe, mozzarella sticks for Abe, chicken fingers for Roni. Ryan just agreed to eat whatever came to the table. The waitress left with their food and drink orders, relieved she didn't have to separate the bill.

Seeing Roni rubbing her arms, Ryan asked, "Are you cold?"

"Just a little chilled. I forgot about them having the air on."

"I have a jacket in my car," he volunteered, rising from his seat to retrieve it from the car.

Roni didn't want to be any trouble. "You don't have to do that, I will be fine."

"Oh, let the man take care of you," Felipe encouraged, "you might like it," raising his eyebrows with the sound of the others snickering.

As Ryan walked by Felipe he whispered, "And you call Effie the devil."

Having someone take care of her was new for Roni; she was so used to being the one taking care of everyone else. It was a sweet gesture for him to care, she thought watching him walk to the door. She noticed his nice build with the slightly bowed legs in his jeans taking in as much of him as possible without being too obvious. Before she could look away, he turned around catching her as he backed into the door to open it. He smiled as if to say, "Caught you."

With his hand over his mouth laughing silently, Felipe stared at Roni. Looking around the table, everyone was smiling as if they knew some secret; even Abe with his shyness was looking at her.

"What?"

Ansari started making kissing noises and for the first time without being prodded Abe chimed in, "Oh, you don't have to do that," laughing so hard he turned red in the face.

"I told you they had it bad for each other," Ansari smiled at Abe.

Embarrassed, Roni stuck out her tongue acting like a child.

"I bet Ryan will know what to do with that tongue," Ansari taunted and they all laughed as Roni gave a shy smile.

"Don't be embarrassed, girl," Effie advised. "He is fine as hell with a nice ass."

"Hey," shouted Ansari pretending his feelings were hurt.

She grabbed his face in her hands. "But I still love your little flat ass." Effie kissed him on the lips lightly, which made Ansari act weak as he slid down in his chair.

"You are all sick," Roni scolded, but knew they spoke the truth.

"Girl, Stevie Wonder can see you two got it for each other," Felipe mocked.

Ansari reiterated, "I told you."

Finally it dawned on her those little rats had set this up. "You three are terrible!" Her friends obviously thought Ryan was a nice person since they were trying to set them up.

Felipe, Ansari, and Abe all smiled like little boys who had done something devilish.

"Both of you would never go past those common pleasantries if we didn't run interference." Felipe smirked, and then seriously continued, "He's not like those other idiots on the team. Ryan was the only one that welcomed me when I joined. Now we didn't hang out or anything, but we sat together on the bus and he didn't act as if I had some disease. Really, he's not your average white guy."

Roni heeded their advice, but had to consider in a few weeks they would both be going their separate ways. If they had another year in school it would be something she might have considered, but very little in a relationship could happen in that short period. *Besides, he probably just wants to try it with a sister to say he has done it before. Why waste my time; I have too many things to do when I get back to New York. I don't need a broken heart to console in the process,* she advised herself.

Ryan opened the door of his jeep, getting his denim jacket from the back seat. As he closed the door, he saw some of the younger guys on the team all following Steve as if he were some God. He tried to ignore them on his way back to the door but was unsuccessful.

"Hey, Ryan," raising an open can of beer to his lips, Steve shouted, "Want a beer?"

"No thanks."

"Oh, come on, we got plenty!" Ryan continued to the door as if he hadn't heard him. Steve was a bulky man, not actually strong, just big. The reason that he was on the team was yet to be seen. As a back catcher, he wasn't too bad, but the guy on the second string was much better at the position and wasn't always hung over.

His eyes were blue when not bloodshot and he had reddish colored hair that was hard to describe. Even though you knew he was a bully you still felt sorry for him, because he was not a man. A man didn't need to put someone down to feel better about himself; he felt good just knowing who he was.

That could be the cause of Steve's problem: He didn't know who he was and tried to label others in order to feel powerful. Unfortunately it showed him to be powerless, causing him to drink more.

Opening the door, cool air hit Ryan in the face. Now he understood why Roni was so cold. Looking at the group, he saw why they were friends. They were different, but somehow had a common bond. Black, Arab, Jew, male, female, New York, Chicago, and the Caribbean; all had something different they brought to the table. With their differences they were willing to share their experiences with each other and him.

Ryan wished he had known them earlier when he was a freshman. Back then, he was too busy trying to be one of the guys. It took him awhile but he finally figured out he was not a follower and could think for himself. During that time, he would have been a fool and would have abused the privilege of these great people. Even Abe with his quiet nature brought something to the table. What could he bring? How could he give something back for their friendship?

Feeling eyes on her, Roni looked toward the door and saw Ryan walking in. He looked deep in thought as he came toward the table. Stepping from the door, Roni thought she understood why. The jerks from the team were behind him giving him reason to be annoyed. *Are they following him? Why do they seem to show up everywhere Ryan went? It is probably just a coincidence,* she reasoned with herself.

Draping the jacket on her shoulders, Ryan asked, "Is that better?"

Roni smiled and said, "Yes, thank you," while the guys snickered like little boys who had put something in the teacher's desk, just waiting for her to open the drawer and discover it.

Thank God! Roni thought as the waitress brought their food. She had bread plates for all of them to get their share, each passing a platter with a different appetizer.

Roni loved hot spinach dip with wafers so that was her first choice to occupy her plate. Seeing her put a hearty helping on her plate Ryan asked, "What's that?"

"Spinach dip." Seeing the funny expression on his face she added, "It's good. You should try it," and using her fork, she put some on a wafer.

"That looks--" and before he could say any more, like a mother she shoved the wafer into his mouth. Ryan hated to admit it but it was tasty. "Not bad, but what would you have done if I was allergic to spinach?"

"Don't worry, mama Roni always has Benadryl in her purse," Felipe teased.

"Well, well, well," Steve snarled as he came near their table, "look what we have here." The stench of beer was heavy on his body as he walked over to Ansari's chair, bumping it trying to antagonize him. Ansari just looked at the others at the table. His entourage behind him laughed at his ignorance as if Steve had just told a joke.

Ansari was used to that sort of harassment, receiving it just because he was an Arab. Even though he knew it was coming when Steve was around it didn't stop the pain of being taunted.

Ryan started to say something, but Roni put her hand on his arm to keep him from getting involved. She knew Ansari could handle Steve and gave him the chance to stand up for himself.

With a little grin on his face Ansari asked, "Are you putting on weight, Steve? You seem to be having a little trouble getting past my chair." Everyone at the table had a little smile on their face and that angered Steve, because he was now the butt of the joke. "Have a seat; they will serve you here even though your IQ is below standard."

"Oh, Steve, go sit down somewhere," Felipe told him because he knew Steve had Ansari by more than fifty pounds.

They all stared at the little entourage as he walked to a table close by. Ansari waited until they were seated before flippantly commenting on Steve's future as a used car salesman. "Hurry down to 'I'm so stupid motors' and buy you a lemon." They could no longer control themselves and all burst out laughing. Hearing them Steve knew he was the source of the humor and didn't like it.

Ryan felt embarrassed by how Ansari was being treated. What had Ansari done other than being born that warranted Steve disrespecting him that way?

"Ansari, why do you antagonize him?" Ryan asked unable to understand.

"Because I have thick skin and I want him to know that. He can say what he wants, it will not make me less of a man. I will never put my head down for anyone, not even a punk like Steve."

Hearing that, Ryan understood why Roni kept him from standing up against Steve. It would have been disrespectful to Ansari to have another man fight his battle. Felipe, on the other hand, spoke up because like Ansari he had been one of Steve's targets when he first came to the team.

Ryan was unaware of the altercation, because they lived in different dorms. Steve had been in Felipe's building, intoxicated from a frat party and pushing everyone around. When Felipe heard him in the hall, he went to the door and asked nicely for him to tone it down. Letting the alcohol speak for him, he called Felipe a jungle monkey and pushed him.

Without thinking of the consequences, Felipe turned in anger, grabbed him by his shirt, slamming him on the floor. Before he could hit Steve, the student advisor intervened telling him to go back to his room. Felipe knew he could have been kicked out of school for that altercation but nothing was ever said about it. Now Steve always walked softly around him.

They soon got back to their laughter and went on enjoying the evening. Roni found herself staring at Ryan often. Why couldn't she stop looking at him? It was so easy to get lost looking into those eyes. His strong jaw line was captivating, accented by his prominent nose. The little mole on the left side of his neck near his Adam's apple sat there as if it were a drop of paint left by an artist as a signature mark for the artwork.

His strong hands with his closely clipped fingernails had small calluses probably from gripping the bat or handling the ball. It was so cute the way he tried to hide his smile by covering his face with his hands. She had no idea why they were laughing but hoped they didn't stop.

"Too much water for me tonight," Ansari said as he left the table for the men's room.

Felipe looked back at the table, making them laugh. "Need a pair of tweezers?"

"No, I'm whipping out mine not yours," Ansari said and again, the table erupted with laughter.

Ryan tried hard not to look at Roni too often, but it became very difficult. His jacket slipped off her arm and he noticed the beauty mark on her shoulder just barely peeking out from under the strap of her shirt. It looked like a white rosebud or maybe a popcorn kernel. One of the things that made her unique; little imperfections that also made her perfect.

Just wanting to touch her, he pulled the jacket up onto her shoulder. The touch of her skin was intoxicating and only made him want more. She turned toward him smiling with those big dimples to acknowledge his touch.

Her cool brown skin warmed at the slight touch of his fingertips. His touch set her body on fire in the cool room and sent the shiver of desire down her spine. There was a deep connection between them that neither had felt before; all they knew was it felt right.

Noticing Ansari had not returned, Felipe glanced over to the other table and saw Steve and some of his friends were missing as well. Looking at Ryan, they both seemed to understand what the other was thinking. Trying not to alarm Roni and Effie, Felipe teased about Ansari being gone so long and that he might need a pair of tweezers after all. Ryan chimed in that he needed to relieve himself as well. Neither said a word as they went down the hall to the men's room. Upon trying to enter, they found that someone was standing in front of the door.

Without haste, Felipe pushed his way into the restroom with Ryan behind him. Steve was holding Ansari by the neck as his little cronies stood around laughing. They moved away seeing the two men come in.

Seeing Felipe, Steve instantly released Ansari allowing him to slide to the floor weak from the lack of oxygen. Ryan rushed over to catch him before he completely landed on the floor. Ryan looked back at Steve not understanding his ignorance.

Felipe pushed Steve back. "Touch him again and I will beat your ass!"

"Oh, he your girlfriend?" Steve mocked breathing a little heavy.

"No, but you can be my bitch with your punk ass," Felipe said as he moved closer while Steve backed away, never removing his stare. You could see his anger from the muscles in his arm growing as his hands clenched. His eyes never blinked as his breathing grew stronger and his chest swelled.

Ansari now being held up, Ryan tried to calm the situation by putting the spotlight back on him. "He should be your girlfriend with that sissy grip of his."

Steve began to put distance between him and Felipe. "Let's get out of here."

"Are you alright?" Ryan asked Ansari.

"Yeah, I will live."

The three men remained in the restroom until Ansari got his breath, but vowed to keep what happened between them private. They didn't want to spoil their evening and Ansari insisted they didn't tell.

"Roni, why are you so coy with Ryan?" Effie asked as they waited for the others to return.

"I don't know. Like I said before if it had been earlier in the school year it would be something I could possibly pursue."

Abe asked, "What are you afraid of?"

"Girl, it is obvious he is into you," Effie teased Roni with a little sneaky smile, "or at least he wants to get into you."

"You are so nasty," Roni blushed.

"Oh, girl please, you know men think with the wrong head all the time. Look at Felipe, always looking for his next conquest."

"Effie, let it go. You knew he was a dog when you met him." Roni put up her hands like paws and started panting. Both women laughed while Abe just shook his head and smiled.

"What y'all laughing about?" asked Ryan.

"How it took two of you to help Ansari use the bathroom," Abe injected as Roni and Effie smiled at the thought of men going to the restroom together. Something not commonly seen, because they had the fear that someone would look at their package.

Ansari had to get into the conversation. "I told you it would take more than me to hold the tiger." In unison, they all laughed.

The waitress came by to collect the check as they all pooled their money and added extra for the tip. Gathering their things Roni looked to Ryan, handing him his jacket. "Thank you, I really appreciated it."

Ryan took the jacket and it smelled just like her. "Any time," he managed to blurt out.

Remembering only the good time they had spent together, they started for the door.

CHAPTER 3

They were all excited to be driving down to Roni's Uncle Walt's for the family BBQ. Since Roni had been in college, she and her friends always went to the family gathering before the end of the school year. Over the years, some of the friends had changed, but Felipe, Effie, Ansari, and Abe had always been a part of it.

This time they had a new member with Ryan, although he was a little nervous about meeting Roni's family for the first time. He really didn't know why but he just wanted them to like him. Driving up to the house Ryan felt a little uneasy hoping he didn't do something stupid and embarrass himself.

Roni's uncle lived in a rural part of the county with the whole family living on the same road, giving the unofficial name of their little neighborhood, Roger's Town.

As they arrived Roni's Aunt Betty came out to greet them. She was very light in complexion with light brown eyes. Ryan originally thought she was white when they first drove up, but was happy he didn't make that known to the others. Betty was a full figured woman with an inviting smile.

Along with Betty came her daughter, Bianca, a beautiful little girl approximately ten or so. She wore her deep brown hair in pigtails hanging off her shoulders. To Ryan, Bianca looked like a younger version of Roni. Although she had her mother's light brown eyes, she had the family trademark dimples that brightened up her face when she smiled.

Ryan didn't really know what to do, because this was his first time meeting her family. With Roni's friends, it was easy because some he already knew. The others were his age accepting him as just another student. Her family wasn't going to be so easy to impress because it was obvious they loved her.

He understood why they felt that way about her, because everyone wanted to be near her. They didn't know why, but once they crossed paths with Roni life wasn't the same without her or at least Ryan felt that way.

"Hey baby, how you been?" her Aunt Betty asked as she gave Roni a big hug.

"Doing good, Auntie," Roni replied, then looked down at Bianca. "How are you, young lady?"

Giggling, Bianca answered, "Fine," reaching up for a hug. Roni swung her around because she knew that was what she really wanted.

"About time you brought your narrow behind down to see us," Ryan heard a deep baritone voice walking toward them. The deep sound of the voice had Ryan a little shaken because he was already nervous. A tall slim man walked over and picked Roni up with a big bear hug. "Girl, you look more like your mama every day," he said, then planted a kiss on her forehead.

"Hey, Felipe, how you been? Roni, I see you picked up a new stray. Hi, son, just call me Uncle Walt," he shook Ryan's hand, "we are all family here." Walt sensed his fear and wanted to put him at ease, because the Rogers were family and no one ever left their home feeling unwelcome.

"Uncle Walt!" Ansari ran toward him with his arms wide grabbing Walt before he could escape.

"Roni, I told you to stop feeding him," he laughed as Ansari laid his head on his chest.

"Oh, Uncle Walt, you know you love me," Ansari joked, and he was right. When Walt had a problem with a project he was working on, he called up Ansari and they discussed it. Ansari gave some insight Walt had not thought about. It was amazing what a fresh pair of eyes did for the project.

Walt appreciated his help so much that Ansari worked as an intern during the summer for him. Ansari lived with them while he was working and they became very close. During that time, he was like a big brother to Bianca and Justin.

"Effie, if I were just a little younger and single, Felipe would have some real competition."

"Oh, Uncle Walt, you are too sweet." Effie gave him a big hug.

Felipe seized the opportunity to harass Effie. "You wouldn't have to fight me for that evil woman."

Walt looked over at Roni. "I see they are still at it," he said, giving a hearty laugh at the two of them pretending not to like each other. "Okay, men, follow me." He turned to Ryan. "Sorry, son, I didn't get your name."

"Ryan, sir," he replied, feeling a little more confident now and falling in line with the others.

Roni smiled at him as he glanced back over his shoulder to look at her. The wind was blowing through her hair and she adjusted her shades to hold it back from her face. Watching her Ryan felt this was going to be a good day and knew he didn't want it to end.

The men walked around to the back of the ranch style home as Walt fell behind putting his hand on Ryan's shoulder. "Where you from, Ryan?"

"Virginia, sir," he said with his Virginian twang.

"So you are the student Roni was tutoring," he cackled because Roni had complained about having another dimwitted jock to tutor. Walt saw Ryan had a puzzled look on his face. "Don't worry, you undoubtedly weren't as dimwitted as she thought."

Ryan had to laugh because he had been a bit of a knucklehead when they first met and she probably did get the wrong impression of him. Over time, things had changed and they were friends, but his heart desired more.

"Okay, men, let's carry this stuff down to the pond. Got to get the fish started or Betty will be fussing and I don't like it when she fusses. Keep her happy, you keep me happy," Walt flashed a smile showing his dimples.

Like soldiers, they carried coolers of fish, cleaned and ready for batter to the pond, setting them near the two deep fryers getting hot with oil. Walt grabbed his apron from the table that had a cartoonish woman on it with the slogan "Kiss the Kook." Putting it on, Walt looked around at his family clapping his hands. "Let the fun begin! Betty, where is that fish batter now? This grease is getting hot."

"I got it, Uncle Walt," Roni handed him a bowl with a cornmeal-based batter.

"Set it there, baby girl," he pointed to a spot on the table.

Ryan couldn't help but notice her sexy legs as she leaned over the bench of the picnic table to set the bowl there. She put her hand on the table to steady herself as she leaned forward lifting one leg slightly for balance. Her white shorts were showing just enough skin enticing him to look. The red tank top she wore showed her stomach when she reached. It was hard for Ryan to look away, but he knew he must or someone would notice.

Damn, that Felipe he doesn't miss a thing. Ryan hadn't figured out he wasn't the only man that saw her beauty; even Ansari was getting an eye full. Without even acknowledging their stares, Roni retreated to the house.

In their daze, they hadn't noticed Walt standing behind them. "Now I can bury you boys out here in these woods, and no one will ever find you," he said, giving them a mean stare before bursting into laughter. All three of them looked at each other laughing because they were caught.

"Hey, dad, where do you want me to put the charcoal?" A teenage boy about fifteen came from the house with a bag across his shoulders. "Ansari, what up? Felipe, Abe, I see daddy has already got you working." Having not met Ryan he walked over and extended his hand, "Hi, I'm Justin, you must be Ryan."

"Yes, nice to meet you," Ryan smiled as they shook hands.

Leaning in close so his dad couldn't hear, Justin whispered, "My sister is telling my cousins about the cute white boy in the backyard. So expect the silly girls to be here smiling in your face all day," Justin told Ryan as if he were giving advice. "Roni says you play baseball with Felipe." He began to speak louder. "Will you guys help me with my catching later?" Both Felipe and Ryan agreed and all started back to the house to pick up more supplies.

They gathered mesquite wood chips for the grills and another large tub with ice and sodas. Felipe and Ryan picked up the one with ice because Abe and Ansari were not the athletic type. Both men wore sleeveless shirts and shorts showing their muscular frames. As they bent down to pick up the tub, they heard the giggles of little girls. Turning back to look at the window where the laughter was coming from, they saw little heads duck down.

"Bianca, ya'll get away from that window with your little hot tails," they heard Aunt Betty hollering at the girls. The sound of their feet on the floor was all Felipe and Ryan heard as they ran to get away. Both thought it was hilarious as the women in the kitchen began to laugh. After all, they had been little girls once.

Aunt Betty waited for the girls to get out of hearing range and looked back at Effie and Roni. "They are fine," she faked fanning herself. Roni and Effie were laughing at Betty's antics as she pretended to faint. "Girl, if I wasn't married to your uncle, hello!"

"You wouldn't wish to be younger, Aunt Betty?" Effie asked.

"Unlike men, women don't have to have youth on their side, if you know what I mean," the women laughed at Betty's comment.

Roni laughed at them both in her shy way, but her mind was drifting back to Ryan with his new haircut that showed off his strong features. When he looked at her, his eyes penetrated her soul and his stare didn't turn away anymore. It was so much easier when she had the upper hand and could make him look away, but now he seemed to challenge her with his eyes.

Ryan was no longer that shy young country boy she had first met. No longer did he have a problem hugging her, and he didn't care if anyone saw them on campus together. Before it seemed he was afraid of what people thought; now he just didn't care what anyone thought. It was funny how people changed before your eyes and you didn't notice until you analyzed them.

"Earth to Roni," Betty snapped her fingers as she and Effie joked with Roni, who was obviously in a stupor thinking about the young man outside. Betty was very impressed by Ryan. He was a very respectful young man, not that the others weren't, but he had that Southern charm about him.

It was also nice to see Roni's attention somewhere other than a book. Betty had never let her know, but she had been so worried about her after Bernice's death. She just seemed to lose interest in her life and concentrated so much on her dad and Laurence. Her decision to attend college in the South was a good choice, because she really had a chance to find Roni again.

When Bernice was first diagnosed, Roni went from being a preteen kid to a responsible adult. Bernice's health had failed quickly, not giving her, much less Roni, a chance to understand what was happening to their family. It was never her intention to put so much on Roni in her young life. Knowing what was to come, Bernice cried many nights at the thought of her baby having to grow up too soon. Now Betty was seeing a spark of the little girl coming back into Roni's eyes while she and Effie prepared things for the BBQ. They seemed to have regained their fire.

The sound of the door opening on the sun porch interrupted the conversation of the women as the shadow of a man came into the kitchen. Ryan entered. "Mrs. Rogers, Uncle Walt asked me to bring him something to put the cooked fish in." The truth was Ryan volunteered so that he could see Roni. Why was he so smitten with her? There was something about her he could not describe or comprehend. She had enough strength to stand alone, but still allowed him to be a part of her life.

"Mrs. Rogers? You call Walter uncle but you call me Mrs. Rogers?" Betty sternly chastised him.

Ryan began apologizing when he noticed the little smirks on the faces of the women and began to laugh with them. Finally, he was feeling like one of the family. It was clear why the others were so excited about coming and told him not to worry. He saw firsthand Roni's wonderful family, feeling they would accept him.

"Ladies, I think he has figured us out," Betty teased as she gave Ryan the aluminum pan. "Don't let any flies in on your way out," she told him as she gently pushed him out of the kitchen as the laughter of little girls was heard in the background. "Bianca!"

Roni had the batter for the hushpuppies in a bowl, setting it in the pan for him to take down to the pond. "Be careful because Uncle Walt will kill you if you drop his batter," she smiled as she looked into his eyes. They say the eyes are the window to the soul. If that were true, what was his soul trying to say?

Over the course of the day, many different members of Roni's family visited and enjoyed the festivities including her grandparents. Doc and Alberta were a lovely couple with fifty years of marriage on their résumé, which Roni's grandpa pretended was jail.

Ryan and Felipe played a little baseball with Justin, both giving him pointers on the game. They even played a game of football with the little ones; well, actually, they carried them around the yard when they had the football in their hands. Which had them giggling all day and keeping them away from the pond and the grills.

Uncle Walt had two grills going. One had hotdogs and ribs, the other had chicken and hamburgers. He always made sure he didn't let the pork get near that grill because of the religious beliefs of Ansari and Abe. Which made Felipe and Ryan very happy; all the more for them.

Those two ate like horses and Betty loved watching them put it away. She wasn't sure what gave her more pleasure: cooking or watching her family enjoy it.

"Mom," Justin got Betty's attention, "can I get a tattoo like Ryan's?"

"Not if you want to live," she advised him.

He started to whine a little. "But mom," he said, very disappointed by her answer.

"My mom reacted the same way when I got mine, but I was twenty-one and it was a gift from my cousin who is a tattoo artist."

Roni hadn't noticed it before, but the artistry of the work was magnificent. "Your cousin did that? Wow, that is beautiful!"

Walt looked on with a loving smile, because that was how Bernice reacted when she saw something interesting.

Ryan's tattoo was a beautiful depiction of a wolf with green eyes perched on a cliff, as a protector with a dream catcher background. The wolf looked as though it was guarding the dreams. Whose dreams was he protecting? Was the wolf keeping something from entering Ryan's dreams or preventing something from coming out?

"Yeah, he does that for extra money at Virginia Beach. I went up last summer and he gave it to me as a present for graduation. I hid it for a week before my mom saw it. She almost flipped, but grew to like it."

"You hear that, Justin? Twenty-one not fifteen." Betty gave Justin one of those just try me looks as she passed the fresh blackberry cobbler Roni had made for dessert.

"That is so cool!" Roni said while rubbing her fingers over the tattoo, feeling the muscles and watching the movement of his arm as she analyzed the details of the work. "I have got to meet him. Human skin is not an easy canvas for an artist." Roni slowly pulled herself back into reality joining the conversations around her.

Ryan felt the burning touch of her fingers as they traced the wolf on his upper arm. He knew what Felipe would say, "Ryan got wood for the girl," which wasn't completely true. It was more than a physical attraction, because the body reacted on what it saw. The heart was harder to explain or see.

"You like blackberry cobbler, I see?" Betty asked seeing how Ryan was enjoying it with the homemade ice cream.

"Yes, it's my favorite."

"Secret family recipe right, Roni?"

"You made this?" Ryan asked very surprised.

"Don't act so surprised," she gently nudged him, "I can cook you know."

"Yes, she can and her baked chicken with stuffing is the bomb," Ansari told Ryan while scraping his bowl and licking the spoon.

"Betty, give that boy some more before he eats the bowl," Walt teased. "I don't know where you put it all, must be in those big feet of yours."

Ansari just danced to his own music at the table not caring everyone was laughing at how he was enjoying his pie.

Roni began to cover the leftovers with Effie helping her. Bianca and her cousins whispered to each other, while looking at the young men as they got up to help Walt take things back up the hill.

They started by emptying out the tubs with the ice, which had dissolved into water, carrying them back to the storage building. Everyone pitched in carrying various items into the house as they all gathered in the kitchen.

"Roni, are you going to take some of this stuff?" Walt asked as he came in with a pan of leftover grilled meat. "You men grab a plate and take some of this stuff with you too."

"Great, I won't have to cook this week." She gathered some of the grilled chicken and ribs that were left from the BBQ. She didn't eat the hamburgers and hot dogs too often, but would have a side salad with the chicken and ribs.

"Ryan, don't be shy," Walt encouraged him as he passed by. "They aren't," he pointed at his friends.

Betty gave Ryan a little bowl with the last of the blackberry cobbler, putting her finger to her lips for him to keep it between them. Ryan mouthed the words "Thank you," as he accepted it.

With their food for later, they went back to their cars. The family walked out with them for their last hugs and kisses. Bianca was so excited to hug Ryan and Felipe that she didn't tell on Justin for looking at Effie's butt.

Walt started back inside before they were in their cars because he hated watching Roni leave. Betty gave big motherly hugs, telling them to drive safely and they were welcome anytime.

"Hey, Ryan," Felipe shouted back as he went to the car with Ansari, "I'm riding back with Ansari; we are both on the same side

of the campus. That way Roni won't have to drive me home."
Felipe knew Ryan would never talk with him around and if he
wanted to let Roni know of his interest, they needed to spend time
alone.

Feeling a little frightened and excited about the drive, his
throat became dry as Ryan fumbled to say, "Okay." He didn't know
what he was going to talk to her about; it was at least an hour's
drive away.

The sneaky grins on their faces were so obvious, but like Ryan,
Roni had her own apprehensions about the drive. Her stomach
began to feel a little queasy at the thought of being alone with
him. What were they going to talk about during the drive? They
had been alone together before but now she had started to see
him differently. Maybe that was why she always invited the others,
to keep from being alone with Ryan. It wasn't that she didn't trust
him; the reality was she didn't trust herself.

Roni turned on the radio as they left her uncle's driveway,
hearing the strong sexy voice of Preston Miles from the speakers.
Normally this would have soothed her, but tonight it made her
heart race.

They had been riding about fifteen minutes without a word,
which made them uneasy. Both began to speak at the same time
but had to laugh at how silly they were being.

"I think my uncle likes you. You seem to know as much about
cars as he does." Roni glanced over at Ryan.

"Yeah, he's really a nice guy and I love that candy apple red
Monte Carlo in the garage. You didn't tell me he was an engineer."

"He received his education while he was in the military and
sent money home so my mom could attend State College. Being
the eldest, he felt she was his responsibility. My grandparents
worked in the mills all their lives but wanted more for their
children. Uncle Walt joined up for my mom and his education."

"Now your Papa Doc is a character. He can say some of the
funniest things without trying." Ryan laughed at the antics of her
grandfather. "Your uncle was doing something with the fish and
your grandpa was telling him how he was doing it wrong. Then he
would look over at us and wink his eye as if he was having fun
harassing him. You have a great family; I could feel the love
there."

"Yes, Papa is a trip. He always harasses Uncle Walt and my dad
when it comes to things like that. For him it is just his way to be

part of the festivities; since his stroke he doesn't help as much. Oh, did he tell you any of his war stories?"

"No. He was in the war, which one?"

"He would say marriage, but really he was in the military during Vietnam. I would hear him talking to my dad and uncle about that war. They both had served during peacetime so the hell of war was something they didn't know. When we came down to visit, they would go in the den and just talk about some of the horrors. I remember my dad telling my mom that he was thankful he hadn't seen the things my grandpa had."

"My grandfather was in that war too. He used to have nightmares about the things he had seen. I remember spending the night with them when I was about eight or nine when he woke up and started crying. That was why he and my dad didn't want me to join the military."

"You wanted to join the military?"

"I looked into it before I received the scholarship to play ball. If I had gone into the military, I would be in Iraq or Afghanistan right now." There was a moment of silence because some of his friends were serving and those that had come back were not the same. They looked the same but their eyes were different as if they had seen the horrors of hell walking among men.

Trying to change to a happier subject, Roni said, "You know my mom introduced Uncle Walt to Aunt Betty."

"You're kidding, really?"

"Yeah, Aunt Betty and my mom were college roommates and sorority sisters. When she and my dad got married, Aunt Betty was her 'Maid of Honor.' Uncle Walt teases her that he was set up, but he wouldn't have it any other way. He always says it's alright to be henpecked if you are pecked by the right hen." They both laughed at how that sounded.

During the ride home, they laughed and enjoyed each other almost forgetting they were alone together, until the radio host announced, "Let's slow it down for all the lovers. Here is Luther with 'If Only for One Night.'" They heard the sound of the music in the background as the mellow voice of Luther Vandross began singing the words their hearts felt but could not speak.

Both refrained from looking at each other, afraid to show the feelings they were trying desperately to hide. Not a word was spoken because the words of the song were so intoxicating it made them afraid of what would come from their lips. For a brief moment, their hearts were free.

"You are greatly missed, my brother," said the voice when the song was over. "You can be angry with the one you love and someone can put on Luther, and instantly you forget you are mad. All you want to do is make up."

As they pulled into the complex, they both felt a little relieved that they would be able to escape the yearning in their bodies.

"We're here!" Roni broke the awkward silence as she parked the Volvo that had been her mother's car.

"And in one piece too," Ryan teased as Roni gave a fake look of shock.

"Thanks, friend," they both laughed as they got out of the car.

"I'll help you carry this stuff in." Ryan went to the trunk getting things out, not wanting the evening to end.

"Thanks." Roni went to the trunk to assist with the food. She carried a box on her hip as if it were a toddler as she fumbled with her keys. Roni prayed she didn't drop them forcing her to bend down and pick them up.

Opening the door to her apartment with little pillows on the love seat and a small table for two in the dining area next to the kitchen, she felt relief. "Just set it on the counter. I will put it away in a minute," she instructed Ryan.

He did what she asked as she opened the fridge, moving things around to make room. Ryan watched her squat down as she restructured the shelves for the bowls. The light from the refrigerator glowed on her legs showing the line on her thigh where her shorts had tightened from her squatting. She rose up, bending at the waist, and looked back at him; Ryan then gave her the dishes he had just brought in from the car.

Her beauty was so alluring he couldn't breathe. Each time she looked back, he handed her a different dish until he got to the small bowl of cobbler Aunt Betty had set aside for him. "Oh, no this is mine. Aunt Betty said so," he taunted her with a mischievous grin.

"Hey, how did you get that?"

"Aunt Betty saved it for me," he teased her with the bowl.

"Not fair!" Roni lunged for the bowl.

Ryan being at least four inches taller than Roni held the bowl over her head as she tried to grab it. Standing on her toes, she tried to pull his arm down feeling the strong muscles. Her fingertips were remembering each line as they traced down from his wrist to his elbow.

His arm was on fire as her fingers slid across his skin. Both laughed at how funny it was to pretend the cobbler was so important. They knew it was only a reason to be together longer.

During their antics, Roni lost her footing falling into Ryan's chest. "You alright?"

"I'm fine," she told him still laughing at how silly they were acting.

"Let me see," he lifted her chin to look at her nose but only saw her eyes looking back at him. Before he could stop, he drew her closer, lowering his head to kiss the lips he could no longer deny himself. His hand was in the small of her back holding her tight. Without thinking, he put the bowl on the counter freeing his hand to stroke her hair as he kissed her deeply.

Her hand rose up to his face feeling the light stubble as she slid her thumb over his cheekbone. For a moment, they were lost in each other. Then as if awakening from a dream, they both stepped back like children caught touching something forbidden.

Embarrassed by allowing his desire to control him, Ryan paced from the kitchen into the dining area. Roni felt equally uncomfortable that she had shown her vulnerable side and folded her arms, not knowing what to do with them.

"Roni, I'm sorry," Ryan stumbled with his words. "I shouldn't have done that."

"It's okay, we've both had a long day." Roni tried not to look in his eyes for fear of being in his arms again.

"I better go." He started for the door but his feet felt like they were encased in cement and he couldn't move. Looking back at her, he realized he was only sorry that he waited so long to kiss her. Her lips were so sweet and moist he asked himself why he had waited.

Afraid to look up, Roni was nibbling on her thumb as she rocked on her feet. She turned her head away from him because she knew his eyes were on her. *What am I doing?* Roni was asking herself knowing she had to look at him eventually. Taking a deep breath, she looked at him standing in front of her. His arms were at his side as he stared at her. Looking away was not an option for her now because the test of wills was over.

"No, I'm not sorry," were the only words Ryan uttered before he pulled her into his arms, feeling her warm soft body as he began to kiss her again. Holding her face, he looked into her eyes and they weren't saying stop. He felt her heart pounding and it was getting hard for them both to breathe.

Again, his lips found hers as their kisses grew stronger to the point of pain. Sliding his hands down her body, he lifted her up by her waist. He held her as she wrapped her arms around his neck and legs around his waist. She ran her fingers through his hair as they kissed each other with an obsession.

He felt the rapid beating of her heart; soon he realized it was his own. Roni loosened her legs from his waist as she lowered her feet back onto the floor. Moving her hands to his face, she held him as she backed away.

Ryan didn't know how to react because both of them were still breathing heavily from the kisses. Staring into his eyes Roni knew what she was feeling, but was it the right thing? Her hands began to move from his face down to his neck then to his chest as if she were inspecting a statue for imperfections.

Ryan searched her face for an answer as he tried to pull her closer, but she wouldn't allow it. Instead, her hands slid down his shoulders reaching for his hands. Bringing them up to her lips, she kissed them gently. The feel of her moist lips only increased his desire, sending fire into his soul.

She saw he wanted her as much as she wanted him. Again, she began to back away holding his large hands in her small ones until she was at arm's length from him. Their eyes were fixated on each other, not moving from their stare as she guided him down the hall.

Unable to withstand being that far from her any longer, he lifted her into his arms, carrying her to the bedroom where he gently set her in the middle of the bed while he continued kissing her lips. Crawling up to meet her there, both were on their knees as they kissed and caressed each other.

Roni reached for the tail of his shirt as she began to remove it. Ryan, in a quick motion, took it off tossing it aside. Rubbing her hands over his stomach, she felt the muscles as they tightened from anticipation. Roni buried her head into his chest; she kissed it softly.

Ryan gently peeled her tank top from her body, tossing it aside. He felt the soft skin as his hands explored her body searching for the snaps on her bra to release her firm breasts. He saw their beautiful shape and color from the moonlight seeping in through the window; cupping them in his massive hands, he moved his head down, kissing them gently as a whimper came from her lips.

Moving his lips up to meet hers again, he lowered her onto the bed. From her lips to her neck, to her breast to her stomach, he enjoyed the sweet smell of lilacs on her skin. Reaching for the button on the waistband of her shorts, he unbuttoned then unzipped them slowly. He exposed her green panties with the cartoon turtles, which gave Ryan a little smile as he pulled them down past her thighs, her legs, and removed them with extreme care.

She lay naked on the bed with her body glowing from the sweat stemming from the heat of their bodies. He could not help but slide his hand up her thigh as he leaned in to kiss her deeply. His body was hard against hers as he held her in his arms, taking in every inch of her. Moving her hands down his body, she felt his firm buttocks as they tightened from her touch.

She rose suddenly, sitting up in the bed causing Ryan to back away. He feared he had gone too far but she slid her hand in the waistband of his shorts to assist him in their removal. Ryan was relieved that he hadn't offended her, allowing her to continue while his body tingled at her touch.

They explored each other's bodies as if they were looking for secret treasure. Gently, Ryan positioned himself between her legs, as he anticipated the pleasure to unfold. Entering her, both released a moan of bliss from their lips. Like the waves of the ocean, their bodies moved in a rhythm only they could feel.

With each thrust, Roni felt him growing inside her. Ryan had never felt the vibration of a woman's body, until now. It became harder with each thrust for him to control himself, but he didn't want it to end. Her body was on fire as she felt each ridge of him inside her until their bodies could take no more. There came an explosion of their souls, as they became one, releasing a loud cry from their lips.

They didn't speak because no words were needed. Wrapping their legs around each other as they fell asleep, they clung to each other attempting to make sure the other would be there when they awakened.

* * * *

It hadn't been easy pretending for the past week that everything was the same between them. Roni didn't want to let the others know about the change in their relationship yet. With so little time before graduation, she wanted to concentrate on the upcoming ceremony. So it was kept as their little secret between them until after graduation.

They were in the student hall picking up their cap and gowns for graduation when Roni began to feel uneasy. She knew all of the families except for Ryan's and that frightened her, even though Ryan had changed from an uncomfortable white boy to a man with whom she had fallen in love.

Even before she came to know him, Ryan had never been disrespectful to her, but seemed uncomfortable at times when they were on campus together. Roni had never worried about what others thought; having grown up in a diverse neighborhood, she always had friends of different races or cultures. Ryan on the other hand grew up in a small town where everyone knew each other and all looked alike.

Ryan was also worried because he knew how some people really felt about those that were different; some were in his own family. Like Roni, he was concerned about his family coming to graduation, but for different reasons. He didn't want them to embarrass him in front of his friends, especially Roni.

Peter, his father, was a quiet man much like Ryan's grandfather. He wasn't as tall as his son, which gave Ryan a reason to tease him about having to look up to him. Hearing that, Pete would give a simple smile before going back to whatever he was doing.

The times Ryan remembered most when growing up were fishing with his dad in the lake behind his grandparents' home. That was their special time together. They talked about anything from cars, to hunting, and even girls. Pete always felt a little uneasy when the subject of women was discussed. Ryan sometimes brought it up so he could watch that look on Pete's face. Mostly Pete would mumble a few words because he didn't know much about them. The one rule he always shared with Ryan was just to stay out of their way.

With his mother, Helen, Ryan knew why that was his father's advice. Helen, being a kindergarten teacher, would sometimes treat everyone like they were five, but she meant well. Her personality was a little rough, even if her heart was in the right place. Always giving advice where none was needed made many enemies for Helen and she definitely had one in her mother-in-law. They couldn't be in a room more than five minutes without a snippy remark from Pearl.

Ryan's grandmother, Pearl, was an exceptional woman. She owned a beauty shop and knew more about what was going on in town than anyone. Pearl had a boisterous personality and told it like it was. If you didn't want her opinion, you had better not ask for it. Of course, sometimes she just volunteered it.

Ryan loved his grandmother because she played ball with him when he was growing up, and for a woman her age, she had a mean fastball. She taught Ryan how to slide into home without being tagged and how to watch a batter for the direction of a ball's path. "It's all in the eyes," she told Ryan. Her grandson was the love of her life. He was precious to her, being the only child of her only child, and he sported her green eyes.

He didn't know how his family would react to Roni, but he knew he loved her. After all, his family loved him and wanted him to be happy. Now they might be a little surprised at first but would grow to love her as much as he did. Never in his life had he ever met a woman like her. She had been a true friend to him and that was hard to find. Most people wanted something from you, but not Roni. The only thing she wanted was honesty in return.

Honesty had been the foundation of their relationship, because they could talk about anything. Even if they disagreed on something, they could at least hear the other's point of view. In some cases, even understand why they thought that way. It didn't mean the other's ideas were right, but they saw it from a different perspective.

Before he met Roni, he had never actually been around black people. Yeah, there were a couple on his teams growing up, but they never socialized outside of practice or a game. Since he had met Roni, his life had become richer. He had met people of different races and cultures and they all wanted the same things: Just to live their lives in peace, raise their families, go to work, and build their American dream.

Looking over at Ryan, Roni asked, "You got everything?" while trying on her gown.

"Yeah, it looks like it," he smiled at her. "I can't believe we are graduating!" After saying those words, reality sank in. *What are we going to do?* he thought to himself. He and Roni hadn't talked about that. There was a job lined up for him back home and Roni was going back to New York. With so many miles between them, how were they going to continue their relationship?

Roni knew what was going through his head, because like him she was wondering about the future of their relationship. Seeing her about to speak, Ryan looked at her with honesty in his heart. "We will figure it out."

Taking off her graduation gown and draping it across her arm, Roni said, "I know we will, but let's just try to get through graduation first and work on that later," hugging each other before they walked to the door.

Coming out of the student hall, the brightness of the sun blinded them as their eyes adjusted to the change from artificial to natural light.

"Ryan!" his name came from a familiar voice. *It can't be*, he thought to himself. The look of shock was in his eyes as he looked at Roni. Confused, she searched them not understanding the look he was giving her. "Ryan!" came again, closer this time from a young attractive woman who was coming toward them. His face turned pale as fear showed in his eyes. Roni looked at him, feeling unsure and somehow angry for a reason yet to be determined.

"Roni," not knowing how to continue, Ryan managed to force her name from his lips. Before he could say any more, the young woman leaped toward him almost knocking him down. As he tried to catch his balance, she kissed him. "I missed you so much!" Now understanding the look in his eyes, Roni's heart sank as Ryan struggled to regain his footing.

He searched for the words to explain. "Roni," he fumbled, but before he could continue with an explanation, the young woman turned to Roni and said, "Hi, I'm Amy, his fiancée," waving the diamond ring in her face.

Roni looked at Ryan in disbelief, but tried to tone down the hurt and betrayal she felt. Part of her wanted to lash out at them both, but Amy had done nothing to her. With the grace of an Oscar-winning actress she turned to Ryan and smiled. "You never told me you were engaged. Congratulations."

Ryan looked uncomfortable, but tried to reassure Roni with his eyes. Roni looked in his direction but showed no emotion. Her demeanor was cordial but he saw the hurt in her eyes as she looked past him at Amy. All he could think was, *please look at me, Roni*, because he needed her to see him.

"Well, I'll let you two catch up." Roni had to get out of there because it had become hard to control her emotions. "See you later," she told him as she turned to walk away with her eyes stinging from the tears she fought to keep back.

Ryan watched as she walked away wanting to run after her, but she needed to be alone. He knew he had to explain and would call her later after he got things settled with Amy. *Why was she there?* he thought, before seeing his parents coming toward them.

Waving her arms frantically Amy yelled, "I found him!"

Feeling embarrassed by her behavior, Ryan broke away and walked toward his parents. Looking sternly at his mother he asked, "Why did you bring her? Never mind!" he scowled, walking past them toward his apartment.

"Pick up, Roni, pick up," he softly spoke to himself as he called her cell phone for the tenth time. "Please, Roni, talk to me," he begged to her voicemail. "I really need to talk to you. Please call me back." Closing his cell phone, he knew she wouldn't call back, but he needed to explain.

Roni heard the phone ringing, but refused to answer. How could she have been so stupid? She should have listened to her head because the heart was a liar by design.

Why had he gone after her? She thought of him as a friend. How could he have lied to her like that? Why lie to her? What did he have to gain? Remembering that night, she scolded herself, "You are so stupid."

The master of ceremonies read from his list announcing the names of the graduates as they crossed the stage to receive their diplomas. Ansari glanced back at Ryan with a happy grin of accomplishment. Undoubtedly, Roni hadn't told him what had happened the day before.

Ryan forced a smile because his heart was hurting. After thirty-two phone calls and twenty-five text messages, Roni had never responded. Looking through the Liberal Arts graduates, he searched for her face but couldn't find it.

"Veronica A. Somers, graduating Magna Cum Laude," the dean called her name as she walked across the stage to accept her diploma. Ryan almost didn't recognize her, because she had straightened her hair. Smiling, she walked by the different professors who once had taught her. The usher standing at the bottom assisted her down the steps. Walking by, Ryan saw her face but she never looked in his direction. She and Ansari gave each other the thumb's up as she passed by. "Please look at me, Roni," he silently mouthed as she continued to her seat.

He couldn't look at her because she was behind him, but he was hoping to see her as he passed the Liberal Arts graduates to receive his diploma. Rising from his seat, he began to search the crowd for her face not caring if anyone saw him anymore. *Look up, Roni!* he wished, as she pretended to read her program.

Roni could feel him staring at her, but the thought made her sick. The hurt was too deep and the wounds too fresh. *The first time I allowed someone into my world, he destroyed it*, she told herself for the hundredth time since yesterday.

That was one of Roni's faults, she was far too critical of herself, not understanding that the heart could sometimes be blind, dumb, and stupid, but it didn't mean it was wrong. She looked up and caught his stare. Damn! she thought as she turned her head to escape his gaze. No matter how hard she tried, her eyes met his. Her heart was beating rapidly. The person behind Ryan had to nudge him so he would keep the line moving. Their eyes remained locked as he looked over his shoulder to burn her beauty into his memory.

The campus quickly filled with graduates and their families taking pictures. Each were happy to be finished with college, but saddened because they might never see each other again. Roni and Ryan had additional reasons for their sadness.

Ryan saw Ansari after they marched out of the auditorium, giving each other a hug. Abe, Felipe, and Effie soon joined them. "Where is Roni?" Felipe asked as he looked around for her.

"She probably hasn't gotten out yet," Effie said, adding, "She was behind me in seating assignments."

"Don't worry, she's coming; probably had to get her camera," Abe chimed in as he laughed with the others.

Holding on to her cap, she came from the auditorium with a digital camera in hand. "Hello, graduates!" she shouted while hurrying to get there for their final picture on campus. Seeing Ryan, she sighed but needed to pretend everything was fine. How could she let the others know what a fool she had been? They all looked up to her and saw Ryan as a friend. Besides this was their last time together and she wasn't going to bring drama to their special day.

Unlike Roni, Ryan couldn't conceal his sadness, but he tried to smile and laugh as they got in line for a picture. Roni looked around to find someone to take the picture for them. An underclassman she knew came by so Roni asked him to take the picture for her.

Getting on the end and smiling, she stood next to Abe. "Move in closer," requested the amateur photographer. "Wait, you need to put the ladies in closer," he instructed as he waved his hand for them to rearrange. Shifting, they lined up Ansari, Effie, Felipe, Ryan, Roni, and Abe. Finally getting into position, they all wrapped their arms around each other and smiled for the camera.

"Perfect!" the photographer said. Walking over to give Roni her camera back, he received one from each of the others. They all gave a jovial laugh as they stood together for one last time to make sure they all got a picture of their college friends. After the last camera was returned, they all hugged saying their goodbyes, each promising to keep in touch, before they returned to their families.

"Roni!" she heard Ryan calling her name. She turned to look at him. Feeling the tears in her eyes, she tried to look away but he lightly touched her cheek, forcing her to look back at him. "Roni, I'm sorry about yesterday," he searched her eyes for what she was feeling. "Please let me explain."

"Don't worry about it. I will be fine," she lied to him as well as herself. Seeing his fiancée coming toward them, she used it as an opportunity to leave. Reaching up to hug him she kissed him on the cheek and whispered in his ear, "Have a great life."

Her hand on his face burned into his cheek as it slid across his skin. The smell of lilac lingered as she released his chin and he saw the tear roll down her cheek. Before he could stop her, she turned and hurried away. "Roni!" he called after her, but she did not return.

CHAPTER 4

The sounds of chatter as people talked on cell phones or to each other was heard when Ryan entered the office building for his interview. Looking down at his watch, he saw he was early. *Great! I have forty-five minutes before my interview.* Holding onto his portfolio, he walked toward the elevators.

Checking the directory, Ryan began to wonder why he was there as he watched people go about their daily business. He could hear his mom telling him he would be all alone in New York. Although she meant well, Ryan knew it was time for him to take his own path in life and Virginia was no longer the place he wanted to be. If he succeeded that would be wonderful, but if he failed, he would just get back up and start all over again.

Those mental pep talks weren't exactly working. Maybe he should just go back home to his job and be satisfied. Unfortunately, that was no longer an option for him, because he wasn't the same since Roni.

Ryan thought about her every day. Then he would be saddened because of the way it had ended between them. He could still feel her soft hand on his face when he thought of her, her moist lips as she kissed his cheek and whispered, "Have a great life." It had been so final and the words were so haunting.

Walking to the elevator, he sighed, trying to shake off the sad feelings. Knowing he couldn't hide his true emotions, Ryan tried to find a happy thought before ruining his chances with the interview.

Standing with the group waiting for the elevator doors to open, he smiled, thinking they were like cattle being herded. That thought gave his spirit a little boost while he laughed to himself as the doors slowly opened.

The occupants began to exit; some were silent while others chatted. Looking up he saw what he thought was a familiar face, but the hair was shorter and lighter in color. She was talking to a tall man standing beside her. Although he only saw her profile, the woman looked so familiar.

He couldn't take his eyes off her as she walked by. Her voice was haunting as she laughed with her companion, then said, "You are so stupid." The sound of her voice gave Ryan chills and before he could control himself, he asked, "Roni?" Ryan felt a little foolish that he spoke to a complete stranger.

The woman dressed in a black double-breasted pantsuit wearing a black overcoat slowly turned to face him. At first, the expression on her face was that of annoyance over a stranger speaking to her, but seemed to lighten once she saw his face. "Ryan," she said as she walked toward him with her arms stretched for a hug. "How have you been? What are you doing here?" she asked then laughed at not giving him a chance to answer the first question.

"Been doing well. And you?" he answered nervously, not sure if she was still angry with him. Hugging Roni, he fought with himself to release her. Stepping away from the elevator, he told her, "You look great."

"Thanks, so do you."

The tall man approached them looking suspiciously at Ryan. "Roni, I'll get the car," he told her before walking to the building entrance.

Ryan felt awkward. "I'm sorry. I didn't mean to intrude."

Roni looked at him, not understanding his reason for an apology and then finally realized. "Now I don't know about Virginia, but we don't do inbreeding." She began to laugh at the look on his face.

"Oh, that's your brother," Ryan felt embarrassed. "I thought you and he were, you know dating or something. My bad," both smiled at his use of slang.

"What are you doing here?" she asked again because he never gave her an answer.

"I have a job interview with Pegasus Designs and Construction on the eighth floor."

"Great company. I've seen their work. They mainly do historical renovations, right?"

"Yes, and some commercial designing." Ryan wanted to impress her.

"Sounds interesting. How long will you be in town?"

"I have this interview today and if it goes well I will have to stay through the weekend for a follow up on Monday." Ryan saw her brother trying to get her attention. Although he didn't want to let her go, he knew it was no longer an option. "I think your brother is trying to get your attention," he told her.

"Here," reaching into her messenger bag she pulled out her business card, writing on the back, "this is my cell number. Call me after your interview and let me know how it went. Maybe we can grab dinner later and catch up. Good luck, don't forget to call me," she smiled like she did before he hurt her.

Ryan watched as she scuttled to the door, not taking his eyes off her until she got in the car with her brother and drove away.

"Who was that?" Laurence asked as he maneuvered into traffic.

"Ryan Grant. We graduated from college together," Roni said, still smiling, thinking how great it was to see him. Even though they ended on bad terms, it still felt good seeing him again. They were young and stupid back then, and both had made mistakes. The ringing of her phone interrupted her thoughts as she fumbled to answer it. "Hello."

"Just wanted to make sure I had the right number," Ryan laughed before hanging up.

Roni couldn't help but laugh at his little joke. Noticing Laurence looking at her, she explained, "It was Ryan being stupid," with a silly grin on her face that she couldn't wipe off.

"Something I should know about here?"

"No," she shook her head coming back to reality about Ryan. After all, he was married now, probably with children. She was just thrilled to see him. It would be nice to catch up, because so much had happened since that day on campus. They had both matured and might be able to put the past behind them.

Roni reasoned that she had too many things going on in her life right now and she really didn't have time to spend with him and his wife if he got the job. With Ryan being such a brilliant architect, he most likely would be hired. Well, at least she hoped he would.

Looking over at Laurence, she asked, "Think we should invite Thuy, Abe, and maybe do dinner at Shondra's? She sings tonight, doesn't she?" Roni's mind was making plans, as her fingers were dialing numbers. "Abe," she paused, "guess who is in town?" not giving him a chance to answer. "Ryan Grant." She listened to Abe talk excitedly. "You want to meet with us later for dinner? Great, I was just asking Laurence if Shondra's would be good, what do you think?" Again, she listened to his answer. "I will say around six, will that work for you? Okay, we will see you then."

"Abe knows this guy?"

"Yeah, he hung out with us during our last semester of college." She wanted to give Laurence very little information about her past with Ryan. "He was one of the students I tutored back then. After his grades went up, he still hung out. It's kind of funny, because he was like a cat, once you fed him, he wouldn't leave." Both laughed at the comparison.

The car grew silent as Roni's mind went down memory lane. She remembered all the details of their past, but had tried hard to forget some. No matter how she looked at it, their lives were intertwined.

Ryan's interview went well, prompting them to ask him back for a follow up on Monday with the director. Now if that went well he would be in New York soon with Roni. Good thing she gave him her cell number; even if he didn't get the job he would still be able to repair their relationship. It might have to be long distance for a while, but it was better than no contact at all.

Pulling out his cell phone, he called her but it went straight to voicemail. Was she having second thoughts about dinner tonight? The tone for a message beeped and he decided to leave one. "Hey, Roni, this is Ryan. Give me a call back when you get a chance." He ended the call, whispering to himself, "Please."

Exiting the building, he signaled that he needed a taxi to the attendant and one was promptly hailed for him. "Steinmark Hotel, please," he told the driver. Feeling the phone's vibration in his pocket, he frantically retrieved it. "Hello?"

"Hey, sorry I didn't answer; I was on another call. How did it go?" A little apprehension was in Roni's voice as she asked.

"It went well I think. I have to stay over the weekend for the group interview on Monday," he sighed feeling a little afraid about his chances.

"Why the long sigh? You will do fine."

"I know, I shouldn't look for the worst." He tried to change the tone of his voice. One of the things he loved about her was she always tried to encourage him.

"Where are you staying?" she asked

"I'm at the Steinmark in midtown."

"I know where that is. It's not far from where you are now, about eight blocks I think. Be ready around five thirty. I will call you when I'm close so you can come down to the lobby."

"Okay, sounds good, see you then." He felt much better now and it came across in his voice.

Hearing the change Roni just giggled softly. "Okay, bye!"

He was excited they would be spending time together because he had so much to tell her. Things he had waited over four years to say. Even though Roni didn't seem angry anymore, he still wanted to apologize for the hurt he had caused her. They say time healed all wounds. If that were true, why did he still feel the pain in his heart? In time maybe he would be able to right the wrong he had done to her, but only time would tell.

Ryan wanted everything to be perfect so he had a fresh shower, a clean shave, and put on a little dab of cologne to make him smell extra special. Wearing his black slacks with a smoke-gray mock turtleneck sweater, he located his shoes then sat in a chair near the window.

Looking out he noticed the city looked so gray. Sort of like when you watched a movie and the colors are dark, not showing much life. Even with the dark cast to the sky, New York was full of life. No wonder Roni loved it so much. He had always heard it was a cruel place, but there are cruel people everywhere; no one place had claim on all of them. Smiling at that thought, he heard his phone ring. "Hello!"

"Hi, we are about four blocks from you. Come down and we will meet you out front."

We, he thought, but refused to let it show in his voice. "Okay, see you in a few." Tonight he was going to spend time with Roni and it didn't matter if it wasn't alone. After all, he would be there through the weekend and they would have time to talk alone later.

Walking past the mirror, he took one last look at himself. Grabbing his overcoat, he headed for the door.

Ending the call Roni had a lost look on her face, not knowing what to feel at that moment. Everything had gone so wrong back then, but she needed to get past it. Their separation could have been positive for them, because now they could be friends again.

As the taxi pulled up to the curb, Roni began to look for Ryan in the lobby. Not seeing him, she asked the driver to keep the meter running while she called him, but before the call went through, she saw him. He was more handsome than she remembered. Maybe it was because they both had matured and were no longer wide-eyed kids. She opened the door, motioning for him. "Over here!" Seeing her, he smiled like a teenager on his first date.

Giving each other a hug, they got into the taxi. "Shondra's on 758 W 145th Street," she gave directions to the driver. "You will love this place. One of my best friends since I was in diapers is the owner and she sings there. Hopefully tonight it won't be too crowded, but she is expecting us."

"Sounds terrific," he said losing his thoughts as he looked at her. "What did you decide to do with your degree in art?" Ryan managed to ask.

"Well, I decided not to do the gallery thing, but opened a little boutique with my own clothing line."

"Wow, that sounds like fun. How is it going?"

"Doing well, had to expand once since I opened and added an online store," she explained feeling very proud of the boutique. Switching the conversation back to Ryan, Roni didn't want to ask, but she had to know. "How is married life?"

Ryan knew that question was going to come up, but really hadn't thought of how he would answer. "Well, that is a little complicated because we didn't get married."

Roni didn't know how to respond to that answer. Should she ask what happened or just allow him to elaborate? "Okay, that was a peculiar answer," she said as she tried to figure out what else to say.

Seeing her uneasiness, Ryan tried to make her feel more at ease. "Long story; I will have to tell you when we have more time." He changed the subject because it was making him feel guilty. "Have you kept in touch with the others since graduation?"

"Yes, all of them." Remembering she hadn't contacted him, she added, "As a matter of fact Abe will be meeting us tonight. I invited him, I hope you don't mind." Searching his eyes, she looked for a sign of his true feelings.

"Abe's going to be there?" Hearing that bit of news made him feel as he had back in college. "It's going to be good to see him."

"He was ecstatic when I told him you were in New York. I'm surprised he hasn't called me asking where we are." They laughed at Abe's excitement.

"Well, how is Ansari?"

"He and Effie are doing well and expecting their first child in the spring."

"What? They are expecting a child? Now you have to back up and tell me what's going on with that."

"Yes, after graduation Ansari took a job with the same company where my uncle works in Atlanta, and Effie was teaching there, so those pretend sparks became real. There was always something sneaky between them, but with Felipe being our friend, they never pursued it. It was so funny when Ansari told him that he and Effie were seeing each other."

Felipe's response still tickled Roni. Putting on her fake Caribbean accent, she mimicked, "God be with you my brother. You will need Him with that devil woman." Both began to laugh hysterically, even the driver joined in.

"Felipe didn't make the wedding but gave them a honeymoon package at the resort he is managing in Barbados. They had a great time. Felipe took them to secret places on the island only the locals knew."

"It didn't bother him that they were getting together?"

"No, Felipe and Effie were never in a committed relationship. They just gravitated to each other because they shared Caribbean roots. Unfortunately that wasn't enough to make a real relationship for them, but it was enough to keep us all friends."

Knowing how he felt about Roni, Ryan wasn't sure he could wish her well with Abe or Felipe. He hoped he would be a better man than that, but right now, he knew it would break his heart.

The taxicab pulled over to the curb, stopping in front of the restaurant. "We are here!" she told Ryan and motioned for him to open the door. "You are going to love this place, I promise." Excitedly Roni paid the driver as Ryan stood on the sidewalk to wait for her.

He could hear the chatter from inside and the aroma of the Creole cuisine made his stomach rumble with anticipation of the flavors. Ryan could only think of one thing that excited him more. "Come on!" Roni put her arm through his as they walked to the door.

Once inside, you not only heard but also saw the enthusiasm on the people's faces. After checking their coats, they maneuvered between patrons as they passed the bar. The beautiful architecture was breathtaking as Ryan looked at the brick walls and the mahogany bar in the center of the room.

Some of the patrons were sitting at the bar still in their business attire getting a drink before they went home. Definitely the Wall Street crowd, Ryan surmised as they gave orders to the bartender. He was well adapted to them, because most of the time the bartender had their order before they could finish telling him what they wanted.

"Hey, Roni!" A very handsome man shouted from the bar waving at them.

"Hi," Roni yelled back hoping that would satisfy him, but it didn't. He wove around the patrons as he walked toward them. Being her usual charming self, Roni gave him a hug. "Greg, how have you been?" she asked without real sentiment.

"When are you going to let me take you out again?"

"Ah," she looked for the words to answer his question.

Ryan saw she needed a way out. "Honey they are waiting for us." Looking at Greg, he said, "Excuse us."

"Thank you," she told Ryan as they walked toward the back where the restaurant was located. "How did you know I needed to get away from him?"

"Well, that shitty grin on your face kind of gave you away," Ryan laughed as she lightly shoved him. During their playful exchange he noticed that her wrap sweater dress fit nicely with her leggings and black boots. The dress complimented her figure as it rested mid-thigh, showing enough skin with the plunging neckline to entice any man in the room.

"Ryan, over here!" He heard a voice coming from the other side of the restaurant. Looking in the direction of the voice, he saw a familiar face. Standing there all smiles, it was Abe. He didn't give them a chance to come to the table before he scurried across the floor, arms stretched for a hug. "How have you been?"

"Great and you?" Ryan hugged him as if he had just found his long lost brother. Abe hadn't changed a bit, but no longer wore his kippah. He had thickened up a little, which matured his look. Now he looked manlier than when they were in college.

"Doing well. I never thought we would see you again." Abe was still in shock that he was there.

"I didn't think so either, but was lucky enough to run into Roni this morning."

"She phoned me right after she saw you. At first, I thought she was playing a hoax. Then she asked me to join you for dinner and I knew it was true."

"Come on, guys, you are blocking the passageway." Roni ushered them back to the table.

"So how did the job interview go?"

"Went well, I have a second interview on Monday." Ryan sat down in the chair next to Abe. "I should get a verdict a couple of days after that."

"How do you stand the pressure of waiting? I would be tied up in knots by now."

"I guess I am just too excited right now to feel the pressure." He looked at Roni as she sat next to him at the table. Ryan would probably be that way, if he weren't concentrating on Roni.

They heard the voice of someone speaking Vietnamese and all heads turned toward the entrance of the dining area. A petite woman with dark straight hair was waving her arms in the air. She seemed to be talking to herself as she hurriedly walked toward them.

"Is he after you again, Thuy?" Roni jokingly asked.

"As always, why can't he understand that not every woman wants him?" This time she spoke minus the flamboyant Vietnamese accent. Seeing others at the table, she apologized, "I'm so rude, how is everyone?" she acknowledged them before taking the seat beside Roni.

"Ryan, this is Thuy. We've been friends since kindergarten."

Thuy peeped around Roni looking strangely at Ryan, making him feel a little uncomfortable. "Hi, nice to meet you." She finally gave a broad smile and he saw her bright eyes. They reminded him of a deer in headlights, but it complimented her look. Her straight jet-black hair was almost blue in the light and her features were cartoonish in appearance. She was the kind of woman that you underestimated because most did not see her as serious.

"Ryan and I went to college together," Roni explained.

"Oh," her face relaxed, "I thought you were that guy she told me about that was trying to push up on her." She instantly became friendlier toward him.

"I didn't tell you? Girl, I had to pull the split personality routine on him." Roni and Thuy giggled like teenage girls in class, losing Ryan in the conversation as he looked on.

Seeing his confusion, Abe injected, "Trust me, you don't want to know," as he looked on laughing at them.

"What up, my people?" Laurence shouted as he walked up to the table. Looking at Ryan, he extended his hand. "Thanks to my sister we haven't formally met. I'm Laurence, Roni's little brother," he introduced himself, while he ignored the look of sarcasm on Roni's face.

Ryan could see the resemblance but thought he must look more like his father. He was a tall man with deep dark eyes. In some ways, he had a Latin look to him with the neatly trimmed mustache and goatee he was sporting. Like Roni, Laurence exuded confidence and it showed in the way he carried himself. "Abe, my man, what's up?" Then he looked over at Thuy. "How is my baby girl doing tonight?"

"Oh please, Laurence, you have too many women in your life," she blushed with her answer, because Laurence was strikingly handsome. When he walked in a room, the women took a second look.

"Oh, but you are my main lady and you know this." He flashed a smile that even men envied as he kissed Thuy's hand.

"Will you two stop that? I am getting ill." Roni made a sick face as they all laughed. Watching them interact, Ryan thought to himself, *she has the greatest friends*.

Coming up behind Roni and Thuy, a woman squeezed them in a group hug. "Hi, Luc wanted me to find out if you had arrived," she told them with her beautiful African accent. "He has prepared a special menu for you tonight," she announced with a beautiful smile. Her dark mahogany skin glowed under the light and her eyes danced like stars in the sky. Looking at Ryan, she said, "Hello, I am Shondra," extending her hand to him with a warm smile. "You must be Ryan; Roni told me you are one of her friends from college. Thank you so much for coming."

"Thank you for having me." Ryan was in awe of her beauty and loving nature. He didn't know why but being around Roni with her friends or family, you felt so much genuine love from them. What made them so loving toward each other and strangers? Ryan really didn't care what it was, he just enjoyed being among them.

"I will get a server for your drinks," Shondra motioned to a young man. "Chris will be serving you tonight. I have to go prepare for my performance, but Luc will be out to greet you shortly." She blew kisses toward the table as she left. Watching her walk away, Ryan saw why she was glowing, because she was expecting a baby.

"She's performing tonight?" Ryan asked.

"Yes, she's an awesome jazz singer." Everyone agreed with Roni.

Shondra's talent as a singer was how she and Luc met. Both worked at the same jazz club, Shondra as a backup singer and Luc as a cook. With Luc, it was love at first sight, but Shondra had to be persuaded. Luc was at least an inch shorter than Shondra in her bare feet, which made her shy away from him. For Luc, it just increased the challenge.

It took a little time but she couldn't resist his Cajun accent and Creole charm. Shondra learned a wise lesson in meeting Luc; he was everything she wanted in a man. She thanked God daily for him, because in the past she hadn't been that lucky with men. Shondra would have missed this one if she had allowed his height to stand in their way.

"Hello, my family," came a strong Cajun accent from a man under five feet, eight inches, but to hear him you would think he was twelve feet tall. He was a comical looking man with a smile one would see on a can of soup for marketing. With his bushy mustache, you only saw the smile in his eyes.

Roni and Thuy hurried over, giving him a big hug. "Now ladies, I know I am a great catch, but this crawfish is already boiled," Luc teased as he received the attention. They all laughed together knowing that comment was coming before they approached him.

"I see we have a new member to our family here. Hello, welcome my friend," he shook hands with Ryan as the appetizers appeared. "Sit back and enjoy." He stretched his arms as if he were trying to hug the whole table.

The young server, Chris, came out with a tray carrying three appetizers of fried chicken wings with Luc's secret BBQ sauce, fried oysters with a spicy sauce, and Roni's favorite hot spinach artichoke dip with fresh sliced vegetables. You could smell the heat of the spices as the servers placed them on the table with the plates. Roni could see Ryan was really enjoying the food so she leaned over and advised, "Save room, Luc has more to come." Seeing Ryan was eating the spinach-dip she giggled to herself.

"How did your case go?" Abe asked Thuy.

"Not so well. This is his first offense and he is only fourteen. I don't want him to end up a criminal in training. Right now he has a chance to turn his life around," she sighed.

Laurence saw she was beating herself up again. "Thuy, you can't save them all."

"I know, but these kids don't deserve jail, well, not all of them. Some are just in the wrong place in life making bad decisions. If he is sent to a juvenile facility, he might end up hard and I don't want that to happen. His mother is working two jobs just trying to keep her head afloat with three other children to support. Hopefully I can get the judge to give him probation and get him in a school program with community service." Getting depressed, she put her napkin on the table.

"Is he from the neighborhood?" Laurence asked with concern.

Picking up an oyster and getting some sauce on it she continued, "Yes, I think that is why it bothers me so. He was getting good grades in school and got involved in a burglary with some friends. Just one of those things, I guess."

"Come on, Thuy, eat. We will figure this out later," Roni told her trying to change the mood. She had worked with Thuy in the past, trying to keep others out of jail. Sometimes it worked and sometimes it didn't, but nonetheless they always tried to give back to the community.

They all turned to a happier conversation, laughing and enjoying each other while the servers came back to the table with their entree. The feast of red beans and rice, shrimp Creole, and Cajun chicken pasta hot from the kitchen was placed on the table. Each grabbed a plate helping themselves from each of the dishes on the table. You could see they were all getting full, but couldn't stop eating the delicious meal Luc had prepared.

Ryan's pants were starting to get a little tight, but everything was so good. When he thought the end was near the servers returned to the table with dessert, the three dishes of bread pudding with a praline sauce, rum cake, and key lime pie. He was happy they were all in bite size portions; even with his being stuffed he could have eaten full portions of the desserts. "Whew! I am about to explode." They all had a cheerful laugh at Ryan because they all felt the same way.

"I told you, Luc will stuff you. He loves seeing people enjoy his cooking," Roni told Ryan.

"How is everybody tonight?" Shondra's voice was heard as she walked up to the microphone with the smooth sounds of the musicians behind her playing softly. You saw the music as it moved through her soul the closer she got to the microphone as the sounds of an angel parted from her lips. She began singing "God Bless the Child" as you would think only Ms. Billie Holiday could perform. Occasionally her hand would touch the child growing inside her as if the baby was singing along with mommy.

Luc came from the kitchen hearing his wife singing and stood there with his hand under his chin as his eyes glazed over with tears. Even the chatter of the bar had quieted as they all were swept away into the mystical voice of Shondra.

It had been a long evening and was getting close to nine o'clock as they all gathered outside the restaurant while they hailed taxis. Abe and Thuy shared a cab; since they were going in the same direction as Laurence, he joined them. That left Ryan and Roni to their own taxi. They said their goodbyes and started on the rides to their destinations.

Roni tried to give the driver directions to Ryan's hotel, but he insisted she go home first. She finally conceded and gave her address, which made Ryan happy that they were able to spend more time together.

"How do you do it?" Ryan asked.

"Do what?"

"Find all these amazing people?"

"We all grew up together. Shondra and I have known each other since birth almost and we met Thuy in kindergarten." She smiled, pleased that he liked her friends. "Thuy was picked on in school because she was smaller than the other kids so Shondra and I protected her. She didn't speak English very well and we helped with translation. It wasn't easy for them moving into Harlem, but her family had just opened a laundry here. It was definitely tough being the only Asian in class, but she wasn't alone; she had us."

"So you've known Shondra since you were in diapers? Now that woman can sing."

She smiled at his joy over hearing Shondra sing. "Yes, we were born two weeks apart. Her dad was working on a construction crew with my father when he first started doing renovations. Mawuli was a hard worker and dad really liked him. Therefore, he sponsored Shondra's father so his family could come here to live, all before we were born. Our mothers were pregnant at the same time, making us friends from the womb." They both laughed at the thought.

"Roni, you and I really need to sit down and have a real conversation about--"

Roni interrupted before he could finish his sentence. "Ryan, let's just leave that in the past and move on to being friends again."

Feeling defeated, Ryan just tried to keep their conversation going and changed to a different topic. "I thought you would be in some tomb in Egypt cataloging artifacts by now."

"Well, when I graduated those were my intentions. I didn't think I would be doing design work, but I am enjoying it. Getting to put a little of myself into the clothing line is fun," she told him as the taxi drove down her street. "Oh, here we are," she said as the driver stopped in front of a beautiful Renaissance-era home that was built before the wars.

The building was at least four stories tall and wide for a brownstone. It may have been the home of some great artist or entertainer from that period. Ryan got out of the cab looking up at the structure because that was one of the reasons he became an architect: so he could design those kinds of buildings.

"Wait here," he instructed the driver.

"You've seen me home. You don't have to walk me in," she joked with him knowing he wouldn't have it any other way.

Walking up the tall steps together, both hated that the evening was ending. "Call me when you get up in the morning. We usually go to the organic market upstate for fresh cheese and milk." She gave him a hug and kissed his cheek.

"Definitely," he told her as he ran his finger across her cold nose. "Good night," he told her as she went in, closing the glass doors behind her. Ryan watched her, cherishing every second he spent with her.

He was still smiling like a kid at Christmas after getting back in the taxicab. Putting his hand on the seat, he found Roni's gloves. She must have dropped them when she was getting out. Tapping on the glass partition, he asked, "Can you take me back? She left her gloves." Ryan could have waited to give them to her, but he would use any excuse to talk to her once more.

Roni was still smiling as she put her coat away in the closet at the entrance hallway. Hearing the sound of footsteps, she turned quickly to find him standing behind her giggling. "What are you still doing up?" She swept him into her arms with him laughing as she tickled him. "You are supposed to be in bed, young man," she teasingly scolded.

"I wait on you," he laughed showing his big dimples.

"Why are you waiting for me?"

"So I can kiss goodnight!" He hugged her neck, laying his head on her shoulders.

"I always come up to give you a kiss when I get home," she told him as she closed the door to the closet.

"Mommy, who is that man?" He pointed in the direction of the door.

"What ma--" Before she could finish her sentence she saw Ryan standing at the door.

CHAPTER 5

Who is the child she's holding? Ryan questioned. *She never mentioned having a child. How can I be so stupid? She is probably married and her husband is inside.*

Still holding the toddler, Roni walked to the door wondering what to say to him. With a sigh, she entered the foyer to the outer double glass doors. "That was quick," she said with a little nervous laugh.

Ryan's eyes were fixated on the child with his head on her shoulder hiding his face. "You left your gloves in the cab, just thought I would bring them to you," he said trying to see the child's face. Hearing Ryan's voice, the child slowly looked toward him only showing one eye, but quickly covered it.

"We only got to the end of the block so I asked the driver to bring me back," he spoke again so the child would look at him and he did. This time Ryan saw the left side of his face, with Roni's dimples and his green eyes. Ryan looked at Roni confused, then back at the child.

"Where are my manners? Ryan, this is my son, Joshua," she smiled at Joshua not wanting to look at Ryan. "Say hello to Mr. Ryan." With the innocence of a child, he glanced up waving before quickly retreating to the safety of his mother's neck. Again, Roni tried to express amusement. "Now you are not shy." Joshua raised his head again to smile at Ryan.

It was like his reflection in a mirror when Joshua looked at him. "How old is he?" Ryan asked, never moving his gaze from the child.

"He's three," Roni told him.

"I be four in Feb rary," the small voice chimed in.

"February," Roni corrected Joshua.

"Feb ru ary," he said, laughing because he loved doing big words.

"Then you are a big boy," Ryan told him as Joshua giggled while trying to crawl up his mother.

Roni knew it was time for the conversation she was dreading. "Ryan, we need to talk. Will you pay the taxi, while I put this little monster to bed?" She tickled Joshua as he laughed louder. Looking at the young babysitter, she requested, "Ciara, show Mr. Grant to the family room when he returns." She put Joshua down. "Come on sweetie, you don't want to fall," Roni told Joshua, holding his hand as he looked back at Ryan smiling.

When Ryan returned to the house Ciara took his coat before showing him into the family room overlooking the garden. It was a comfortable room completely glassed-in with an excellent view of the little cobblestone path that led to a garage. The soft natural light of the stars shone down on the little bench along the path with the small flowerbeds that were hibernating for the winter.

"Thanks, Ciara, I appreciate you agreeing to babysit on such short notice," Ryan heard Roni speaking to the teenager.

"Any time, he is no trouble. Sorry he wasn't in bed. I was about to take him up when you came in." She felt the need to apologize for Joshua not being asleep.

"No problem, he can be very persuasive at times." Roni walked down the hall to the family room. "Ryan, I'm going to watch Ciara walk to her house."

Ryan was silent but acknowledged that he heard her. As he stood at the window, he wondered what he was going to say when she returned. Afraid of where their conversation was leading, he felt lost. Not just for words, but of thought.

He heard the door open, then closing; the footsteps on the hardwood floor sounded distant to him but they were very close. While he stood at the window looking out not wanting to look at her, he heard the doors as they slid shut. Ryan continued to look out into the darkness not knowing what else to do.

Trying to figure out how to start their awkward conversation, Roni rubbed her arm as she walked toward Ryan. She knew he saw her because her reflection was in the glass.

Seeing her reflection, he asked, "When were you going to tell me?" His emotions were uncertain because he didn't know how to feel. There was a feeling of nothing in his heart. If he could have just been angry, maybe that would have given him something, because that feeling of nothing was too painful.

Roni didn't know what to say. Like Ryan she didn't know what to feel, but knew she needed to give an answer. Unfortunately, nothing she thought of seemed appropriate. Rubbing her temples, she hadn't noticed Ryan looking back at her. The look on his face was one she hadn't seen before and she didn't know how to respond. Even searching his eyes had no answer for her. Before she could stop, she asked in a challenging tone, "Tell you what?"

"This is not the time to play games, Roni!" Remembering the child was just upstairs, Ryan tried to control the tone in his voice. "When were you going to tell me?"

Roni sat on the edge of the brown leather sofa, putting her face in her hands before finally looking up to see him staring at her apparently angry at her secret. This instantly put Roni on the defensive, a place she didn't like to be, and that angered her as she cut her eyes at Ryan, repeating, "Tell you what?"

Ryan knew he wasn't getting any answers and came straight to the point. "Is that my son?" Walking in her direction, she moved away from him not knowing what his intentions were. "Roni!" he called her name to bring her back to reality.

"What do you want me to say?"

"Just answer the damn question!"

She tried to walk away, but he grabbed her arm, forcing her to look back at him. Seeing the anger in his eyes, she opened her mouth but no words came out.

Ryan loosened his grip because he saw he was frightening her. Trying hard to soften his look, he searched her face for answers. "Why didn't you contact me? It has been over four years, you knew where I was."

"Why do you feel he is yours?" she asked because she didn't know how to explain Joshua.

"Roni, he will be four in February; besides you are not that kind of woman."

Feeling insulted that there was a certain kind of woman to have a child, she sarcastically asked him, "What kind of woman?"

Having to walk away, he turned to face her. "Don't be cynical, you know what I mean." He saw the look of hurt on her face then added, "Roni, I was the first man you had ever been with and even if you met someone after me the probability of him having green eyes is unlikely."

She hated to admit it, but he was right. Four years ago, she was caught up in the moment and didn't protect herself; now she was tied to Ryan with Joshua. She felt the tears burning in her eyes, as the lone tear escaped down her cheek.

He sat beside her on the sofa. "I don't mean to upset you, but why didn't you contact me when you found out?"

"Ryan, we didn't separate on good terms. I knew you were getting married and didn't want to bring this into your life."

"Bring this into my life? Roni, we are talking about my son." Hurt and not understanding why she felt that way Ryan asked, "When did you find out you were pregnant?"

"First of July." She stopped but heard nothing from Ryan so she knew she must continue. "When I found out, I wasn't sure what I was going to do. I looked into terminating but decided to finish out my pregnancy. Considered adoption, decided against it when I saw his tiny face." She smiled as she thought of the first time she saw Joshua, then she remembered that she was still talking to Ryan, adding, "The one thing I knew was that I couldn't tell you, because I didn't want to cause problems with your pending marriage."

"I didn't get married."

"Yes, I found that out today, but at the time I knew those were your plans."

"Roni, you wouldn't talk to me! I never told you those were my plans." He looked into her face seeing the weaker side, the side he knew she didn't want him to see. Looking away, he asked, "Were you ever going to tell me?"

"If I hadn't seen you today, I would have probably waited until Joshua asked about you." Knowing the thought wasn't complete she added, "But I was planning to talk to you about him this weekend while you were still here in New York."

Although Roni felt an apology was needed for not telling him, she searched for words to express her feelings. "Ryan, I am truly sorry for the way you found out and that you are hurting right now, but I will not apologize for not telling you before." A look of disbelief was on his face. "I did what I thought was best for Joshua at the time and will not apologize for that."

"Roni, what gives you the right to make decisions for me?" Feeling angered again, he argued, "I have already missed three years of his life. He doesn't know who I am, Roni!" Fighting back tears, he said, "I am a stranger to my own son. You don't understand how that hurts?"

He looked at Roni. "I don't want to miss another day in his life. If I don't get the job, I will still be a part of his life. It will be hard, but I want us to know each other," Ryan rambled to himself as if Roni were not in the room. It finally settled in his head, he had a son and a warm feeling came over him. An emotion he had never felt before.

"I know and you should be a part of his life." She saw the pride in his face. "But let's wait until you get the job before we tell Joshua who you are."

"Roni, why?" he asked in disbelief at her request.

"He is three and has never asked about his father. I want him to have a relationship with you before we just tell him. Joshua needs stability and he may feel you are abandoning him when you leave on Monday." Trying to find words to explain her position because she saw the confusion on Ryan's face, she clarified, "Joshua needs to establish a stable relationship with you so he won't be confused about who you are."

She noticed the time. "Look, it's late and you won't be able to get a taxi this time of night. Just sleep in the guest room on the third floor." Roni trusted him, but didn't want to give him too much access to her son. After all, she was all Joshua knew as a parent and part of her liked it that way.

"I don't agree with this, but I will try to understand why you feel this way." That feeling of hurt crept back into his soul. "Three years I've missed, and they can't ever be given back to me."

Going to the built-in cupboard, she opened one of the cabinets. Pulling out a book, she brought it to Ryan. "This is yours." She handed him a book with animal designs and Joshua's name on the cover. "I made a duplicate copy for you." Roni knew Ryan would come up someday and wanted him to have mementos of Joshua's life, but never dreamt it would be this soon.

Ryan turned the pages with the care of a father holding his child for the first time. As the emotions began to overwhelm him, he could no longer hold back his tears.

Sleep didn't come easy for Ryan, but he finally dozed off after one A.M. He and Roni had talked more about Joshua as he looked through his baby book with her, giving the stories behind the pictures. She had even made DVDs for him to see Joshua in action.

Ryan was excited to see those loving pictures of Joshua, although his heart was heavy because he could never be the man holding him as he took his first steps or helped him blow out the candles on his first birthday cake. In the pictures, Roni's father was there along with Laurence, but it was not the same as him being there with his son.

Looking at the pictures, he saw that Joshua was a happy, loving child and Roni had done an excellent job raising him alone. He couldn't make up for the past, but he would definitely be a part of Joshua's future.

When he and Roni looked in on Joshua before going up to the guest room, he didn't want to leave. Ryan stood in the doorway of Joshua's room with the mural of a mythological horse behind the bed and the star nightlights on the ceiling watching him. A tiny hand scratched his nose as he slept in his bed with the little cartoon characters on the sheets. His arm stuck out showing the little pajamas with the funny dinosaurs on them. Ryan began to understand why Roni hadn't told him. He had only known for a few hours that he was a father, but he would kill anyone who tried to hurt his son.

Ryan was between sleep and wakefulness when he felt someone in the room. Slowly he opened his eyes and was startled by a pair of little hands on the edge of the mattress with a pair of eyes staring at him. Ryan jumped in shock as Joshua ran from the room laughing.

"Joshua, behave!" Roni scolded him. Coming into the room, with some clothing and toiletries, Roni was smiling as if relieved Ryan knew about Joshua. "Here are some of Laurence's clothes." She laid the items on the dresser. "You two look about the same size. Some clean towels and a toothbrush as well."

She looked at Ryan in the mirror on the dresser. "Did you sleep well?" Turning around to face him, she got a little embarrassed because she hadn't seen him in the morning since that night they spent together and nothing had changed.

Coming back into the room still smiling, Joshua clung to his mother's leg as he looked at the strange man in the bed. "Come on, munchkin, let Mr. Ryan get dressed." Roni scooted him out of the room as Joshua turned around and waved. Smiling, Ryan waved back at him as Roni closed the door behind them. Ryan didn't move until he no longer heard their voices.

"Now be on your best behavior, young man," she advised Joshua. "We have company today, okay." She held out her pinky finger for him to hold with his.

"Okay!" Joshua shouted loudly as he made the usual pinky promise that was almost immediately broken.

Joshua sat on the stool watching his mother prepare breakfast, occasionally playing with the little action figure in his hand. The smell of bacon and eggs filled the kitchen as his mom cut up fresh strawberries, cantaloupes, and honeydew melons that she bought at the Asian market on Fifth Avenue and James.

He watched her as she carefully used the knife, cutting the fruit into small chunks for him to eat. Getting down to the last piece of the fruit, she gave it to Joshua. He quickly grabbed it, putting it into his mouth and catching the juice with his hand. Seeing him, Roni reached for a paper towel to wipe his mouth. Joshua hated when she wiped his mouth, because her hands moved too fast.

Taking the towel, he began to do it himself, still chewing the piece of cantaloupe he had been given. "Mommy, can I play with Mr. Ryan today?" He knew to ask her because he had been taught that just because they were mommy's friend didn't make them his. Therefore, Mr. Ryan was a stranger and could possibly be dangerous. He hoped his mother would say yes because he liked Mr. Ryan.

"It's fine with me if it is okay with him, but don't worry him like you do Uncle Lar," she warned Joshua, a rambunctious three-year-old, but smiled as a sign of permission.

Hearing footsteps on the stairs, she knew Ryan was on his way into the kitchen. Grabbing a mug from the cupboard, she poured his coffee. "Good morning! You still take it black?" The expression on Ryan's face made her laugh because she knew what he was thinking.

With a devilish grin, he said, "Yes, thank you," before glancing over at Joshua staring up at him. "How are you this morning?"

"Fine," he giggled and squirmed in his seat. Ryan watched carefully, not wanting him to fall and get hurt.

"Here you go." Roni placed their plates on the counter for them. "I'm going upstairs to get dressed." Walking past them, she leaned Joshua back and kissed his forehead as he munched on a piece of bacon. As she walked by, Ryan had a look of helplessness on his face. "He is only three, don't be afraid," she whispered to encourage Ryan.

"I be four in Feb rary," Joshua said, letting his mother know he heard her.

"I will be," she corrected him.

"No, you not be, I be," Joshua said not understanding she was correcting his grammar.

Ryan saw a chance to start a conversation with Joshua. "So you will be four soon?" he asked reaching for a slice of bacon.

"Yes, I get to have a party," he bragged with a mouth full of eggs and cheese, then looked over at Ryan. "You coming to my party?" he mumbled, looking up at Ryan, waiting for an answer.

"Well, I will have to see, because I won't know if I have a job here in New York until Monday. Will it be okay for me to tell you then?"

Still chewing his food with less in his mouth now, Joshua nodded his head in agreement. Reaching for his sippy cup, he drank some of the fresh orange juice. "Ah!" he sighed as he put the cup back on the counter.

"Why do you want to be four?" Ryan asked wishing he could keep him a child forever.

Cupping his hands around his mouth, he tried to whisper, "I just want to have a party," and threw his head back as he laughed at his own joke.

Ryan couldn't help but join in with the laughter as they both finished eating their breakfast.

"Joshua, come get your shoes sweetie!" Roni called out to him.

Seeing him struggling to get down off the stool, Ryan assisted him. As soon as Joshua's feet hit the floor, he dashed for the stairs. "Slow down," Ryan called out to him sounding like a parent, smiling that he and Joshua were getting along.

Ryan heard Roni's footsteps walking back into the kitchen. "So, what do you think?" she asked while clearing away the dishes.

"He is amazing," Ryan smiled giving her credit. "You have done a wonderful job raising him."

"Thank you." She really appreciated that compliment coming from him. Although she had help, it was very hard being a single mother and an entrepreneur. Smiling, she told Ryan, "I think he likes you. He asked if he could play with you." Both laughed at Joshua thinking Ryan was a toy.

Looking at Ryan, she saw that he and Laurence were close in size. Laurence was a little larger across the chest, but close enough that the clothes didn't hang improperly. If Ryan only knew what she had gone through with Laurence to get the clothing, he would be hysterical with laughter.

First, Laurence had wanted to know why he had to stay overnight. Roni explained that he had seen Joshua and they ended up having a long discussion very late. Then he wanted to know where Ryan had slept. Why did Laurence make it so difficult? She had to laugh at him pretending he was riding a bucking bronco when asking where Ryan had slept. Then he had sounded disappointed finding out it was in their dad's old room on the third floor.

It had only been a few months since his death from heart failure, but Roni felt it was more from a broken heart. After she returned from college, Roni knew he was still missing her mother deeply. Her parents had had a relationship that was unique. Not to say they didn't have their differences, but they were able to talk about it and her mom won. She smiled at the thought, but was still saddened by his unexpected death.

When she found out she was pregnant, her dad never judged her or even asked who the father was. The only thing he told her was maybe that was God's way of giving them someone back to replace the life gone.

From the day Joshua was born, her dad spent every moment he could with him. Even when he was a newborn, her dad was in the nursery before Roni's feet were on the floor. Joshua missed him tremendously, but not as much as his mother.

"I'm ready!" Joshua shouted as he jumped off the bottom step.

"Okay, here's your coat." Roni handed Joshua his coat from the hall closet.

Joshua turned to Ryan for help putting it on. Without asking questions, Ryan held his little coat as he put in first his left arm then his right. While buttoning it up he noticed Joshua hadn't taken his eyes off him. Ryan looked up, winking at him, which made Joshua giggle.

"Will I have to put you two in time out?" Roni teased. "Okay, let's move it."

Grabbing Ryan's hand, Joshua looked up at him as if he were ten feet tall while walking out to the garage. If only Joshua knew right then Ryan felt much taller.

"Okay, little man," Roni looked in the backseat at Joshua sitting in his car seat, "you have your gloves?"

"Check!"

"What about your shades?"

"Check!" Joshua slid on his little play shades. "You got your belt, mommy?" he questioned about her safety belt as Ryan watched and listened to them with pride.

"Check! What do you want to listen to?" she asked, locking the doors as she turned on the engine.

Almost jumping out of his car seat he shouted, "Uncle Charlie the baby song."

"Uncle Charlie it is," she agreed as she switched to that CD and played track three. The smooth sounds of Charlie Wilson came from the speakers as Roni raised the garage door, backing into the alley in her Volvo.

Roni wasn't a creature of change, favoring the Volvo because that was her mother's car of choice. To be honest it made her feel like her mother was advising her with the decision.

She saw Ryan looking at her mouthing, "Uncle Charlie?" Roni pointed to the CD player. Now he understood that was a favorite singer of Joshua's. Ryan was surprised that it was an R&B singer and not a goofy kiddy song, hearing the chords when the music began as the mellow voice sang about meeting a woman at the mall. Mixed in with the singer, they heard the voice of Joshua as he sang along getting only a couple of words to the song correct.

Pulling down the visor and using the mirror to watch him, Ryan saw Joshua in his own little world bouncing in his car seat moving his head from side to side. Then with a burst of energy at the top of his lungs, he sang, "There goes baby!" which tickled Ryan, making him chuckle. Roni started to laugh with him, but Joshua was still in his own world and continued to sing the baby song.

Their drive to the organic farm was long with Joshua falling asleep about halfway there. Ryan had enjoyed watching him, as he sang along with CDs during the drive. Joshua saw him watching and tried to wink his eye like Ryan, but blinked instead.

With the car quiet, Ryan felt it was a time they could talk more about their lives since college. He wanted to tell her the reason he didn't get married, but Roni just wanted to forget about it. That puzzled him because he wanted her to know the truth. Ryan didn't understand that for Roni talking about it only reopened old wounds and the healing wasn't yet complete. Therefore, he changed the subject. "What made you go into clothing design?"

"When I was pregnant with Joshua, I couldn't find baby items that I liked. So my dad suggested I make my own. With time on my hands, I came up with patterns for comforters, sleepers, diaper shirts, etc. By the time he was born, Joshua had a whole wardrobe of one of a kind items.

"We would be at the park and other mothers would come up and ask where I purchased them. I told them they were originals, but would take orders giving them a copy of my design. Those mothers would get the same response from their friends and thus 'Joshua's Closest' was born."

She smiled at the story, remembering how her dad had supported her with that venture. It was not what she had planned, but circumstances changed, so her dreams had to accommodate the changes. If she could go back and alter any event in her life, she wouldn't. All the things Roni had been through created the woman she saw when she looked in the mirror and she liked her.

Wanting to take the attention off herself she glanced over at Ryan. "Tell me what you've been up to."

"How do I follow that story?" They both laughed at Ryan's shyness. "After college, I went to work for a log cabin manufacturer doing floor plans for prefabrication." Hearing it out loud was boring even to Ryan. Roni glanced back, wanting to hear more because she loved creating things no matter what it was. "Roni, this is so boring," he smiled, embarrassed.

"No, it isn't, keep going," she encouraged and flashed that tutoring smile he remembered when they first met.

"Well, I designed homes made from logs. What do you want me to say?"

"Yes, you designed homes made from logs, but what excited you to go to work each day?" That had always been his weakness, telling someone about himself.

He didn't want to tell her that for the past four years he hadn't been living, just existing and that wasn't a life. After her the simple things just weren't enough anymore. Her energy was what he missed and longed for during their separation. Ryan tried to think of something to add. "Well, a paycheck is nice," he laughed as he stared at her.

"Come on now, you know you love what you do."

"Okay, I do enjoy doing the floor plans making sure you have enough bathrooms and closet space," he lied. It had been tedious for him, but he needed to do his internship somewhere. "Well, I have learned that doing house plans isn't as easy as it looks. My designs were sometimes a little Antebellum for the log homes so I would have to go back to the rustic feel.

"Worked with Habitat for Humanity designing houses for the elderly and saw I wanted to do more with renovations. I guess that's why I decided to come to New York and learn more about older buildings. They seem to have more history attached to them and that makes them real." He smiled to himself; Roni had a way of getting things out of him.

Turning onto a secondary road, Roni called back to Joshua, "Wake up baby, we are here."

Ryan looked into the mirror as Joshua stretched his arms yawning while he wiggled in his car seat. The little shades were twisted on his face; as he became lucid, he reached up to straighten them.

The Steely Farm had been family owned and operated for two generations, with acres of plants and livestock. They not only sold to individual families, but also to restaurants. Luc was one of the farm's frequent customers for their restaurant. The Steelys' livestock were fed all natural grains, which gave them a much better taste. You didn't have to worry about steroids or sick animals served as your meal when you bought from them.

Ruth prided herself on her preserves and Jim made the best apple cider around. That was one of the reasons Joshua liked the farm, but he actually loved to pet the animals more. His favorites were the horses because he could sit on them. Timmy, their youngest son who was deaf, always brought a horse around for Joshua to pet and taught him simple signs so they could communicate.

During the winter months the farm was not very busy because the garden harvest hadn't come in. They mostly sold livestock during that time of year and Roni always called ahead with her meat orders.

Seeing them as she came out of the barn, Ruth treaded through the snow. Vapor came from her mouth because of the mixture of her warm breath in the cold air. Ruth was a stout woman, with red cheeks and glassy eyes from the cold. Pulling off her gloves, she came to hug Roni.

Ruth was so happy when Roni started coming back to the farm. After her mother passed, her dad didn't get up there much. Then Roni went off to college, but she had become a regular customer after returning to New York. She had been there for Roni during her pregnancy, giving her advice on foods to eat and those to avoid, creating a valuable friendship. "Well, I see you couldn't stay away from us," she smiled looking like she could be Mrs. Claus with her red nose. It had been hard convincing Joshua she wasn't until he saw Jim, because he was a thin man and looked nothing like Santa.

"You know I can't stay away too long." She hugged Ruth.

Ruth watched as Ryan helped Joshua out of his car seat, smiling at the fireball about to be unleashed. Running around the car, he gave her a big hug and then started looking for Timmy. Ruth knew who he was looking for. "Don't worry, he's in the barn feeding the horses, but he knows you are here." Seeing the stranger with them, she looked at Roni.

"Oh, where are my manners? Ruth, this is Ryan Grant, a friend of mine from college."

Feeling a little nervous meeting more new people, he smiled but before he could say anything, he felt a tug on his coat. "Come on, Mr. Ryan. There is Timmy, he got horse." Grabbing his hand Joshua dragged him in the direction of the barn while the two women laughed at the funny expression on Ryan's face as a three-year-old yanked him around.

Entering the market, Roni loved the country feel with sawdust on the floors. It was like being at the feed store back in South Carolina when she visited as a child. The hardwood floors made that sound of giving under her weight as she walked on them. She loved the scent of peppers and fresh spices in the air as she filled her basket with the stringed peppers. Roni put both the hot and banana peppers in her basket; the combination was great for stews.

She also made sure to purchase thyme, ginger, and cinnamon. Tomorrow would be Sunday so an apple cobbler might be good for dessert. Sniffing the spices for freshness, she asked, "You have any oregano, Ruth?"

"Sorry, hun, I am all out this week, but I will save you some for next time."

"You have sweet butter? Oh, and I need three dozen eggs; Joshua eats them quicker than I can cook them." They both laughed at his appetite.

"We just got the cheese he loves ready." Ruth knew how Joshua liked his cheese and made some special for him. "You want just sweet butter or both?" she asked before going into the cooler.

"Both," Roni requested as she grabbed a scoop and bag for the coffee. The rich aroma filled the air when she disturbed the beans; the natural oil could be seen as she put them in the bag. Glancing out the window as she continued to fill her basket, Roni saw Ryan and Joshua with Timmy walking back from the barn. Joshua was trying to do sign language as Ryan looked on proudly. They looked so comfortable together; maybe she had been wrong keeping Joshua a secret from him.

Ruth saw them coming inside and had already warmed Joshua's cider for him because she knew that was his next stop. Like a whirlwind, he came in heading straight to the counter for his cup. With his little gloves on, he reached for the cup, licking his lips and blowing on it because he knew it was hot and needed to be tested.

Being an old hand at raising kids, Ruth only slightly warmed it. Children never tested anything, they just went through the rituals of it being too hot. "Now don't drink it too fast, sweetie," she instructed Joshua. Handing Ryan a cup of cider, she said, "No one leaves without trying Jim's cider."

"Thank you." He accepted the cup from her. "How long have you had this place?"

"Oh, this place belonged to my husband's family. They mostly sold locally, but Jim and I expanded it over the years." Ruth looked through the window proud of their accomplishments. "We just recently started being open year around." Noticing his accent, Ruth asked, "You are not from around here are you?"

"No, ma'am, Virginia."

"So you're used to being around farms."

"Yes, ma'am, my grandparents had a small farm, but nothing like this. We had just the garden, with a couple of horses, which in Virginia is considered a farm." Ryan smiled at the comparison. "We mostly gardened for the family but did both deer and turkey hunting."

"Rifle or bow?" Jim asked as he brought in wood for the stove.

"Bow, sir; have to give the animal a fighting chance." They both laughed.

"Jim this is Ryan, Roni's friend from college," Ruth introduced them.

Jim removed his glove and extended his hand. "Nice to meet you. What part of Virginia are you from?"

"Small town called Wolf's Hollow. We only have one traffic light," he joked about the number.

"So you hunt with a bow?"

"Yes, sir, my grandfather taught me. The hardest part was remembering the breathing sequence." Even though they had rifles at their home, his grandpa felt it was an unfair advantage when hunting. In his eyes, a good hunter had to have skill and it didn't take much to point and shoot. Ryan remembered those hunting lessons with him; they went out long before deer season for tips on tracking, with the one rule for a hunter, "Don't kill what you can't eat."

Ryan really missed his grandpa, because they would sit on the porch during the summers with jars filled with ice and homemade lemonade. Once when he was thirteen his grandpa tried to teach him how to chew tobacco, but he swallowed instead of spitting. It made his grandpa laugh at how green he turned. Hearing his grandpa laugh was a rarity, as he was a serious man, much like Ryan's father. Sometimes he would look at Ryan and ask, "Want some tobacco?" then roar with laughter.

"Yeah, I used to hunt some too, but we are busy now and I don't have the time." Jim took off his cap revealing the bald spot on top. "How you like that cider?"

Before Ryan could answer, Joshua shouted "Great!" as he gave his cup to Ruth for more.

"I know *you* think it is great." Jim picked up Joshua as he giggled.

Ruth poured more cider for Joshua. "Here baby." Looking at Jim, she asked, "Would you get Roni's meat order for me, please?"

Jim took orders with a smile and went to the cooler, grabbing the cloth sacks with the fresh bacon, beef for stewing, a ham, lamb roast, and whole chickens. Seeing she didn't have any steaks in her bundle, Jim stuck his head out, "Roni, you didn't need any steaks this time?"

"You have some already cut?"

"No, but it won't take but a minute," he replied, waiting for an answer.

"Yes, please, if you don't mind."

"Rib Eye or New York strip?"

"Ryan, which do you prefer?" Roni asked

"Rib eye; okay with you?"

Before they gave him an answer, Jim said, "Rib eye it is," and he twirled back into the cooler, putting on his apron.

Signing to Timmy, Ruth told him to help put the stuff in Roni's car. Then she proceeded to ring up Roni's order, giving her the total. Roni reminded her about the steaks, but she refused to take payment for them. Jim and Ruth knew Roni would be back in a few weeks to make more purchases, because she was a loyal customer and brought in new customers. Loyalty and new business were worth more to the farm than a few steaks.

Their drive back to the city was a pleasant trip. Before falling asleep, Joshua told his mommy about the horse he saw. Then he asked Ryan many questions about deer and bow hunting, which fascinated him.

Ryan hoped someday he would be able to teach his son some of the things he learned as a child. Those life lessons had made him the man he was. Even though they had a late start, Ryan was willing to take the time to be a real part of Joshua's life, ushering him into manhood.

Sitting in his hotel room, Ryan was already missing being with Joshua and Roni. With Joshua being so young he and Roni thought it best that he didn't spend the night there again. However, Ryan hated to admit his spending so much time in the home might be confusing for Joshua.

Ryan pulled out his laptop, putting in one of the DVDs Roni had made for him entitled "Joshua the Beginning." He heard the voice of a man he had not heard before and thought it might have been Roni's father. The joy of the voice was unmistakably of someone who loved both Roni and Joshua, as he lovingly gave instructions on how to present Joshua for the camera while Roni proudly held the baby. She asked her father to get more shots of the baby instead of her because she hated cameras.

Seeing Joshua just hours after he had come into the world saddened Ryan, because he hadn't been there. The reason why didn't matter, he should have been there. Dismayed that he hadn't been, Ryan vowed not to miss another birthday or any other event in Joshua's life.

Hearing the phone, he answered trying not to show the sadness he felt.

"Hey, Ryan, where you been all day?" Abe asked, completely aware he had been with Roni and Joshua.

"Spent some time with Roni," Ryan said, trying not to be antagonistic, but he needed to know if Abe was aware that Joshua was his son. "Abe, I want the truth. Did you know about Joshua?"

Abe wasn't surprised by the question, because he had asked himself what he would tell Ryan if he saw him again. "Yes," he paused choosing his next words carefully, "but I wasn't aware you were the father until he was born."

"What do you mean? Roni never told you?"

"She still hasn't. The first time I saw him I knew, but she never acknowledged to anyone who the father was. She didn't mention you and I didn't ask questions. I figured when she felt like telling me, she would. To be honest during graduation I felt something was different between the two of you. Just couldn't put my finger on it, but I knew it was different."

"Why didn't you call me or write me about Joshua?" Ryan asked.

"It wasn't my place," Abe sighed. "Roni never confirmed what I felt about Joshua and I wasn't going to bring you into a situation where you may not have been needed."

"Abe, if it had been the other way around..."

"You would have done nothing," Abe finished the statement before Ryan lied to himself with his false sense of loyalty. "Like me, you would have respected Roni and Joshua. Not everything is black and white, Ryan."

"I understand that, but..."

"But people's lives are involved and that's not something you toy with. To be honest I wish you could have been there." Understanding the reason why he hadn't been, Abe elaborated, "It just wasn't my choice to make, sorry."

"How much do you know about what happened?" Ryan needed to know how much Roni had told him.

"To be honest, we never spoke of you until she told me you were in town."

"Wow, that hurts." Ryan wasn't joking because it cut deep to hear she hadn't talked about him. It was as if she had pretended he didn't exist.

Sensing his pain, Abe couldn't tell him that she would always change the subject if he brought up Ryan's name. He felt it was easier if Ryan thought that they didn't discuss him. "Did you have fun with our little Simba?" Abe felt the need to change to a happier tone.

"He is awesome." Ryan experienced such joy when he talked about Joshua. "Roni has done a great job raising him. She said she had help from her dad, Laurence, and you. Thank you for being there and helping her." Being a man, Ryan couldn't understand the pressure of a woman raising a child alone and was happy to see Roni had positive men in Joshua's life. His only regret was he hadn't been one of them.

"Well, with Joshua we are not enough." They both laughed thinking about him.

Abe and Ryan talked for more than an hour. He gave Abe all the details of the day he had spent with Joshua, while thumbing through the scrapbook Roni had made for him. Pictures filled each page; some had locks of hair or shoestrings. The one thing that excited him most was the footprints taken the day he was born. Looking at how tiny they were, he rubbed his finger across them trying to feel the ridges. Ryan was thankful Roni had thought to make him a book. Now he had a piece of Joshua's life.

That Sunday, everyone was excited to be together for dinner. Roni prepared a lamb roast using a rosemary and thyme marinade but enhanced the flavor by adding garlic and white wine. The asparagus and scalloped potatoes with sage and Asiago cheese were delicious. Accompanied by the Cabernet Sauvignon from Napa Valley, it was only upstaged by the apple cobbler for dessert. Luc gave the meal four-and-a-half stars, because if she got five she would be a chef.

Shondra was thrilled watching Ryan and Joshua together sharing secrets during dinner. It was like looking into a mirror with the images of an adult man looking at a view of himself as a child. There was no mistaking they were father and son.

CHAPTER 6

Ryan was very excited about his interview and hoped to get the job, but he was determined to keep trying if he didn't. On Friday it was just about him, but today it was about him being with his family. His family, he liked the sound of that.

The outcome didn't matter, because he wasn't going to miss Joshua's birthday party. It would be next month and Roni was setting a date so he could to be there. He laughed to himself that he would be getting a lot of frequent flyer miles.

Exiting the elevator on the floor of the firm, Ryan walked over to the receptionist's desk, giving his name before joining the other two candidates. Ryan hadn't been this nervous on the original interview, but there was now more riding on the outcome to put him a little on edge.

"Good morning gentlemen, I'm Miguel Cruz. Please follow me." Walking down the corridor to the boardroom, Ryan felt his heart beating in his throat. He knew he needed to relax, but his only thought was being in New York with Joshua and Roni.

"Hello!" Roni quickly answered her phone when she saw it was Ryan calling. Before he could return the greeting, she asked, "What's the verdict?"

"Hello to you too." Ryan prolonged his answer to her question.

"Oh, cut the crap! How did it go?"

"Very well, but they will call me later with their final decision. Sorry I don't have an answer yet."

"That's fine." She sighed because now it would be more difficult for him and Joshua to develop a relationship. "What time does your plane leave today?"

"I need to be at the airport no later than five thirty; the plane leaves at seven o'clock. You have to go through an act of congress to board," he chuckled wearily. "Headed back to the hotel to get my luggage, the concierge is holding it for me."

"I'm heading out now, so we can pick up Joshua together. I should be there in about twenty minutes," she told him as she grabbed her keys and purse to leave.

"Okay, see you then." It wouldn't be much time but at least Ryan would get to see them before he left. In his heart, even one day was going to be too long away from them. With Roni trying so hard to make sure he was a part of Joshua's life, he wanted to savor every moment.

The thought had crossed his mind about him being a part of Roni's life as well. Time and distance hadn't changed his love for her, but he couldn't rush back into her life. Mistakes had been made in the past and Ryan was determined not to repeat them.

Watching her pull up, Ryan grabbed his bags so she wouldn't have to be double-parked. Seeing him come out, Roni opened the back of the SUV so he could load his things. Neither of them really said much, just went through the motions, not knowing what to say.

"You know he is going to ask if you are coming to his party." She broke the awkward silence as they drove in traffic.

"Yeah, I know." He felt a little down, but continued, "Just make a date and I will be there." Ryan living in a different state wasn't going to make it easy for him to be a father to Joshua.

"Well, this year his birthday falls on a Saturday, so we will be having it on his actual birthday. Maybe we can check for flights back while we are at the airport?" Roni suggested, hating the thought of the long distance relationship between father and son. How was she going to help Joshua to understand why Ryan was not there all the time? Well, Joshua still didn't know Ryan was his father, so they didn't have to explain that to him yet.

Seeing her turmoil, Ryan reassured, "Don't worry, Roni, we will figure this out. It will be a little difficult at first, but we will make it work." He didn't know what else to say to assure her that he was going to be there for Joshua and her, if she allowed him.

After picking up Joshua, they went out to lunch. Joshua didn't eat much because he knew Mr. Ryan was leaving. Even Ryan promising to come back for his birthday party in February didn't make it easy, because that was a month away. As they drove to the airport, he still wasn't saying much but he held Ryan's hand as they went inside.

Ryan lifted Joshua up in his arms to look at the flight listings, showing him which plane he was taking back to Virginia. Joshua only nodded his head in agreement, not actually listening. Even when Ryan hoisted him up at the ticket counter, Joshua didn't say much.

They all walked to the security checkpoint in silence. Due to the national security measures, Roni and Joshua couldn't go beyond that point. So Ryan picked Joshua up, giving him a big hug and telling him to be good for his mommy; the usual chitchat, because Roni had stopped listening to them.

She was trying to figure out how they were going to manage the two of them being able to spend time together. Maybe they could meet halfway at least once a month to spend the weekend. He wasn't big enough to travel by himself so Joshua going to Virginia alone was out of the question for now. Those trips would have to wait until he was older and knew that Ryan was his father.

"Hello?" Ryan said, trying to get her attention.

Walking closer, Ryan hugged her. "Thanks for everything." Before letting go, he kissed her cheek. "I will call you when I get home." Looking down at Joshua, he urged, "You take care of your mommy until I get back." Joshua gave a big grin in agreement.

After walking through the metal detectors, Ryan turned around to get one last look at them before going to his gate. Seeing Roni and Joshua waving, he waved back before continuing on to board the plane.

Roni knew the ride home was going to be quiet because Joshua hadn't said much since they left Ryan at the airport, although she knew in a couple of hours, Joshua would be feeling better and running through the house like a tornado. The silence was broken when they heard the cell phone ringing. She answered, putting it on speaker.

Hearing the voice on the other end was Ryan, Joshua immediately perked up. "Hey, just wanted to speak to you before I boarded the plane. I'm going to miss you guys."

"We're going to miss you, too," she sighed.

"Joshua, are you there?" Ryan asked.

"Yep!" he yelled almost jumping out of his car seat.

"You can tell now."

Completely confused Roni glanced in the backseat. "Tell what?"

With all the excitement he could muster, Joshua blurted out, "Mr. Ryan got job, will be back in two weeks. Yeah!"

Ryan was grateful after returning to Virginia to find his job didn't require him to work the normal two weeks before leaving his position. Unfortunately, the company wasn't getting many orders, forcing them to cut back, so his finding other employment allowed them to keep at least two of the skilled laborers on the job. With the downturn in the economy, new home construction was down and prefabricated log homes were taking a big hit as well.

Ryan's mother was a little upset about his moving to New York, but she would have to get used to it. With the way she reacted when he told her about Joshua, Ryan didn't care.

How could she question whether he was the father? Joshua looked just like him at that age and they both had green eyes. Ryan tried to understand her reaction with the defense that she was just being protective. Now that he himself was a father, he understood how as a parent she wanted to protect her child, but it didn't make her right.

Pete was his usual self when Ryan told him: no expression, just a sly smile when he looked at Joshua's pictures from the baby book. Ryan saw him touching the lock of Joshua's hair, sliding his finger slowly across it. Sometimes Pete would glance up, looking at Ryan and then back to the pictures of Joshua.

Helen refused to even look at the pictures. That angered his father, but Pete said nothing. He just left the room, going outside to walk, which was something Pete did when he was troubled.

Now Ryan and his grandma watched the entire DVD twice. Mama Pearl laughed so much she had tears coming from her eyes as she watched Joshua running down the hall naked with nothing but soap bubbles for cover. Roni tried grabbing him as he giggled while slipping through her fingers because he was wet. Laurence had to corner him, but like his father, Joshua was quick.

"I believe he will be a better shortstop than you," Mama Pearl teased Ryan.

"I sure hope so," Ryan agreed as he proudly smiled at Joshua.

"When are you going to tell him you are his father?" Mama Pearl asked, not mincing words.

"Soon I hope, but I need to be a stable person in his life before telling him."

"Roni seems like a nice girl. Why didn't she contact you about him before now?" Pearl asked.

"Mama Pearl, that's complicated. She thought I was getting married and didn't want to bring Joshua into a situation where he might not be accepted."

"Why did she think you were getting married?"

"Remember graduation when Amy came?" Ryan asked, feeling ashamed. "She made sure Roni knew we were engaged."

"Oh, did you explain that situation to her?"

"I wanted to but she wouldn't talk to me. Matter of fact when I ran into her again, I wasn't sure if she would talk to me then, either." He paused to reflect back on when he saw her getting off the elevator. "But I am glad she did."

"Well, good thing you didn't marry Amy." Mama Pearl lowered her voice as if someone could hear them. "That baby she got ain't her husband's."

"Mama Pearl," Ryan scolded, "do you women do anything in the shop besides gossip?"

"Yes, what we don't know we make up." Both had to laugh at her comment. "Ryan, when are you going to let me meet the little fellow?"

"Soon I hope." He gave her a sarcastic smile. "You think you can keep up?"

"I kept up with your little butt, didn't I?" Getting serious, she looked at him. "I wish your Papa Pete could've seen Joshua. He would've loved watching him run through the house. I never told you but he loved it when you came on the weekends and spent most of the summer here with us. The only thing he cared about was what the two of you were going to do." She laughed at the memories.

Ryan saw she was getting a little sad thinking about his grandpa, because he was too. Reaching over to her on the couch, he said, "Yes and he would have turned Joshua off of tobacco for life." Both smiled remembering that episode in history.

"Now, you have been talking about Joshua and you, but what about his momma?"

"I don't know. I guess it is too early to tell." Ryan felt helpless when it came to Roni. "Mama Pearl, so much has happened, I just don't know," he wearily told his grandma.

"What do you mean you don't know? You knew for at least one night how you felt or was she right in her thinking?"

Getting defensive, Ryan denied, "No, she is not right. I tried to talk to her; I called all night and she wouldn't answer the phone." Feeling as powerless as he had four years earlier, he lamented, "I should've just gone to her apartment and stood at her door until she talked to me. How could I have been so stupid? I just let her walk out of my life."

"Are you finished kicking your own butt?" She paused, looking Ryan in the eyes. "Do you love her?"

"Yes, I never stopped," he smiled at the thought of Roni.

"What is it you love about her?" His grandma walked into the kitchen as Ryan followed her. Pearl set the kettle on the stove to boil water for tea as she looked back at Ryan for an answer.

Ryan sat at the table trying to pull his thoughts together. "Well, she's different."

"Of course she is. She's black, but that isn't the reason you love her." Looking in the cupboard to get the little teapot with the tea bags, she set it on the table. "When you love someone it isn't about what others see, it is about what you see. Now let's start over. What is it about her that makes you love her?"

Thinking back to the first time he saw Roni and how he got to know her by becoming her friend and then growing in their relationship to the point he knew he loved her, he listed, "Her independence. Her loving nature. You don't have to ask Roni for help, she gives it willingly even if she gets nothing in return. She has this ability to make you feel important, just by walking into the room." Hearing his list of reasons, this was the first time Ryan understood why he loved Roni

"See, not one thing you mentioned was physical." Hearing the kettle whistling, Pearl got cups from the counter, placing them on the table. "It is obvious you truly love her and I am pretty sure she still loves you."

Putting a tea bag in his cup as Pearl poured water, Ryan asked, "Why do you think that?" understanding Mama Pearl didn't know Roni and how stubborn she could be.

"Because she has been thinking of you for that child's entire life." Grabbing the cookie jar filled with peanut butter cookies, she placed it on the table. "Even though you weren't there she made sure you have mementoes of him. If she didn't care about you, she wouldn't care if you knew anything about Joshua. How many people, myself included, would go through that kind of trouble for someone they didn't care about?"

Biting into one of her homemade cookies, Ryan felt she was right, but was still afraid she could be wrong. "You're probably right."

Pearl sat down beside him. "You know I am," she told him then leaned over, kissing him on the cheek.

When Ryan returned to New York, he was thrilled but also a little nervous. While back in Virginia, he had kept in contact with Roni and Joshua daily. Their constant contact prompted Roni to suggest he stay with them as a guest until he could find an apartment close by.

His finding an apartment in that area was going to be expensive, because Harlem real estate over the years had greatly increased in value. All he needed was a studio, until the details could be worked out about Joshua spending the night with him. Although Ryan really wanted to be within walking distance of them, the expense would be enormous. Laurence joked that *they* wouldn't be in that neighborhood if their parents hadn't bought the property before they were born.

Roni had gone with him to look at several places, which were either too expensive or in a less than safe area. She knew that coming from a small town, being in the city could be overwhelming and dangerous for Ryan. Unfortunately, the apartments that were affordable were too far away and Ryan wanted to be able to see Joshua every day.

They had been together the past week, waking up, having breakfast, and reading stories at bedtime. The two of them had even fallen asleep together on the couch watching a movie. Roni had only smiled, draping a blanket across them before she went up to bed.

"Roni, how far is 125th St.?" Ryan asked. She walked up behind him to look at the apartment on the Internet.

Before she could answer, Laurence chimed in, "You don't want to know. Still no luck with apartment hunting?"

"By subway, maybe thirty minutes; cab, depending on the time of day could be as much as an hour," Roni solemnly answered. After closely inspecting the photos, she told him, "Those are demo photos so there is no guarantee that the place will look like that."

Laurence came to take a peek. "Those are definitely not the actual photos."

"How do you know?"

"Ryan, it is seven hundred square feet in the description. Those photos are of a much larger apartment." Walking back into the kitchen, he added, "Unfortunately they do that sometimes."

Putting her hand on his shoulder, Roni agreed, "He's right that does happen."

Coming back into the family room, Laurence plopped down on the sofa with a bowl of ice cream. "Roni, you know he won't find anything close that is affordable."

"It doesn't look like it." She and Laurence discussed Ryan as if he weren't in the room, although Roni tried to put a positive spin on it. "You don't have to report to work until Monday so we have the rest of the week to find something and you can stay here as long as you need to."

"That's a great idea!" Laurence sat up on the sofa.

"What?" Ryan asked.

"You can stay here." He looked at both Roni and Ryan. "He's already staying in the third floor apartment that was Dad's." Getting a stare from Roni, he defended, "Hey, sounds like a good idea to me."

"Thanks, Laurence, but don't put Roni on the spot like that."

"Look, you want to be able to spend time with Joshua and he enjoys having you here." Adding a little of his own selfish nature, he cajoled, "Besides I won't have to worry about them needing a man around the house when I am not home."

"Since when has that ever crossed your mind?" Roni gave him a callous look.

Shuffling his feet and dancing like a little kid, Laurence said, "It just makes perfect sense to me." He licked his spoon and made a silly face at Roni as he passed her to go back into the kitchen.

"Roni, I know Laurence means well but don't let him force you into feeling--"

Before he could finish, Roni admitted, "Laurence is right, it would be easier for you to be with Joshua. To be honest I didn't know what we were going to tell him when you moved," she nervously laughed.

"Are you sure about this?" Ryan didn't want to intrude but was happy to be in the same house as Joshua and Roni.

"Yeah, it will be fine." She gave him her big smile of approval.

"Thanks!" He hugged her before he could stop himself. "Ah, sorry."

Roni had to laugh at him as he pulled back from her so quickly, but that was the reason she hadn't suggested he stay with them before. It was obvious that she still had feelings for him. The past week had been wonderful with them becoming close again.

She felt it might be an awkward situation, especially if he started dating someone. Roni didn't want him to feel she had to be a part of his life for him to be with Joshua. Deep inside she knew it was best for Ryan to be in the house with them, but she was afraid of her own feelings. The heart can forget many things; unfortunately, pain wasn't one of them.

It still hurt deeply when she thought about their past. Now she was allowing her heart to rule her head again. With their parting on bad terms, Roni was still feeling the hurt. She reminded herself that Ryan had tried to explain, but she had been too angry to hear. Roni knew she needed to stop living in the past. It wasn't about her and Ryan anymore. It was about Ryan and Joshua. They should have each other and she wouldn't stand in their way.

Ryan couldn't stop smiling because he was going to be a consistent part of Joshua's life. Each day he felt them growing closer and Joshua was so comical. He experienced such delight being with them. Although the main reason for his being there was Joshua, he still loved Roni.

Part of him just wanted to throw caution to the wind and take her in his arms, kissing her passionately. A smile came over his face thinking about her slapping him silly for doing it. Then he laughed to himself about it being worth it.

Ryan wished he could tell her how he felt, but she would think it was because of Joshua. He wanted to make her understand that he loved her too and even if there were no Joshua, he would still love her. It would take time, but Ryan would prove to her that she was the only woman he wanted in his life.

Knocking on the door, Roni called out to Ryan, "I brought you some clean towels."

"Thanks! Roni, are you sure you are all right with this? I mean I don't want you to feel obligated."

"Ryan, I wouldn't have it any other way," she smiled, handing him the towels.

Standing in the door, he watched her until he couldn't see her anymore.

Roni refused to look back knowing her heart would show through.

CHAPTER 7

Life couldn't have been better for them. Joshua had his party with his little friends from the playgroup. Family, both blood and extended, came to the party at the pizzeria with the funny characters and games. Although Joshua was playing with his friends, he frequently came back to the table to make sure Ryan wasn't feeling neglected. Everyone thought it was sweet that he didn't want to hurt Ryan's feelings.

Roni hadn't given her permission for Ryan to tell Joshua that he was his father. Nor had Ryan asked to reveal the secret. What was he going to say to Joshua? "Oh, by the way I am your dad." It sounded like something from an old movie with the birds singing, the sun shining, and everybody dancing. Unlike a movie, they were real people that could possibly be hurt. He had hurt Joshua's mother in the past, and he didn't want to do the same thing to him. As long as Joshua didn't ask, Ryan wouldn't have to explain where he had been for the past four years.

Maybe he could just wait until Joshua asked about his father to have that conversation, were his thoughts. In reality, Ryan knew he was only kidding himself, because they needed to tell Joshua he was his father. He just didn't want Joshua to hate him for not being there before. It wouldn't be fair to put Roni in the middle of it, because her only intention by not contacting him was to protect

Joshua. This was something Ryan felt he should explain to Joshua for both of them.

Besides, he could hear Roni now, exclaiming, "You are afraid of a four-year-old? Oh please!" No, he wasn't afraid of a four-year-old, but he did fear Joshua would hate him. Ryan would rather die than hurt Joshua or Roni. They both meant so much to him.

It was obvious the desire between Roni and Ryan was growing stronger. Roni kept her distance; usually after dinner she went upstairs to work on her designs. Ryan knew she was just avoiding him. In his heart, nothing had changed in the way he felt. He was still in love with her and just wanted to show her that he could be trusted with her heart again.

After dinner, Shondra called to tell Roni she wasn't feeling well. That deeply concerned Roni, but Shondra assured her she was fine, just having some indigestion. The doctor had taken Shondra off her feet because she was retaining fluid, causing him to fear she would go into early labor. Hearing that she was sick, Roni tried to convince Shondra to allow her to sit with her until Luc came home. Shondra declined the offer promising to call if things worsened.

Ryan could see Roni was worried and suggested she phone Luc so he could check on Shondra. At first, she wanted to respect her friend's wishes but decided Ryan was right that Shondra shouldn't be home alone. Luc greatly appreciated her call because he knew Shondra wouldn't have wanted to worry him.

Roni asked Luc to call her when he got home to let her know how Shondra was doing. He promised to keep her informed about Shondra's condition through the night. That eased Roni's mind, but only a little.

"Ryan, do you think I should just go over there?"

Trying to comfort her, Ryan said, "That's up to you, Roni. Just give Luc time to get home first. She might be right and it's only indigestion." Ryan wasn't comfortable giving her advice on such matters because he had never been around pregnant women to know the problems they faced.

"Okay, I will let him get home before I call. She's not due for another month; it could just be something she ate," Roni tried to convince herself.

An hour had passed and Roni still hadn't heard from Luc or Shondra. "Ryan, I am getting worried."

He saw the troubled look in her eyes. "Have you tried Luc's cell?"

"No, I've been calling Shondra's." She quickly picked up the phone to dial Luc. "No answer." Roni began to pace. "I'm going crazy!"

"I know it is hard, but calm down; he will call when he gets a chance," Ryan tried to reassure her.

Roni knew he was trying to ease her mind but right now, she didn't want to hear that. When the phone rang Roni quickly answered, "Hello!" From the smile on her face, Ryan knew it was Luc on the other end. "Okay, call me back after the ultrasound and give her a kiss for me."

Ryan could tell the news wasn't as bad as she had anticipated so he waited for her to tell him how Shondra was doing.

"She's okay. When Luc got home, her abdominal pain had worsened so he took her to the emergency room. They are doing an ultrasound now to make sure the baby is fine." Roni reached over, hugging Ryan. "Thanks for trying to calm me down. Sorry if I snapped at you."

"You didn't snap. Growled a little, maybe," he laughed as she playfully shoved him.

"I'm going to bed. Good night!"

"Good night." Ryan watched her as she walked up the stairs, still smelling the lilacs from her perfume. He went through the house turning off the lights and the television in the den. Sleep should come easy tonight because he smelled her on his clothes and could pretend she was there with him.

Deep in sleep, a knock on his door awakened Ryan. He couldn't remember if he had told Roni to come in or not, but she was sitting beside him on the bed.

"Ryan, Luc just called. Shondra is in labor." A very concerned look was on her face. "I'm going to pick up Thuy, and we are going over to the hospital."

"Now?" Ryan questioned.

"Don't worry, Laurence will be with us." She paused, "I hate to ask, but will you watch Joshua and let him know where I am?"

"Roni," he gave her a look that made her smile.

"I'm sorry, I know you will." She kissed him on the cheek. "Thank you."

"No problem." He could still feel the burn of her kiss on his face as she left his room.

Ryan started downstairs to look in on Joshua when he heard his voice. "Mommy, can I go?" By the sound of his voice, Ryan knew he was half-asleep when he asked that question.

"No, baby, Ryan is upstairs if you need him." She kissed him. "Go back to sleep, sweetie." Seeing Ryan on the stairs, she had a nervous look on her face. "I will call you as soon as we find out something," she said and forced a smile.

"You ready, Roni?" Laurence asked from the hall. He was waiting for her before going out to the garage.

"Ryan, can I sleep with you?" Joshua came to the door, rubbing his eyes.

"Sure." He squatted down so Joshua could get on his back.

Joshua laid his head on Ryan's back as he held onto his neck. "Ryan!"

"Yes?" he answered

Joshua let out a little yawn. "I love you."

That was the first time Joshua had said that to him. It took Ryan by surprise as he felt a lump in his throat. "I love you too, Joshua." The two climbed the stairs in silence.

Ryan didn't sleep much after Roni and Laurence left. He was concerned for Shondra and the baby, because she and Luc had become good friends of his since he had returned to New York. From the first moment he had met Shondra and Luc, they had treated him like family. With Ryan being new, that meant a lot to him.

True, he was worried about Shondra but the little monster in the bed next to him wasn't making it easy to sleep either. Joshua's little legs and arms were flopping all over the place; Ryan had to smile at his wild sleeping antics. During the night, Ryan moved him, trying to make sure they both had room in the bed, but Joshua moved back, snuggling up against Ryan. After a couple of tries, Ryan just gave up and savored the time with him. It was as if he needed to feel Ryan close by, making sure he didn't leave.

The phone rang, waking both Ryan and Joshua from their sleep. Ryan looked at the time before answering the phone. It was almost six A.M. and he would be getting up soon. "Hello," he managed to get out while Joshua squirmed next to him.

"It's a girl!" the screams of Roni and Thuy were heard.

Moving the phone from his ear, he waited for the shrilling voices on the other end to calm. "Great! How are Shondra and the baby?" he asked after moving the phone closer to his ear, feeling it safe.

"Doing well, but Shondra is a little tired after the delivery. The baby weighs six pounds, four ounces and is nineteen inches long. Ryan, she is beautiful."

He looked over at Joshua. "I'm sure she is. How is Luc?" he asked to change the subject, regretting not being there when Joshua was born.

"He is walking in circles, speaking so fast we can't understand him." They both laughed over such a vision. "How is Joshua?"

"Oh, he's fine. Sleeps like a wild man, but okay," Ryan teased as Joshua giggled in the background. "You want to talk to your mommy?" he asked, giving the phone to Joshua.

"Hi, mommy. Is Shondra still got baby in her stomach?"

"No, the baby is out now and she is beautiful," Roni told him

"Yucky, a girl!" He made a face. "Can I see her?"

"Yes, I will be home shortly to get some sleep but we will come back this evening. Will that be okay with you, mister?"

Smiling from ear to ear, he asked, "Is Ryan coming too?" He looked at Ryan, trying to wink his eye.

"Definitely, we are going to wait until he gets off work. Let me speak to him again."

Joshua gave Ryan the phone. "Ryan, we will pick you up from work this evening before we come back to the hospital." She didn't give him a choice, which Ryan appreciated. It made him feel like she wanted him to be a part of her life, not just Joshua's. "We're going in to visit with Shondra a few minutes before leaving. I should be there before you leave for work, but just in case I'm not, I've called Eva and asked her to come early. I don't want you to be late."

"Well, don't worry about that. I will stay until one of you gets here. Kiss Shondra for me and tell Luc congratulations!"

"Will do. Ryan, thanks again for everything," she told him before hanging up.

Feeling good about talking with Roni, Ryan looked at Joshua who was smiling up at him. "What are you smiling about?" he asked, making Joshua giggle.

Looking at the time, Ryan decided he would just go ahead and take a shower. He left Joshua alone watching cartoons in the bed. As he stood under the shower, the warm water felt good running over his body. All he could think about was Roni and how he wished he could have been there with her when Joshua was born.

She would have been so beautiful pregnant. Her face was glowing in the pictures he had seen of her, sharing big smiles with Shondra and Thuy like sisters. He knew Shondra had been there the night Joshua was born just as Roni was during her delivery.

Even though the shower felt good, he needed to get out and see what Joshua was doing. Coming back into the bedroom, he saw Joshua had found his pictures of Roni when they were in college: the picture after the game when they went out to eat, pictures from the BBQ, and the group photo at graduation.

He had them spread out on the bed and was shocked when he saw Ryan looking at him. Ryan could see Joshua was afraid he had done something wrong, so Ryan walked over and sat beside him. "What are you looking at?" he asked as he leaned over Joshua's head to look at the photos with him.

"Pictures of you and mommy," he smiled.

She was so beautiful. "You got her dimples," he told Joshua. Feeling nostalgic, he knew he needed to get away from the pictures. Messing up Joshua's hair, he kissed him on the head. "Come on, let's go get some breakfast." Joshua jumped on his back as they made their way to the kitchen.

"What do you want for breakfast?" Joshua sat on the stool at the counter.

"Eggs, bacon, and cheese," he requested.

"What, no fruit?"

"No, but don't tell mommy," he pleaded.

"How about I cut you some orange slices? I'll eat them with you."

"Okay." He laid his head on the counter.

"It's not that bad," Ryan teased him.

"Ryan, can I have that picture?"

"What picture?"

"At the restaurant." He looked up inquiringly at Ryan.

Not knowing how to respond, he continued preparing their breakfast. "Why do you want that picture?"

Shrugging his shoulders, Joshua said, "I don't know. You just look happy."

Ryan had to admit they were happy then. "Will it make you eat your orange slices?"

Nodding his head and grinning, he shouted, "Yep!"

"Okay, it's yours. Now eat!"

Roni made it home before Ryan had to leave, giving him a chance to see the picture on her phone of the baby new to the world with her tiny little fingers placed on her face and her eyes still shut. Her mother held a little pink cap on her head as Luc looked on. They were a beautiful family.

Ryan needed to break the weird silence that came over the room. "Have they named her yet?"

"Yes, but Shondra refuses to tell us until you are there this evening." Touching his arm, Roni continued, "She wants you to be a part of the celebration and I agree with her. You are part of the family and need to be there for the baby's proper introduction to the world."

Feeling at a loss for words, Ryan said, "Thanks, I appreciate that," then tickled Joshua while he laughed. "Let your mommy get some rest. See you guys this evening." Picking up his messenger bag, Ryan left for the subway.

The workday could not end fast enough for Ryan. He kept looking at his watch wishing time would hurry along. The best part of the day was when he got a chance to talk to Roni and Joshua. They called after lunch, because Roni was going to the store to check on things before picking him up. She promised not to be late and as always was on time.

Arriving at Shondra's room, everyone was there except for them. Laurence couldn't resist taking a dig at them for being the last to arrive. He let it be known even Thuy was there before them, asking if they made any stops along the way with a devious smile.

Ryan purposely ignored Laurence as he lifted Joshua up to look at the baby girl. Although she was a girl, Joshua decided she was pretty. Then he wanted to know when she could play with him. Shondra explained it would be awhile before she could play, which disappointed Joshua, but he was encouraged to treat her like a little sister and protect her. Joshua was excited at the thought of being a big brother.

"Gather around everyone," Luc instructed. "Time for the proper introduction."

"Family, today Luc and I would like to introduce you to Hadiya Bernice LeBeau."

Roni couldn't hold back her tears. "Shondra, you don't have to do that."

With tears in her eyes Shondra explained, "Roni, your family has given so much to mine. Luc and I talked about it and thought we would honor the memory of your mother with our daughter."

Forgetting Hadiya was in her arms, Roni hugged Shondra as they both cried.

CHAPTER 8

Ryan couldn't believe how big Hadiya had gotten. She was only a month old, but already starting to show personality. It had been great visiting with Luc and Shondra last night. Even though he enjoyed visiting friends and having them visit, tonight he just wanted to be with Roni and Joshua.

She must have been very busy, because Roni hadn't called nor answered when he called earlier. Ryan knew they were doing inventory and buying merchandise for the winter line. It just seemed abnormal for her even with a busy day; they usually would have spoken at least once. During breakfast she appeared distant, but Ryan felt she had a lot on her mind.

Getting to the brownstone, Ryan skipped up the steps still whistling as he opened the door. "Hello!" The house was silent as Ryan walked in. He laid his keys in the dish on the cherry wood table before he walked to the foot of the stairs. The silence was starting to scare him until he saw Joshua coming down the hall. "Hey!" Ryan saw something was wrong. "What's going on?"

In a solemn voice, he told Ryan, "Nothing."

"What's wrong?" Looking around, he asked, "Where is your mommy?"

"Upstairs in her room." Laying his head on Ryan's shoulder, he said, "Mommy's blue today."

"Hi, Mr. Ryan. Ms. Roni asked me to stay until you got here," Joshua's nanny, Eva, told him. "She is feeling a little down, been here most of the day." Eva looked at Joshua, instructing him to be good as she left for the day.

Ryan asked Joshua to go to his room while he checked on his mother. Knocking on the door, Ryan called her name. There was no response, so he knocked again louder. "Roni, are you all right?" Not waiting for her to answer, he cracked open the door. When there was still no response from inside, he opened the door fully. Roni was curled up on the bay window seat. He could tell she had been crying. Not knowing what had happened he rushed over to her. "What happened?"

She shook her head, telling him, "Nothing," as she forced a smile. "Just a little blue today." In reality, she was finally grieving her parents. Although she had lost her mother many years earlier, her dad had passed away only a few months before. Losing him was like losing her mother all over again.

During both deaths, she had to be the strength of her family. Her grief had to be put on hold because she had Laurence to take care of after her mom's death, and then Joshua during her father's passing. Roni felt as though she was trapped in a room with no exit, only able to look out, seeing her pain without the ability of letting go.

So many nights she just wished she could have screamed, letting go of the loneliness she was feeling, but if she broke who would fix her? No one could because no one knew; Roni wore her mask well.

"Roni, what's wrong?" Ryan was very concerned because he had never seen her this way.

She knew he wouldn't leave her alone until she explained. "I guess I am finally realizing I am alone."

"How do you mean?"

"Both my mom and dad are gone. I just feel like I have no one."

"Roni, you shouldn't feel like that." Ryan sat beside her. "You are not alone. You have Laurence, Joshua, and me. We are here for you, but you have to let us in."

"I know," she told him, but letting people in was hard for her. Any time she trusted someone, she was disappointed. Then she just had something new to get over.

Roni was so tired of carrying the weight of her family on her shoulders. Today her shoulders couldn't hold anymore. Before she could stop herself, she turned to Ryan and began to weep.

Holding her, he tried not to speak. Roni needed to let go, but her pain was deeper than he could imagine. "Let it out," he encouraged her as she cried in his arms. Not saying another word, Ryan just held her. This was the first time she had been able to cry to someone other than herself.

Regaining her composure, she apologized, "I'm sorry I got your shirt wet." She tried to make light humor of her moment of weakness. "I'll get it cleaned for you." She wouldn't look up, not wanting him to see her pain.

"Don't worry about the shirt. I will just put it back in Laurence's closet." Roni had to laugh at Ryan's wit. "Joshua is really worried about you," he told her.

"I need to check on him." She tried to get up from the seat.

"Oh no, I will take care of Joshua. You get some rest." He kissed her on the head. "I'll take Joshua and we'll pick up dinner from Gino's. What would you like?"

"Farfalle with the red wine marinara sauce," she said just to give an answer. "Thank you," she told him, feeling embarrassed by her moment of weakness.

"I will call in your order, Signorina," Ryan smiled and bowed before leaving the room.

Ryan went by Joshua's room to tell him that his mommy was fine and they would be picking up dinner after he changed. That excited Joshua, because he liked going out into the city, and Gino's was only a couple of blocks away so they would walk. Joshua loved strolling through the neighborhood. It came alive during the spring and their neighborhood was special with many different people from different places. To him it was like a walk down Sesame Street; the only thing missing was Elmo.

Ryan went upstairs to change his clothes. While putting on his jeans and a T-shirt, his mind went back to Roni. He just didn't know what to do about her. For a brief moment, she had needed him. Although he didn't know how long she would need him, he loved being there for her. Knowing Roni by the time they returned, she would be fine, not requiring his support anymore. That thought saddened Ryan. Not because she would no longer be upset, but because she would no longer need him.

Joshua was so excited to be walking down the sidewalk with Ryan. They would talk and Ryan always listened to him. He would tell Ryan the jokes he had heard on the kid shows that day and he would tell him stories at night to help him sleep. Ryan was his best friend, and it was great.

Their relationship had grown stronger, and Ryan cherished every moment they spent together. He watched his son grow daily, reminding him of himself as a child. Ryan didn't want their relationship to change because of his secret. Even though Joshua needed to know he was his father, he couldn't risk telling him. Death would be easier than having Joshua hate him.

After picking up dinner, Ryan wanted to do something nice for Roni. Thinking it might cheer her up, he decided to buy her some flowers. There were many beautiful colors: orange, yellow, red, and purple. It was so hard to choose from the arrangements. Even Joshua was having trouble finding something for his mommy with so many choices.

As they walked deeper into the market, Ryan smelled a familiar fragrance. The aroma seemed to be coming from the deep purple flowers. When a clerk walked by, Ryan asked her what they were. She informed him those were fresh lilacs just brought in. Picking Joshua up to smell the blooms, he explained they smelled like Roni. Joshua laughed because his mommy wasn't purple.

Roni showered while they were gone, putting on a little dress that was bright orange. She was hoping the bright color would keep her from feeling so down. The sleek soft material clung to her body showing her curves. Seeing the color against her skin reminded her of springtime, a time for new beginnings.

Looking into the mirror, she pulled her hair back but decided against it. She felt it showed too much of her face and today she just wanted to hide. Noticing the freckles across her nose had multiplied, she smiled because they were a hereditary trait from her mother. Then she was saddened knowing her mother would never see the woman she had become, but knew she would have been proud of her daughter.

There was a knock very low on the door. "Mommy, dinner is ready," Roni heard Joshua say, then the sound of small feet rushing down the stairs. She heard Ryan telling Joshua to slow down and not to run down the stairs. Opening the door, she smelled the scent of fresh flowers. Looking at the floor, she saw the beautiful purple petals strewn on the hardwood floor trailing down the stairs.

Walking on the petals, her feet felt like they were on a natural carpet of spring. As she walked to the top of the stairs, she saw the purple candles glowing as they cascaded down the steps. Feeling the slight warmth of the flames as she descended the stairs warmed her spirit.

The trail continued until she reached the dining room where the two of them sat snickering at what they had done for her. She felt full inside because of the lengths Ryan had gone to make her feel better. "You two, thank you." She smiled as they stood and held the chair for her. "What's for dinner?" She acted surprised at the menu.

"We got bow ties!" Joshua shouted. "Did we surprise you, mommy?"

"Yes, you did; the flowers and the candles smell so sweet." She touched them both. "But not as sweet as you two." Both Joshua and Ryan blushed seeing the bliss on her face.

Ryan hadn't seen such happiness on her face in a long time. He watched her as Joshua told whose idea it was for the candles and why they put them on the stairwell with the petals from the lilacs. He gave Ryan most of the credit for the idea but was letting it be known he did most of the work pulling the petals from the flowers. Joshua was very animated with his hands while dancing in the chair. They could barely eat watching the performance.

Ryan began clearing the table before Roni tried to do it herself. As she started to help, Joshua put his hand on her arm, "No, mommy, we got cannoli for dessert."

"Cannoli, that's my favorite." It really wasn't but she knew Joshua liked it.

Ryan smiled at Roni. "That was all his suggestion."

"I couldn't ask for a better son." She reached over and gave him a hug and kissed his chilled little nose.

"You have to kiss Ryan too, he helped."

Both felt a little awkward at the suggestion, so Ryan gave her a sad puppy dog look, while she and Joshua laughed at the face.

"Oh, come here." She grabbed his face and kissed him gently, taking him by surprise.

"Yuck! Cooties," Joshua screeched at them kissing.

"So that's why you wanted your mommy to kiss me, so you could say cooties," Ryan teased as Joshua laughed at them kissing.

"I'll get dessert." Ryan went into the kitchen, looking back at Joshua and pretending he was going to give him a black eye. That only made Joshua grin because he had said cooties.

Dessert was Joshua's favorite part of the meal. He didn't get to eat sweets often, but enjoyed them when he did. Joshua had more cannoli on his face than in his mouth, with ricotta cheese and powdered sugar all over. No one was sure how he got powdered sugar on his forehead, but it ended up there. It was one of those moments they wished they had a camera.

Roni got up, starting to clear away the dishes before Ryan. "This has been the best dinner I've had in a long time, thank you," she paused letting them think they were safe, "but who is going to clean up the hallway?"

Ryan looked at Joshua signaling for him to be quiet as they both got out of their chairs. Each pretended to tiptoe around the table for a quiet getaway. She saw their antics yelling back at them, "I see you!" Ryan ran around the table grabbing up Joshua as they scurried down the hall. You could hear Joshua laughing as Roni reminded them, "I know where you live!"

"All finished," Ryan came downstairs to tell Roni.

"Thank you so much for tonight, I really appreciate it."

"No problem." He tried not to show his delight at hearing her say that. "I will get Joshua ready for bed."

Roni smiled to herself thinking about how sweet Ryan had been as she finished putting away the dishes. Turning off the lights, she took one last look around the kitchen making sure she hadn't forgotten anything.

Walking upstairs, she heard the laughter of Ryan and Joshua during his bath. Ryan was telling Joshua how he fell from a tree house almost breaking his leg. If it hadn't been for his cousin, Jake, breaking his fall, he would have broken something besides Jake's bow. She imagined Joshua would be like him when he got older, always into something, then laughed because he was already like Ryan in many ways.

Roni went into Joshua's room to turn down his bed. As she pulled back the sheets, a photo floated to the floor. She picked it up, seeing it was a picture of her and Ryan when they were at the Doug Out, back in college. How had Joshua gotten it? she wondered. Hearing them coming from the bathroom she put the picture behind her, not wanting Joshua to see she had it. "All clean?" she asked.

"Yep," Joshua shouted as he passed her going to his bedroom.

Seeing Ryan coming behind him, she stepped into his path showing him the picture. "I found this in Joshua's room; did you know he had it?"

"I had forgotten about it. He saw some old pictures of mine when you were at the hospital with Shondra and asked if he could have it. I didn't think it would be a problem, sorry."

"Oh, no problem, I just didn't want him getting stuff out of your room without you knowing about it."

"Will it be alright for him to keep it?" Ryan asked, hoping she would let Joshua have the photo.

"Sure, just tell him to keep it out of his bed." She smiled as she went to her bedroom.

Joshua was frantic looking all around his bed. "What are you looking for?" Ryan asked.

"My picture," he said almost in tears.

"Hold on, your mommy found it on the floor."

His little eyes were afraid. "Is she mad?"

"No, no, she isn't mad. Just wanted to make sure I knew you had it." He gave him a reassuring smile. Giving the picture back to him, he asked, "What was it doing in your bed?"

He shrugged his shoulders not wanting to tell him, but saw Ryan didn't believe him. "I sleep with it under my pillow." He refused to look up at Ryan.

"Why under your pillow?"

"Ty says if I sleep with it under my pillow, my wish will come true." He slowly raised his head to look at Ryan. "Will it?"

"We will just have to see." Ryan didn't have to ask what Joshua's wish was, because he had the same one.

Ryan had to tell Joshua more of his favorite story, which was about Ryan's childhood in Virginia. He wanted to hear about the horses and Ryan fishing with his dad. Those stories excited Joshua being from the city; the only time he saw animals was at the Steelys' farm once a month or at the zoo. The two of them would always lie on the bed as they looked up at the star nightlights on the ceiling until Joshua fell asleep.

Roni figured Ryan and Joshua were finished with their story time. Knowing Joshua would be deep in sleep, she wanted to check on him before she went to bed. She opened the door, trying not to make it creak too loudly and wake Joshua. She smiled seeing his leg hanging off the edge of the bed as he held onto his pillow for comfort. Moving him back onto the bed, she pulled the covers up around him. He was sleeping so hard that he never even felt her moving him or kissing him good night.

Walking back into the hall, she was still smiling at her little jewel on the other side of the door. As she went back to her room to retire for the night, she noticed that Ryan had left the towels for his room on the table by the stairs. She decided to take them up before he got into the shower.

Hearing the radio, she tried knocking but he couldn't hear her over the noise. Roni didn't want to invade his privacy so she just opened the door slightly, calling his name, but she received no response. Seeing he was not in his bedroom, she could hear the water running in the shower as the music played. Laughing at how his music choices had changed, she smiled. Ryan had developed a love for Luther, listening to one of her favorite CDs. Luther was singing "A House Is Not Home," which was her parent's favorite love song.

She walked to the doorway of the bathroom seeing the steam from the shower. Roni felt she could put the towels on the counter so he would have them when he got out. He would never know she was in the room. Feeling the cool granite tiles under her feet, she walked across the floor to the counter to place the towels there.

On her way out, she looked up to see his reflection in the mirror. Washing his hair, he didn't notice her but she certainly noticed him. The way the water ran down his body was intoxicating. She watched the bubbles from the shampoo as they slowly moved down his body, first down his neck to his shoulder where they seemed to stop.

They were toying with her, making her look as they began their journey across his arm then down his side, picking up momentum until they reached his waist. There they slowed in pace, sliding down to his thigh, which was long and muscular, seeming never to end. The bubbles reaching his knee stopped, like a rollercoaster car when it got to the top of the track and rocked, before speeding to the bottom disappearing in the water.

Remembering she was intruding she turned to walk away and saw Ryan staring back at her in the mirror. His eyes were fixated on her; neither of them could look away. Embarrassed by her actions she mouthed, "I'm sorry," as she turned to leave the room.

Ryan wasn't sorry that she was there, but wished he could have said something. Her reflection in the mirror had been so captivating he'd been hypnotized by the moment. Why did it have to end?

Suddenly he felt the tips of her slim fingers. They burned on his skin as she slid them from his shoulder to the middle of his back. Afraid to turn around fearing he was dreaming, he felt her soft breast on his back as her lips kissed his shoulder. Her hair was wet from the shower and rested on his back along with her dress that was now clinging to her body.

"Roni," he called her name, but received no response. Each time she touched him his body ached with desire to the point he could no longer resist her. Ryan turned to face her, pulling her into his arms. He waited for her to say stop, but the words never parted from her lips as he held her soft warm body close to his.

Tired of waiting for him, she pulled his head down, kissing his lips. All the passion of the past five years came to the boiling point, and they couldn't stop themselves. Her dress was completely soaked as he guided her against the granite wall at the back of the shower. Sliding his hand up her thigh and under her wet dress, he found her panties and with one quick jerk they landed on the shower floor.

Only one small faint sound came from her lips as he entered her. Their bodies were on fire with only one way to put them out. With one arm, he held her body as he caressed her. With the pain of pleasure, she bit his shoulder. Each thrust coming more rapid until she could no longer contain her scream. Looking into each other's eyes they knew their love had never died, but had only grown stronger.

CHAPTER 9

The sheets were damp from their bodies as she looked over on the nightstand for the clock. It was two A.M. and she didn't want Joshua waking up to find her missing. With her head lying on Ryan's chest and his arms wrapped around her, Roni knew she needed to go back downstairs, although she didn't want to leave.

Trying not to wake him, she slowly tried to move his arm, but his grip only tightened. "Where do you think you are going?" he asked, giving her the devilish grin of a child up to mischief.

"I don't want Joshua to wake up and find me gone." She laughed looking at the smile on his face. "Come on, let me up," she said as she pretended to wrestle away from him. Both were giggling at how childish they were acting.

Caressing her face, he pulled her close kissing her tenderly. He looked intensely into her eyes as he confessed, "You know I never stopped loving you."

"Ryan," she called his name, afraid to allow those words to part from her lips much less her heart.

"Roni, you don't have to say it to me. I know you are still hurting, but I hope in time you will heal."

Hugging him, she whispered, "Thank you for understanding." She saw the sincerity in his eyes as she climbed out of bed. "I am going to borrow your robe if you don't mind."

"Wash it before you bring it back," he teased her. "Roni," he called her name as she started for the door.

She looked at him as he motioned for her to come back. Roni sat on the bed answering, "Yes?"

"I need to tell you about that day on campus with Amy."

"You don't have to..."

Before she could finish he put his finger on her lips. "I am telling you hoping that will help to put it in the past for us." Looking into her eyes he began, "Roni, I was engaged." He saw her anger beginning to build. "It happened before we met. During Christmas break, I got engaged. Not because I wanted to be married, just because I felt it was what I needed to be doing. Coming from a small town that was just what you did. You graduate high school, learn a trade or in my case go to college, get a job, and get married."

Dreading having to tell the story, he continued, "Amy and I grew up together and started dating when I was home for the summer. I knew I would be graduating in the spring and thought why not. Easy gift idea. So I got engaged."

He knew he had to finish the story because he could see the hurt in her eyes, something he had hoped he would never see again. "Looking back it was a mistake, because after meeting you I knew I didn't love her. For the first time in my life, I actually felt real love. Not that stuff you say in high school when you are trying to get laid." He nervously smiled remembering his foolish antics of the past.

"When I met you, my whole world changed. Never had I met someone that made me feel so alive." Taking a deep breath, he said, "Once I knew I was falling in love with you, and this was before anything happened between us, I broke off the engagement because I couldn't pretend that I loved her any longer. Even though I never told Amy that I loved her, foolishly I asked her to marry me."

Pulling her back as she tried to get up from the bed, he implored, "Please, let me finish. It was a terrible thing to do but I told her over spring break that it was over and I didn't want to marry her. I didn't get the ring back because she was hurting and I didn't want to hurt her anymore."

"If you broke off the engagement, why did she come to graduation saying she was your fiancée?"

"After I went back to school, she would go cry on my mother's shoulder. Even had my mom calling me asking me to work it out. I told my mom the same thing I am telling you, that I didn't love her and never did. I felt it was unfair to her to lie about my feelings or intentions. My mom thought she knew best and brought her to graduation."

Not sure if she believed him, Roni asked, "Why would your mom do that?"

"She meant well, but that doesn't excuse me. I take full responsibility for the situation, because I created it when I asked Amy to marry me knowing I didn't love her." He tried to get his thoughts together before continuing. "It was a horrible mistake. One I have to live with. Amy is really a nice person, but she wasn't the woman I loved."

His eyes were burning from the tears. "I needed to tell you I am sorry for what I put you through." He searched her eyes for a sign. "If you allow me back into your life, I promise I won't ever hurt you again."

"Don't say that," she stopped him, "because it is a promise you can't keep. We both have made mistakes," she confessed, remembering how she had kept Joshua away from Ryan, hurting him in the process. Caressing his face, she felt the stubble of a beard. She smiled at the roughness of his face. "I will forgive you, only if you forgive me. We both need to leave that behind us and move forward."

She kissed him gently on the lips. "I need to get back downstairs before Joshua misses me." They both held on to each other for as long as possible.

Walking to the door, she turned to look at him. "Ryan, we need to tell Joshua you are his father soon. He is a smart child. I don't want him getting confused about our relationship," she smiled. "I want him to understand that we are his parents."

Ryan knew the day would come and he would have to tell Joshua, but he felt his stomach getting sick.

"We can tell him together," she assured him.

"No, I need to tell him myself. It is something I need to share with my son," he said as he tried to figure out how to tell him.

"Okay." She didn't know why but she understood how he felt.

After the door closed behind her, Ryan pulled the pillow over his head, wondering, *What do I say?*

In separate beds, neither could sleep thinking about the night of passion they had shared. Ryan was smiling to himself thinking about making love to her. Getting the past off his chest had lifted the strain on his heart. He felt like he could be a part of her life now and they could move on.

Breakfast that morning was normal. Roni and Ryan were their usual selves in front of Joshua. Roni wouldn't let him have eggs because she wanted him to eat more fruit. Instead, she gave him yogurt with berries and granola. At first, he didn't want it but the flavors were so delicious he ate it all.

"Drink your juice, sweetie," she told him.

"Okay," he obeyed, grabbing his cup.

"Now, go get dressed; Eva will be here shortly," she told him when he put his cup on the counter.

"Okay." He looked to Ryan for help getting down from the stool.

Ryan watched closely as Joshua went back upstairs. When he was sure he was out of sight he went around the counter. Grabbing Roni as she pretended to try to get away, he said, "I couldn't sleep after you left last night."

Looking to see if Joshua was around she said, "Me either," kissing him gently. "What are you going to say to Joshua?"

Backing off, he remembered his task. "Roni, I really don't know what to say to him."

"I can be with you..."

"No, this is something I have to do." Hearing Laurence coming through the family room Ryan moved back around the counter. They didn't want Laurence to know about them yet, because Joshua didn't know.

"Good morning, my people." Laurence came in singing a song, but stopped in his tracks. Looking at Roni then Ryan as he continued to the coffee maker, he asked, "How you two doing this morning?"

"Fine," Roni answered suspiciously because of the way Laurence was acting.

"I better get to work." Ryan tried to find a reason to leave the room. "See you tonight."

"Ooh! You did it!" Laurence pointed at them.

"What are you talking about?" Roni asked afraid of his answer.

"You two should be ashamed." He lowered his voice so Joshua couldn't hear. "My poor little nephew up there asleep down the hall and you two up there bumping uglies."

"Will you keep your voice down?" Roni tried to control her brother's laughter so Joshua wouldn't hear.

Getting serious, Laurence questioned them, "When are you two going to tell him who Ryan really is?"

"That is what we were discussing before you come in," Ryan told him.

"There was no discussion going on there. A little tongue wrestling maybe, but no talking." Seeing the looks on their faces, he said, "Oh, I saw you from the hall."

Throwing a dishtowel at Laurence, Roni exclaimed, "You are terrible!"

Feeling defeated Ryan just blushed. "He is your brother," he said before turning to go upstairs. "I'm going to say bye to Joshua."

"Roni, all jokes aside, when are you and Ryan going to tell him?"

"Tonight, Ryan is going to tell him tonight," she said with a worried look.

"Joshua is still a child and he won't care where Ryan has been or why he wasn't here in the past. Just happy that he is here now." He took a sip of his coffee. "I bet he won't be as happy as his momma this morning." Laurence giggled as Roni tried to choke him.

It had been the longest day for Ryan. All day he had been trying to think of a way to talk to Joshua. He tried to think back to when he was a child. How did his parents tell him something important? Unfortunately, he couldn't think of a single time that he was told something as important as what he had to tell Joshua.

They had told him his dog, Buster, had been run over by a car when he was six, but that didn't compare. When Buster was killed, they just bought him another dog. If this didn't go well, what could he do to make it right? Tonight was not going to be easy.

He concentrated on what to say on the subway ride home. What if Joshua was angry they'd led him to believe Ryan was just a friend and not his father? Joshua was only four but a wise child. He actually thought things through and that was what scared Ryan, but also made him proud. The way he would ask questions about everything, everything except who was his father.

Why had he never asked about his father? Did he not care or was he just too busy being a kid? He probably *was* too busy being a kid to care. Ryan smiled thinking about Joshua smiling up at him, hoping Joshua would always look at him with that spark in his eyes. With what he had to tell him tonight, he wasn't sure he would any longer.

Walking up the steps of the brownstone, he stopped midway. His head was pounding from all that thinking about the conversation to come. "Get your head together, Ryan," he told himself. Regrettably, the little pep talk wasn't working. It was not a game and if Ryan lost, he didn't get to play again.

Continuing up the steps, he put his keys in the door. Looking up he saw Joshua running to greet him. Knowing what he had to tell him tonight become secondary as Joshua leaped into his arms without worry he would catch him.

"Whoa, you are getting heavy!" Ryan teased him.

"Too much fruit," he whispered to Ryan as they both laughed. "Why are you late?"

"I'm not late." Looking at his watch he realized he was actually five minutes late. "Well, I guess I am," he smiled at Joshua as he carried him down the hall.

Joshua spoke low so his mother couldn't hear. "You going to ask mommy if you can take me to a baseball game?"

Ryan had completely forgotten about the promise he had made to him. "I will if you eat your vegetables at dinner tonight." He gave a stern look but followed it with a smile.

He carried Joshua into the kitchen where Roni had her menus spread out on the counter. "Okay guys, Thai, Indian, or Italian?"

Pretending to care if he ate, Ryan picked up a menu looking at Joshua. "Is this one okay with you?"

"Yep!" Joshua yelled ready to agree to anything Ryan said.

"Thai it is," he agreed as he gave Roni the menu back.

"What do you want?"

"You and Joshua can pick," he smiled. "I got a bit of a headache tonight so anything will be fine." He kissed Joshua on the forehead. "I'm going to take a shower and clean up before dinner."

"Hold on, mister, have you eaten today?" Roni asked.

Not remembering if he had or not, he said, "I had breakfast this morning."

"You are probably just hungry." Looking in the cupboard, she got a box of crackers and retrieved some cheese from the refrigerator. On a small dish, she cut slices of cheese and put out crackers for him. "Eat this before you go upstairs."

He smiled because he knew there was no arguing with her. Getting one and handing one to Joshua, they both ate cheese and crackers. Although he hated to admit it, his head was feeling better after eating the crackers with Joshua. "Go ahead and call the food in while I take a shower." He went up to his apartment on the third floor as his mind thought through the task ahead.

Roni ordered stir-fried beans and mushrooms, fried shrimp with basil leaves, and baby kale and pork. Not forgetting Joshua's sweet tooth, she ordered tua krop kaew, a Thai dessert of caramel peanuts with sesame. After hanging up the phone, she remembered the scared look on Ryan's face. Joshua didn't know who he was but loved him like a father anyway. It would be okay she reassured herself. In her heart, she knew Ryan didn't want Joshua to feel they had betrayed him. She wished he would let her be with him for support, but he was determined to do it alone.

Roni heard the voices of both Joshua and Ryan coming downstairs. "Ryan, can we watch Mrs. Piggle Wiggle? I like the one about the radishes."

"Sure, go get the DVD." Ryan waited for him to leave the room before talking to Roni. "I am so scared. I don't want him to hate me after this," he confided in her with panic in his eyes.

"He won't hate you," she tried to reassure him, but she felt afraid for both of them. Caressing his cheek, she soothed, "It will be okay. No matter what, we will work it out."

Kissing her hand, Ryan said, "I know we will," then left to join Joshua.

Dinner was delicious for the most part. The caramel peanuts with sesame dessert was too sweet for Roni, but Joshua ate his with gusto. At dinner, Joshua had tried to teach Ryan how to eat with chopsticks, but laughed when he kept dropping his food. Joshua encouraged him by telling him that it took practice. Finally, Ryan gave up and grabbed his fork. They all laughed when Ryan pretended to pull his hair out.

After dinner, Joshua wanted to finish watching his show, so he and Ryan retired to the family room. The episode he liked was almost over when Roni came in to tell him it was bath time. Pouting he slid off the couch, starting for the door. "Come on, Ryan!"

"Joshua, Ryan isn't feeling well tonight. I can give you your bath."

"No!" he shouted. "You're a girl!"

Not wanting him to hear her, she giggled quietly. "I was giving it to you before Ryan came."

"Yeah, that's because there was no boy in house," his little face very serious about not letting her see him naked.

"Don't worry, I will give you your bath." Ryan looked over at Roni and smiled.

"You sure you feel up to it?" Roni asked, no longer talking about the bath.

Pretending to pull up his pants, he winked at Roni. "It's dirty work, but somebody has got to do it."

Bath time was not nearly long enough for Ryan as he dried Joshua off and checked behind his ears. "Alright, munchkin, get your PJ's on." After he was all dressed for bed, Ryan knelt down for his piggyback ride. *No need to run now*, Ryan thought to himself, it was time.

Playfully he tossed Joshua on the bed and sat down beside him. "Story time," he announced to Joshua. "What do you want to hear tonight?"

"Can you tell me about the tobacco stuff again?"

"Don't you get tired of that story?"

"Never!" Joshua shouted.

"Well, how about I tell you the story of how I know your mommy?"

Joshua's eyes lit up, because he had never heard that story before. "Okay."

"You know we went to college together, right?" he asked, pausing so Joshua could respond. "Well, we never told you how close we were. Much like your mommy, Shondra and Thuy, we were good friends." He glanced over at Joshua as they lay on the bed looking at the stars on the ceiling. Both had their hands behind their heads as if they were lying in the grass looking at the night sky.

"I met your mother when she had to help me with African American history. She was my tutor and during that time we became close." He could see Joshua was listening to his every word. "You see, when you get to be your mommy's and my age, girls are not quite as yucky."

They both laughed at the thought as Joshua made a stink face. "Like I said as you get older they won't be yucky." Getting lost in thought, he quickly remembered what he had to tell him. "We became very close, like in the picture you have of us. I guess you could say she was my girlfriend." Joshua turned to look at him. "Joshua, I want you to understand that I loved your mommy then and I still do."

"You want her to be your girlfriend again?" Joshua asked excitedly.

"Well, yes, do you give us your permission?" Enjoying the broad smile on Joshua's face, Ryan took a deep breath. "What I am trying to tell you is," the words began to stick in his throat so he tried a different approach. "Our love was so strong that we made you." Seeing the puzzled look on his face, he elaborated, "Joshua, your mommy and I want you to know that I am your father." Ryan became a little nervous because Joshua didn't say anything. "Do you understand what I am trying to tell you?"

Nodding his head yes, he said, "I know that."

"What do you mean you know? Who told you?"

"Nobody, I figured it out."

"How did you figure it out?" he asked, thinking Joshua might have seen them the night before or earlier that morning.

"You took my eyes." Joshua smiled up at Ryan, seeing his face had a confused look. "It's okay, we can share them."

Squeezing as tight as he could, Ryan said, "I love you."

"I love you too," Joshua returned, hugging his father as he patted him on the back. "Does this mean I can call you daddy now?"

"That would make me very happy, Joshua."

"Okay."

Getting control of himself, Ryan urged, "Now you go to sleep." He pulled the covers up around Joshua and kissed his forehead before he started for the door.

"Good night, daddy!"

"Good night, son." Ryan pulled the door closed before allowing the tear to roll down his cheek.

CHAPTER 10

There was a different atmosphere around the house with the cloud of secrecy no longer hanging over their heads, keeping them on edge. Joshua had no problem going from Ryan being his friend to his father. For Ryan it was heaven for Joshua to call him daddy and listening to him explain to his little friends that it was okay for him to be his father, but also his best friend.

Both Roni and Ryan could relax and be honest with their feelings. No longer did they need to steal looks at each other. They could now be a real family. Friday was date night for Ryan and Roni. Saturday was their family day when they took Joshua to the park and a matinee. Sunday was the day they all relaxed from the hectic week before and prepared for the one to come.

Even Laurence joined in on the Sunday unwind making it a relaxing time for all. By two P.M., they gathered in the family room on a couch or chair to take an afternoon nap.

The phone awakened Roni. After answering it, she found it to be Ryan's father, needing to speak with him immediately. Hearing the urgency in his voice, she took the phone to Ryan waking him from his nap. At first, he was still groggy from sleep but he awakened quickly as he spoke with his father.

"When?" he asked his father. "How is she?" he continued to gather information. Joshua had been lying on him sleeping and was awakened by the movement of his father. "Yeah, ah, let me make some calls and get back to you." There was panic in his voice as Ryan spoke to his father.

"Baby, is everything okay?" Roni asked afraid of the answer.

Laurence sensed Ryan and Roni needed to talk without Joshua in the room so he took Joshua outside to play catch.

Waiting for them to leave the room, Ryan turned to Roni. "My grandmother had a stroke earlier today." He tried to keep calm but hearing himself say it frightened him. "This can't be happening. She has never been sick with more than a cold."

Roni moved toward him. "Is she okay?" She knew strokes came in different degrees of severity.

"My dad was calling from the emergency room. The ambulance had just arrived with her so he doesn't know anything yet." Not knowing what else to do he put his head in his hands.

Roni was all too familiar with what Ryan was feeling. She put her arm around his shoulders, letting him know she was there and he could lean on her. "You feel you need to go see her?" She wanted to make a suggestion without sounding as if she was giving orders. Without trying, she would sometimes step into a situation and take command. It was just her nature to feel she had to fix things, but she wanted to be there for Ryan.

"I don't know," he said, looking to her with the vulnerability of a child. "This is the first time I've been in this situation." Ryan didn't know how to react. When his grandfather became ill, he was close by. Now he was at least a seven-hour drive away. "Roni, what should I do?" He knew she had been through more illness than he could imagine.

"Call your boss and let him know your grandmother is ill. I will check on flights leaving tomorrow."

"A flight for tomorrow?" he asked.

"Yes, even if she is better than expected you need to go check on her and see for yourself."

"Roni, I haven't been on this job that long, I don't want to jeopardize it," he said, feeling worried about asking for time off.

"This is more important. Now you can argue with me or you can call your boss letting him know about the family emergency." Roni looked at flight schedules for Monday. "It might be best for you to leave after lunch. You will probably want to go to the office before leaving."

Ryan called Miguel letting him know about his grandmother being in the hospital. Before he could even ask, Miguel told him to take as much time as needed. If they needed him, they would call. Even after Ryan offered to come in to catch him up to speed Miguel told him they could manage; most of his projects had been stalled because of weather, and there was a forecast for rain early that week. All he wanted was for Ryan's grandmother to get better.

"Hello," Ryan answered the phone. "How is she?" he nervously asked.

Roni only heard his half of the conversation and was a little uneasy that the tone in his voice hadn't changed. Still looking on, she was showing signs of worry in her face.

"Oh, okay, so they will be keeping her?" Ryan asked. "I'm planning on coming home tomorrow." He and his father began a discussion. "Dad, there won't be a problem. Stop worrying, I have already discussed it with my boss. It will be fine."

Hearing the conversation, Roni gathered that the stroke wasn't as severe as they had anticipated. The doctors would probably keep her a few days for observation. Still, Ryan needed to go and check on his grandmother because he wouldn't feel she was better unless he saw her himself.

"It's final, dad, I will be there sometime tomorrow." He looked at Roni with surprise in his eyes. "Mama Pearl," he shouted, "so I see they can't keep you down." The fear in his heart began to subside. "Well, I am looking at coming tomorrow for a few days. I know I don't have to, but I am."

During all the chatter Roni compared flights looking for the best choices, narrowing them down before she involved Ryan. She even looked for car rental options along with the flights. The closest airport to his hometown was at least forty-five minutes away and Ryan's father shouldn't have to worry about picking him up; someone needed to be at the hospital with Mama Pearl. Just in case the doctors come in to speak to her or the family about her condition.

Ryan finished his call telling his grandmother he loved her and would see her tomorrow.

Laurence had kept Joshua outside for as long as he could, but Joshua was curious, wanting to come back inside. Seeing him, Ryan began to explain his grandmother was ill and he needed to go back to Virginia to check on her. Joshua's eyes got big, not fully understanding why his father had to leave him. The look in his eyes told Ryan he thought he wasn't coming back. "Don't worry, I will be back in a few days," he reassured him.

"Can I come too?" With wide eyes, he looked up at Ryan.

Not knowing how to respond, Ryan looked over at Roni then back at Joshua. "I will be back by the end of the week, I promise." He looked again at Roni for her help in answering the question.

Roni was not sure how to respond, because she had never thought about Joshua having another side of the family. "Joshua, your daddy is coming back," she tried to reassure him. She could see he was afraid of losing Ryan.

"Ah, Joshua, go upstairs and let your mommy and I discuss this, okay?" He was beginning to understand why Joshua was scared of him leaving. Ryan waited for him to go upstairs before turning to Roni.

"I know what you are going to ask," she interjected before Ryan could ask, not feeling comfortable allowing Joshua to be that far away.

"Roni, it will only be for a few days and I promise I will take care of him," he said, letting her know he understood her concerns. Since he came back to New York, he hadn't talked much about his family and their response in finding out about Joshua. The only person he ever mentioned was his grandmother and how delighted she was when she had found out. He even left the baby book with Pearl so she could look at the pictures anytime she wanted.

Feeling he needed to make his point, he said, "Roni, this may be the only time she ever gets to see him," not telling her that Mama Pearl had asked if Joshua was coming.

"He has never been around people that don't want him there. I'm not sure he should be at his age." She expressed the fear of most parents when it came to their children. Roni knew how cruel people could be when someone was different. "We both know not everyone can appreciate our relationship."

"I know, Roni, but they are his family too." He felt hurt that she thought he would allow anyone to harm Joshua. "Trust me, no one will hurt him or disrespect him."

"I think it would be a great trip for him." Both had forgotten Laurence was still in the room. "This would give you two time to bond without Roni being there." Taking a cue from Roni's face, he said, "That's just my opinion."

Even though she didn't want to admit Laurence was right, she had to agree with his assessment of the situation. "Ryan, I know you will take care of him, but I just don't know how the rest of your family will react. There is a difference in knowing about him and accepting him." She understood that without Ryan having to tell her that some in his family wouldn't be so accommodating toward Joshua.

"Roni, I will respect whatever decision you make." He understood her position, but was still hurt that she didn't trust him to protect Joshua.

"I know you will and that makes it harder." Rubbing her temples as if she was getting a headache, she made her decision. "Promise me you will let nothing happen to him. I don't want him hurt physically or emotionally. He will have enough of that growing up in this world." Roni knew Joshua would have to experience life, but wanted him to retain his innocence as long as possible.

"I promise." He pulled her close, hugging her. Ryan knew it was a very hard decision for her. In his heart, Ryan was also worried about certain family members who might even deny Joshua's existence.

Roni asked Joshua to come down so they could give him the news about the trip. He was very excited about going to Virginia, flying for the first time and doing it all with his daddy.

CHAPTER 11

Joshua was thrilled to be in Virginia because he wanted to see the tree that Ryan fell from only to land on Jake. For him it was like going into a bedtime story and seeing the characters come to life.

Not only would he get to meet his grandparents, but also he would get to meet Mama Pearl. When Ryan called home Joshua would get to speak with her, but now he would get to see her in person.

Ryan was still a little nervous about bringing Joshua home. He knew Mama Pearl would love him and so would his father. Frequently Pete asked about him when Ryan called home, but his mom just pretended he didn't exist. How could she be so cruel to a child? She acted as if Joshua was a pair of shoes that had been given to her, but she thought them to be ugly and refused to wear them in public.

It was as if she felt that if she just ignored him, he would go away. Ryan had made his mind up that he wouldn't force her to see Joshua, but would allow contact if she initiated it. He loved his mother but couldn't understand how she could love him and not love the child that was part of him.

"Joshua, wait up, we need to get our luggage," he called out to him so he wouldn't walk off too far. Joshua stopped in his tracks so his dad could show him where he needed to go next. Taking his hand, Joshua smiled up at his dad while adjusting his backpack on his small shoulders. Ryan looked down, giving him a little wink, and like always, Joshua tried to wink back.

While they waited for the rental car, Ryan called Roni to let her know they had made it and were fine. She spoke with Joshua briefly about his first plane ride. He loved being up above the clouds but didn't like the takeoff or the landing. It made his stomach feel queasy. The flight attendants were very nice giving him his own pair of wings. One kept smiling at his daddy so he didn't really like her.

Roni thought it was so cute the way he was so protective of his father. She told him to keep Ryan out of trouble until they returned to New York and Joshua agreed. Ryan laughed that he had a snitch on his hands and would have to buy him off.

After getting their bags loaded in the car, Ryan felt the need to call the hospital to check on his grandma and to tell them he was on the way with Joshua. He hated feeling a need to warn them about his son, but he wanted to make sure no one would be shocked at seeing him. Dialing the number, he felt a sinking feeling in his stomach, which only intensified as he waited for someone to answer.

"Hello?" Pearl's voice on the other end was a welcoming sound.

"What are you doing answering the phone? I thought you were sick."

"Ryan!" she screamed. "Where are you?" Looking toward Ryan's mother, she mouthed, "It's Ryan."

"On my way from the airport," he laughed at Pearl's excitement. "I got a little surprise for you."

Pearl sat up in the bed. "You've got Joshua with you?" she asked, putting her hand on her cheek as she grinned at the thought of seeing her great-grandson.

"I'm not telling," he glanced back at Joshua in his booster seat. "You will have to wait and see."

"You just hurry here with that baby. See you soon, sweetie." Looking at Helen, she told her, "They are on their way from the airport."

"He's bringing that child?" Helen asked with a sneer

"No, he's bringing his son." Pearl's tone changed from joy to stern.

"How does he know that is his son? That child could belong to anyone and she is just pinning it on Ryan."

Shaking her head and trying to hold her tongue because she didn't want to be upset when Ryan got there, Pearl said, "You know, Helen, you may need to leave." She spoke slowly so Helen would understand she was serious.

"I'm just saying. What do we know about this...this woman?"

"Helen, you need to go!"

"Pete expects me to be here when he gets back."

Pearl wasn't one to play with her words; Helen wasn't going to be there when Joshua came in. "I will say this once more, get out."

Finally, Helen looked up from her book, and she could see Pearl was serious. "Well, I know when I'm not wanted."

"I don't know how you got to be so uppity. You barely had shoes when Pete met you."

Still trying to make her case, Helen argued, "I'm just saying she's probably trying to trap Ryan with this child. He has a bright future and needs a woman more like him."

"Why don't you just say it, Helen. White."

"Well, yes, white." She got up from her seat, gathering her things. "Those people are not like us."

"You're right, they're not and thank God for it."

Helen, feeling defeated, stormed to the door. "Tell Pete I went home."

Pearl wondered what Pete ever saw in her. She wasn't like that when they first married, but got that way after she started teaching school. How could she deny her own grandchild? Pearl tried to control herself but she was so angry she could bite nails. She had to calm down before they came because Joshua wasn't going to see her upset.

Helen could make Satan in hell scream, with her nose always up in the air. If a good rain came along, she would drown. The thought of her drowning brought a smile to Pearl's face and started her back to thinking about getting to meet Joshua for the first time.

She got up from her bed, happy they had taken out the IV earlier that morning. She went to the little closet, pulling out her overnight bag that Pete had brought her. Shuffling through the things, she found a tube of lipstick; not her favorite color, but it would have to do. Primping in the mirror, she tried to fix her hair because it was flat on one side from lying in the bed.

"You don't have to fuss for me."

Hearing Ryan's voice, she froze but knew she had to turn around. Pearl closed her eyes as if she were making a wish on a birthday cake before she turned to face them. Grabbing her face in sheer delight, she exclaimed, "Ryan!" as she hurried to hug him. "I am so glad to see you. Who is this young man?" she asked teasing Joshua.

He peeped from behind his father's leg with a shy smile at the woman he had been talking to on the phone. "This is Joshua," Ryan introduced him. "Say hi to your grandma."

Stooping down so she wouldn't frighten him, Pearl said, "Hi, Joshua. You are as handsome as your father." Getting closer to him, she corrected, "Actually you are better looking." That made Joshua laugh as Pearl stroked his tiny face making him feel at ease. Not wanting to frighten her grandson, she guided him closer to her until she had him in her arms.

"Hey, come on, get back in bed now. You are still sick," Ryan instructed his grandmother.

"You're not so big I can't turn you over my knee," she playfully scolded him. She felt that if she never saw another day, this one was worth a lifetime.

Feeling a tug on her robe, she looked down to Joshua holding a bag. "This is for you, grandma." Joshua was handing her the bag with a little teddy bear. "So you won't forget me."

"Sweetie, I will never forget you." Grabbing him up in her arms she showered him with kisses, hearing the laugher of an angel in her ear.

CHAPTER 12

Joshua made himself at home with Mama Pearl. They sat on the bed together as Joshua showed her the dinosaurs in his book and told her about them. He was a smart child, very articulate when speaking, and often tried to use words beyond his years. Pearl was so excited to be able to see another generation that she couldn't take her eyes off him.

Ryan sat in the chair next to her bed and didn't say anything when Joshua crawled from his lap onto the bed with his great-grandmother. He just smiled watching them interact. It was true that a child knows your heart because Joshua knew right off that Pearl loved him.

While he was concentrating on Joshua and Mama Pearl, Ryan didn't notice his father coming into the room. "Well, look at what the cat dragged in," Pete teased Ryan as he came into the room. Seeing Joshua sitting on the bed with his mother, he smiled trying not to startle him.

"Hey, dad." Ryan stood up, shaking his dad's hand. "Well, I leave and ya'll try to fall apart."

"This can't be Joshua." Pete looked at the little boy sitting on the bed. "He is much smaller than this young man."

"I am Joshua." Joshua smiled because he knew Pete was teasing.

Pete couldn't take his eyes off him; it was amazing that he looked so much like Ryan at that age. With the exception of the dimples, they could be twins. "Yeah, he is definitely yours," he told

Ryan without looking in his direction. Joshua glanced up, smiling as if he understood what he was saying. Moving past Ryan, Pete sat in the chair next to the bed so he could talk with Joshua more. "What you got there?" he asked Joshua.

"My dinosaur book, want to see?" He moved the book closer so Pete could see what he was showing Pearl. Joshua began telling Pete about dinosaurs and which one was his favorite. "Oviraptor means egg robber and I like eggs, so we are a lot alike."

"Oh, you like eggs?" Pete asked.

"Like is an understatement," Ryan added.

"If I remember correctly," Mama Pearl reminded Ryan, "so did you," giving him one of her looks.

"Perfect timing," Ryan said as his cell phone rang. "Hello?" Looking at Joshua, he told him, "It's your mom," then spoke to Roni on the phone. "I called you earlier to let you know we were at the hospital. Oh, she is doing fine. Joshua is telling her and dad about the dinosaurs." Seeing him with Joshua reminded him of the times he spent with his grandpa. "Mama Pearl, Roni says hello."

"Ask her why she didn't come with you," Mama Pearl inquired.

Ryan ran interference. "She had to do inventory and they are getting ready for the fall season."

"Hush up and give me that phone," she said, taking the phone from Ryan as Pete and Joshua watched smiling. "Hi, Roni, how are you?" she asked to soften her up for the harder questions to come. "Oh, I'm doing fine now, especially since I got my great-grandson here. He is such a joy to be with," she told Roni as she fawned over Joshua sitting beside her on the bed. "I must say you have done an excellent job with him. He is well mannered and smart as a whip."

Feeling she had gotten Roni's guard down, Pearl asked, "Now when are you coming down so I can get a look at you?" her tone getting serious. "I've seen you on the DVD Ryan had but it's not the same as being able to look you in the face and talk with you." Pearl was tickled as she saw Ryan fidget, not knowing what she would say next. "I understand you had to work and will forgive you this time." Thinking of a new strategy, she said, "Ryan had mentioned coming back to do some deer hunting with Jake in the fall."

The look on Ryan's face was priceless because he hadn't talked with Jake since he arrived. Pearl just kept talking. "That would be a great time for you to come. The store can run a few days without you, can't it?" Joshua snickered watching his daddy trying to get the phone back. "Well, I will plan to see you then."

Pearl saw she needed to pull out the big ammo. "It would do an old woman's heart good to meet you." Ryan was just shaking his head because he knew she was embellishing. "Okay, sweetie, you think about it and I plan to see you in October sometime." Looking down at Joshua, she added, "Here is Joshua, he wants to talk to you," then gave him the phone.

Pearl made sure not to look at Ryan, knowing she had stretched the truth just a little. Well, when he saw Jake, they would talk about deer hunting. It had been a couple of years since Ryan last hunted with Jake and he needed to come back to check on her. Oh, who was Pearl kidding, she had won!

Getting the phone back from Joshua, Ryan gave Pearl a shame on you look. "Yeah, she's doing fine. Joshua and I will be leaving shortly to go to the hotel. We need to check in."

Hearing that, Pearl interjected, "What hotel? You are not taking this child to a hotel. He can sleep in your old room and you can have the guest room; they are right across the hall from each other." Pearl was determined that he wasn't going to a hotel when her house was right there with plenty of room. "Pete, you let them in, and Ryan, you know where the spare key is so get it for you and Joshua. Stay in a hotel. Poppy cock!" she blustered, forgetting Joshua was listening as he giggled at her excitement.

"It looks like Joshua and I will be staying at Mama Pearl's," he told Roni. Knowing Pearl's mind was made up Ryan didn't argue. "This will give us a chance to spend more time with her when she gets home. I will call you later when we get there." Beginning to feel a little embarrassed by what he was about to say he started to speak lower in the phone. "I love you. Talk with you later."

Turning around, he saw all eyes were on him. His face was red from embarrassment, making him feel like a teenager being caught telling a girl he liked her.

Pearl looked at Joshua. "Are they that mushy all the time?"

"Not all the time, just when they think I am not looking," Joshua laughed.

Now Ryan really felt like he was thirteen again. "Okay, don't make me separate you two."

"You just try it, buddy. I still know how to swing a switch." Her threat was futile, but Pearl just loved making Joshua giggle.

Knowing he must, Ryan asked, "How is mom?"

"Oh, she's fine. She was here earlier sitting with momma waiting on the doctor to come in." Pete knew why Helen had left but didn't want to discuss it in front of Joshua. "I guess she had something she needed to do."

"Hump!" Pearl, like Pete, didn't want to discuss it, but she was still upset at Helen's behavior. What had Joshua done for her to be so evil toward him?

Even though Ryan knew why she had left, it still didn't keep it from hurting him. "You're probably right," he told his father. "Tell her I asked about her." No matter how foolish Helen acted at times, she was still his mother and he loved her.

The room grew silent as if they were having a prayer session until the doctor came in. Pearl's doctor was an elderly gentleman who probably went to school with her, but was maybe a couple years older. He reminded her that she needed to take her meds and wanted to keep her for one more night just to be sure.

That didn't go well with Pearl; she wanted to be at home with Ryan and Joshua. Ryan assured her they would be there until the end of the week and she would have plenty of time with them. Hearing that helped Pearl but she still wanted to go home, especially when Ryan and Joshua kissed her goodnight before they left for the evening.

It was a long drive to the country; as usual, Joshua fell asleep on the way. Peter decided to follow them to Pearl's house to spend more time with his son and grandson. As they drove up the driveway to the house, Joshua awakened to see the beautiful cabin just off the lake. It was the biggest house he had ever seen and he was excited to see a house made of logs. It was like in the stories his dad had told of the house on the lake when he was growing up.

Getting out of the car, Joshua was mesmerized by all the trees and the big yard. To him it looked like the park without all the people. "Daddy, daddy, where is the tree?"

"It's farther down in the woods," he smiled at the excitement in Joshua's eyes. "Come on let's get our things into the house." He handed Joshua a small bag to carry. Gathering the rest of the things, they went to the door with Pete holding it open. "Thanks for your help, Dad," Ryan teased his father.

"Anytime, son," Pete expressed his amusement as he walked over to the cupboard. Pete retrieved the extra key for Ryan while looking at Joshua and said, "Make sure he doesn't lose it." Pete ruffled Joshua's hair as he looked at the house with amazement.

"Ryan, I think he likes it here." Pete patted his son on the shoulder with pride.

"He should; I have to tell him the stories every night about growing up here. Do you think we can take him fishing before we go back?"

"Absolutely, after we get momma home and settled we can take the boat out."

"Yeah," Joshua heard their conversation. "Grandpa Pete, we going fishing in the lake outside?"

"Yes, sir! Maybe as soon as tomorrow, but I can take you down to look at it now if you like."

Looking to his father, Joshua asked, "Daddy, can I?"

"May I," Ryan corrected.

"Not you, me."

Giving up on his son's grammar, Ryan agreed, "Sure. I will take our things upstairs while you two have fun." Seeing his dad with Joshua and wanting to show him the lake reminded him what it was like with his grandpa. When he was growing up, Pete was working most days but his grandpa would take off sometimes just to spend time with him. They would fish or he would teach him to use a bow. Now his dad could do those same things with Joshua that he hadn't been able to do with him.

Going back into the kitchen, Ryan began to look in the fridge and the cupboards because he knew he would need to prepare something for Joshua. Hearing the doorbell, he abandoned his search for dinner to answer the door. As he opened the door, he was almost knocked down by a big burly man with tattoos from head to toe.

It was Jake and his family with dinner. Ryan was lifted off his feet as he tried to put Jake in a headlock. Watching their child's play, Sara teased them that they were such babies, giving Ryan a hug.

Sara was a small-framed woman that upon first sight made you think she was Amish, because she wore her blonde hair long and straight. If she didn't speak, she would vanish in a crowd. No one would think she would be married to Jake, but they had been together for over fifteen years. Together they had two children: a daughter, Libby, age thirteen, and a son, little Jake, fourteen. Both came in behind their mother with food and a gallon of sweet tea. Each gave Ryan a hug as they took the things into the kitchen.

Breathing hard, both Ryan and Jake started talking at the same time, then laughed because they were doing it. "Well, how you been?" Ryan asked Jake. "I can see you haven't lost any weight."

Hearing Ryan's comment, Libby giggled at her father while he rubbed his belly. "Well, I love to eat, what can I say?" Patting his tummy, he drawled, "I see you are still scrawny like a stick."

"I can still take you." Ryan acted as if he were ready to box.

"Boy, I flush things bigger than you."

"Jake!" Sara admonished.

"You're in trouble," Ryan laughed.

"Daddy, you should." Joshua stopped in his tracks, seeing all the unfamiliar faces, and retreated to his father after looking up at the big man that looked like he had come out of a wrestling match.

Jake grinned at Joshua. "So that's little Ryan?" Looking around at Joshua, he asked, "Your daddy tell you how he fell on me from that tree?"

"You're Jake?" Joshua laughed. "Did it hurt?"

"I still have nightmares." Jake pretended to wipe away a tear, but couldn't control his laughter.

"Jake, you're going to scare him. Hi, Joshua, is it?" Sara came closer to him. "I'm Sara, and these are your cousins, Libby and little Jake." Both kids smiled and waved at him.

Shyly Joshua waved back and came from behind his father. "Jake, will you show me the tree?"

"Sure, if it's okay with your daddy."

"Yes, if you eat all your dinner tonight," Ryan gave permission before Joshua could ask. He knew they weren't leaving Virginia until Joshua saw that tree.

Sara had prepared a chicken potpie casserole with fresh green beans and cut tomatoes. Ryan looked down at Joshua and his plate was almost clean. He was sitting between Libby and little Jake chatting away. No matter where Joshua was or who was with him, he always seemed to be at home.

After dinner, the men went outside and sat on the porch to reminisce on days past as little Jake taught Joshua to catch fireflies. Jake smiled because he remembered teaching Ryan when they grew up.

Pete felt a little devious. "Ryan, have you talked to Jake about hunting yet?" snickering as he asked.

Jake looking at Ryan confused. "What about hunting?"

"Nothing, Mama Pearl told Roni you and I had talked about us coming down for me to go deer hunting in the fall."

"You know that ain't a bad idea. We can go bow hunting. It will be like old times." Jake was excited thinking about the prospect of them hunting again.

Seeing his father's amusement, he realized he had fallen into the trap. How was he going to explain it to Roni? "I have to see if I can get the time off first," he said for cover. Although he had to admit, it would be nice to bring Roni to Virginia and let her see where he grew up. Looking at his father, he lamented, "Between you and Mama Pearl I won't be able to go back home." Both Jake and Pete laughed, watching Ryan squirm.

"Pansy," Jake called him.

"You hear that, Sara?" Ryan shouted, looking into the doorway.

Jake jumped from his seat. "Honey, I didn't say..." Seeing she was not behind him, he complained, "That was cold." Pete and Ryan mocked him for being afraid of his little woman.

During their evening chatter, Helen drove up, making them grow silent. Ryan didn't know how to react at her showing up, because he thought she would stay away while he was there with Joshua.

"Hi, all!" she said coming onto the porch as if she were walking into a church picnic.

Ryan got up to hug his mother. "Hi, mom, how have you been?"

"Doing well." Looking at Pete, she said, "I was wondering where you had been all evening," as she gave him a sarcastic look. Hearing the laughter of the children, she saw Joshua trying to catch fireflies in a jar with holes in the top. "Is that him?" she sniped, looking at Joshua.

"He is my son, Joshua." Ryan felt anger at her comment.

"I don't think he looks..."

"Helen, I will be home shortly," Pete interjected because he was embarrassed by her behavior, wanting her to keep those thoughts to herself. "I will see you then," he told her firmly.

Helen looked at Ryan. "You look well. How long are you staying?"

"We will be here until Saturday, taking a noon flight back to New York." He tried to be cordial to mask the anger that was building inside him.

"Good, I hope to see you again before you leave," she said nonchalantly.

"Yeah, sure." Ryan tried to remember she was his mother and must be respected.

"Well, I best get on home," she announced with a nervous laugh. "Good night all."

In unison, all three said goodnight to her. Once she stopped on her way back to her car to look at Joshua again, but he never even noticed she was there. He was too busy having fun.

"Ryan, I'm..." Pete tried to apologize for Helen's behavior toward Joshua.

"Dad, you don't have to apologize for Mom. That is something she must do for herself."

"Well, she never liked me either," Jake interjected. "Always blamed me when you got in trouble."

"No, just when you gave me the tattoo," Ryan reminded Jake. "By the way, it needs to be touched up," and both forced a little laugh.

Ryan was grateful that Joshua hadn't witnessed the scene on the porch. He and little Jake were running all over the place. Although Ryan knew he would have to protect Joshua, he hated the thought of it being from his own family.

CHAPTER 13

They didn't have to tell Mama Pearl twice that she could go home. She was dressed and packed when the doctor came to check on her. Dr. Fenkle, doing his rounds, came in to release her, but had to tease her a little about being packed.

Before he could get the words out of his mouth, Pearl was walking to the door with Joshua. He had to stop her because she needed to be in a wheelchair when she left. Ryan told her he would get the car, leaving her with Joshua and the nurse. Pearl was in heaven as they rolled her out to the front of the hospital. Joshua was close by, as if he was in charge while his father was away.

Roni called while he was walking to the parking lot, giving Ryan a chance to have her alone for a conversation. It was uncanny the way they both really missed each other. In the past months, they had gotten used to seeing each other daily and felt emptiness when they were apart. "Hey, sweetheart," Ryan couldn't contain his smile, "how is work?"

Hearing his voice gave Roni comfort. "Work, what can I say. What are you up to?"

"Joshua and I are picking up Mama Pearl from the hospital. Dr. Fenkle is sending her home."

"I know she is ready to get out of there." Roni remembered how depressing hospitals were. "Joshua isn't giving you any trouble, is he?"

"Oh, no, he is having the time of his life. Mama Pearl is spoiling him rotten. I'm afraid we're going to have to deprogram him when he gets home." Both were happy Joshua was having a good time meeting his family.

"Has he met your mom yet?"

"No, not yet," Ryan reluctantly told her. "I don't think he will this trip."

Afraid to find out what he meant by that comment, she asked, "What's going on, Ryan?"

"Baby, it's nothing. She's just being a little aloof about Joshua." Ryan didn't want to go into much detail about Helen's behavior. "Please, let's just discuss this when we get back."

"Ryan, I don't..." She tried to find the words to explain how she felt.

"Roni, he is my son too, and no one is going to hurt him. Not even my mother," he tried to reassure her. "We suspected she would be this way, but everyone else is being so good to Joshua he doesn't even miss her."

She felt helpless being so far away. "I know you will protect him, but it just frustrates me," she said as she tried not to feel angry toward Helen.

"Don't worry, Joshua is fine." Ryan added a little humor to the conversation, "If mom gets too out of line, Mama Pearl will drag her back."

She had to giggle envisioning that. "As long as Joshua met Jake, the trip has been a success for him." Remembering the conversation with Pearl the day before, she questioned, "Oh, did you get a date set with Jake?"

"What date?" Remembering them hunting, he said, "No, not yet, but he said it would be in October sometime." Having her ask about the hunting plans made it easier for him to think about bringing her to Virginia. "I have to check with work and make sure I can get the time off."

"Okay, just get me a date as soon as possible so I can maneuver some things around."

Seeing Joshua and Pearl on the curb, he pulled up. "Oh, they are waiting for me. Want to talk to Joshua before you hang up?" Ryan smiled because he knew the answer.

"Put my baby on the phone." She was eager to hear his voice.

"It's your mommy." He gave the phone to Joshua as he put him in the back seat, while the nurse assisted Pearl into the passenger seat. He heard Joshua telling Roni about meeting Jake, going to the lake with his grandpa, and catching fireflies with little Jake. Joshua was telling the story so fast he wasn't sure Roni heard it all.

Finishing his conversation with his mother, Joshua gave fake kisses before giving the phone back to his father. "Don't work too hard, sweetie. I will call you later, love you." He was now comfortable saying those words in front of his grandmother because he truly loved Roni. Seeing his grandma motion to him, he told her, "Oh, Mama Pearl says hi." He gave Pearl a wink as she smiled back at his consideration for Roni.

On the ride home, Mama Pearl enjoyed listening to Joshua tell her about the lake in her backyard and meeting his cousins. Joshua was so excited when he told her about the fireflies he caught with little Jake he almost jumped out of his booster seat. "They didn't live long but Libby told me we can catch more tonight," Joshua explained to his great-grandma.

Arriving home, Pearl was ready to get in the kitchen. Ryan tried to get her to rest but she wouldn't listen as usual. Getting her apron from the pantry, she started putting things on the counter to make cookies for Joshua. She gave him the little apron she had for Ryan when he was a kid, which fit perfectly.

"What kind of cookies do you want to make, Joshua?" Pearl asked him.

"Chocolate chip," he looked at his dad because Roni didn't let him eat much chocolate.

"Sure, you are on vacation." Joking with Joshua, he said, "Just don't tell your mommy."

"You want pecans in your cookies, sweetie?" Pearl asked.

Joshua had never had pecans in cookies before but he was willing to try them. He sat at the counter eating chocolate chips from the bag, watching Mama Pearl get the ingredients for the cookies. Ryan had to remind him that they needed to save some chocolate chips for the cookies.

"Oh, leave him alone," Pearl told Ryan as she placed a bowl in front of Joshua so he could add the ingredients. Adding them one by one, he stirred until his dough was ready for the cookie sheet. While they enjoyed their first baking session, Ryan took Joshua's picture with flour on his face. Joshua looked so cute baking cookies with his great-grandma, Ryan smiled at their loving image.

It didn't take long for the house to fill with the aroma of baking cookies. You could smell the chocolate as it melted into the cookie dough. Joshua was so thrilled he asked Mama Pearl to leave the oven light on so he could watch them bake. Those were the longest eight minutes of his life. When they were done, Ryan poured them all a mug of milk as they sat at the table eating warm cookies.

Pete called Ryan to let him know he would be out after lunch so they could do some fishing. The garage wasn't busy that day so he could get away to spend time with them. Jake agreed to stay at the shop, but would be over later so they could make plans for the pending hunting trip.

Little Jake and Libby came by to see if Joshua could go hiking with them in the woods around the house. Ryan was a little skeptical at first, but knew they would take care of him. They probably knew more about wildlife than he did; after all Jake was their father. "Ya'll be careful and don't go near the lake. Joshua can swim but not in moving water," Ryan informed them because there was an undercurrent in the lake that would sweep him under.

"Parents, they take all the fun out of being a kid." Pearl was amused at Ryan being the parent.

"Not trying to take the fun out of it, Mama Pearl," Ryan smiled as he watched Joshua walk down the path with his cousins. "If anything happens to him, Roni will kill me." In reality, he knew if something happened to Joshua, Roni wouldn't have to kill him, because he would probably fall dead on the spot.

After hearing the phone ring, Pearl answered it. "Ryan picked me up this morning," she informed the caller. "You don't have to come by. I'm fine, will probably take a little nap in a few minutes."

Looking at Ryan, she put her hand over the mouthpiece and whispered, "It's your momma." Neither of them wanted her to be around Joshua. "What do you mean you are on your way?" Pearl shrugged her shoulders. "Well, Helen, if you're that close I will stay up until you get here, bye." Turning to Ryan, she informed him, "Your mother will be here in a few minutes."

"You know what she insinuated last night?" Ryan asked his grandmother as he became angry thinking about it. "That Joshua is not my son," he repeated, shaking his head. "Can you believe that?"

"Don't get yourself all worked up over your momma. She means well, but in this case she's dead wrong." Pearl rubbed his back. "Eventually she will have to admit she is, but you know your momma. She will argue with the devil himself just for the sake of argument."

He knew Mama Pearl was right as usual. "I just wish she would stop being so evil about Joshua. She acts like I don't know my own child." Ryan thought back to the night he first saw Joshua. "When I saw his face the first time I knew he was mine." He had to smile at the thought. "He looks just like me when I was that age. Anyone with eyes can see that."

"Sometimes people see only what they want to and she doesn't want to." Pearl knew if Helen kept acting spiteful, she was going to push Ryan away. Feeling Ryan's pain Pearl tried to change the subject, asking Ryan, "Your daddy taking you and Joshua fishing this afternoon?"

"Yeah, it will be like old times." Thinking back, he reminisced, "Remember when Papa Pete and us would go fishing out back?"

"Do I? It took an act of God to get you three to come in off the lake," Pearl laughed at the memory.

"Remember..." Ryan was interrupted by a voice at the door. Just when he was beginning to feel better, he heard his mother's voice.

"Where ya'll hiding?" she asked coming into the kitchen. "Pearl, you just got out of the hospital. What are you doing cooking? Pete isn't going to like this."

Pearl whispered to Ryan, "She's still bossy," then looking back at Helen said, "I'm fine, Helen. Besides Joshua and I had to bake cookies."

"Hump, I still don't know about that," she snarled while moving about the house as if she were looking for something.

"Excuse me," Ryan questioned his mother, "what do you mean?"

"I'm just saying how can you be so sure?" Helen wouldn't make eye contact with Ryan. "He is a handsome little boy, but..."

"Are you crazy, mother?" Ryan was infuriated by her comment. "I am not stupid. I know he is my son and I don't need your approval."

"Ryan, you haven't seen that woman in over four years. That child could..."

"Roni, mom, her name is Roni. Try using it."

"Roni," she sneered. "She knows a good catch when she sees one. Those people..."

"Those people..." Ryan was so heated he paced across the floor. "What do you mean those people?"

"Well, she latches on to a white man and her social status increases."

Ryan gave her an angry laugh. "Is that what this is about, some fictional social status in your little mind?" Throwing his arms in the air, he stated, "I give up! You are hopeless." Walking to the door, he turned to face her. "Until you can respect my son, don't talk to me."

"He has gotten so disrespectful since he found out about that boy," Helen complained.

"Joshua, his name is Joshua. Why do you have to be such a bitch?"

Helen gasped, "Pearl!"

"Pearl, my ass. Keep this up, Helen, and not only will you not have a grandson, but you will lose your son in the process."

"Pearl, I just don't want him getting attached to a child that may not be his. Pete even called that boy grandson; what is wrong with ya'll?"

"We use our eyes and see Ryan in Joshua. Helen, he has green eyes for God's sake." Pearl ran her fingers through her hair. "Regardless of what you think, Ryan loves his son and if he has to choose, it won't be you." Pearl could no longer stand being in the same room with Helen and she didn't want to hear any more of her off color comments. "I'm going to take my nap, damn it!"

CHAPTER 14

Since returning from Virginia, Joshua hadn't been able to talk about anything other than his trip. He caught his first fish with the junior rod and reel his Grandpa Pete gave him. Ryan had bought him a bike so he could ride with little Jake and Libby, but the most fun was when his dad taught him bow safety.

At his age, he wasn't able to steady his hand with the bow and arrow, but Ryan had encouraged him that would come in time. The little beginner's set was more of a toy than an actual bow and arrow, but it served the purpose to teach him to respect it as a weapon.

Joshua had loved being with his dad's family and being at the cabin with his great-grandma just as Ryan did growing up. When Ryan was little, Pearl allowed him to be a kid. He had climbed trees, chased frogs, and caught fireflies just as Joshua had done during his visit. Joshua had played so hard during the day that he would take his bath and fall dead asleep without having a bedtime story.

Ryan and Pearl used the time after Joshua was asleep to talk about the past, the present, and the future. One of their discussions had been about his relationship with Roni and his plans for their future. Although Ryan had never discussed it with anyone, he was afraid to ask Roni to marry him. She was so independent that he feared she wouldn't need him for anything. What did he have to offer her? She had her own home, a career, and business ventures. It was hard being a man in a relationship with such a strong woman.

He sometimes wondered how his grandpa had done it with Mama Pearl. In many ways, she and Roni were similar. They knew what they wanted and succeeded at obtaining it. Maybe that was what he saw in Roni: the strength of his grandmother. Both women were from different worlds but were alike in many ways.

Just before he left, Pearl had sat him down for one of their little discussions and questioned him about his plans for a future with Roni. For the first time he was able to tell someone he was afraid she would say no. Pearl hadn't believed her ears. "What are you scared of?" She couldn't understand his answer.

"That she doesn't need me." He felt ashamed at the thought but it was his true feelings.

Pearl saw the heaviness of his heart. "Ryan, you don't want her to need you. You want her to love you. There is a difference."

Not really comprehending what she was saying, he asked, "What do you mean?"

"Honey, when someone needs you, they are only there until you can no longer supply the need. Now, when someone loves you, they will be there always. Through good times or bad times, they will stand with you."

"It is just hard to be the man with Roni. She has so much strength on her own that I feel incompetent around her." Ryan didn't want to make Roni sound like a bully, so he continued, "Don't get me wrong, she allows me to be the man in my son's life, and yes, in hers too, but I can't help feeling inadequate."

"Sometimes a woman has to be strong not because she wants to, but because it is for her survival." A feeling Pearl knew too well. "Didn't she lose her mother when she was young?" Pearl asked him.

"Yeah, I think she was around fourteen."

"She is the oldest, right?"

"Right," Ryan began to understand what Pearl was saying. "Her mom was sick for awhile and Laurence is four years younger."

"So she had to take the bull by the horns to keep the house going?" Understanding the responsibility of losing a parent, Pearl analyzed the situation. "Sounds like she had to become an adult before she could be a child."

Ryan hated to admit it but his grandma had been right about Roni. She hadn't had the luxury of being a kid, because she'd had to be stronger than her peers and wear her game face all the time. That had given her the ability to multitask, but had stolen her ability to be dependent on anyone other than herself.

"What did she say when the two of you talked about your future?"

Feeling foolish, Ryan shyly told her, "We've never discussed it."

"You haven't spoken to her about a future together?" Pearl had been shocked at his response. "How do you expect her to trust you when you make no effort? If you don't let Roni know you want a future with her and Joshua, how is she to know you do?"

"I don't know," Ryan groaned at the thought. "For me right now the fear of her saying no is worse than not knowing."

Since that conversation with his grandma, Ryan had been trying to approach the idea of marriage to Roni. Each time he tried to bring up the subject, he got a lump in his throat and the words wouldn't come out.

Although they lived in the same house, they still had separate rooms out of respect for Joshua. He knew they were his parents and their not being married wasn't something Joshua cared about at his young age. The only thing he cared about was that they loved him, and they did.

Ryan knew he had to talk to Roni about her feelings for him and if they had a future together. However, approaching the subject was difficult for him. Should he just blurt it out in the middle of a conversation? *Why is this one thing so difficult? We can talk about anything but our feelings for each other. I love her and I feel she loves me. Why can't I just ask her if she wants a future with me? Who am I fooling, I want to marry her, and it scares the hell out of me that she doesn't want to marry me*, Ryan reasoned with himself.

After that fiasco with Amy, Roni might not trust him enough to say yes. Ryan had broken off an engagement in the past, so how did she know he wouldn't do it again? How would he get her to trust him with his past engagement ending badly?

He hoped she would understand that she was the reason he hadn't gone through with his prior engagement. When his heart couldn't bear being without her, Ryan knew he couldn't marry Amy.

It had been a couple of weeks since they had returned from Virginia and he still hadn't gotten the courage to speak to her about marriage. Ryan would always convince himself that the timing wasn't right, but tonight after making love, he knew it was time.

"Roni," she turned her head to look at him and he saw her soft features in the moonlight, "can I ask you something?"

"Sure," she answered, not knowing what the question would be. She tried hard to keep suspicion from appearing in her eyes.

Again, the words seemed to stick in his throat. "How do you feel about us? I mean, do we have a future together?" His words just rambled without real meaning.

"I'm not sure. I guess I haven't thought past the present." Not only was she lying to him but she was also lying to herself. Like him, she was afraid of the answer to this particular question.

"Well, we love each other," he sighed because he knew he must finish his thoughts, "and we have a beautiful son together." Again, he struggled to find words to express his feelings. "Don't you want a future for us as a family?"

"I think we have a family, maybe not in the traditional sense, but a family nonetheless."

"True, and I love being here with you and Joshua. You both mean the world to me and I don't want to lose either of you." He caressed her cheek. "Roni, even if there was no Joshua, I would still love you and want to be with you."

She couldn't respond because it felt good to hear him say he would love her even if Joshua wasn't there. For her it meant he wanted to be with her and Joshua was not the reason he stayed. "Ryan, I really don't know what to say. I mean, what are you asking?"

"I guess I am asking you to spend the rest of your life with me." He searched her face for an idea of what she was thinking. "You don't have to answer right now, because it isn't very well thought out. I mean, the way I am asking you, but will you marry me?"

Roni's words were stuck in her throat and she didn't know how to answer the question.

"Look, I haven't gotten a ring or anything, but I felt I had to ask." Still not getting a response, he pleaded, "Come on, Roni, work with me here."

The man she loved was asking her to marry him and she was frozen in thought. "Right now my head is spinning, I don't know what to say." She finally showed a smile. "I can't believe you are asking me this."

"Why not, Roni, don't you deserve to have someone love you, too?"

"Yes, I do," she smiled at him with the radiance of joy on her face.

"Yes, you deserve someone to love you or yes, you will marry me?"

"To both," she could hardly breathe because Ryan had pulled her close, kissing her passionately. Getting her breath back, she asked, "Have you spoken to Joshua about this?" Roni didn't know how he would react. Although they all lived in the same house, Joshua knew his daddy lived upstairs. How would they explain it to a four-year-old? Their family was just normal to him. His friends had both parents in the same house and so did he, but marriage to him didn't mean anything.

"I will talk to him," Ryan volunteered for the task.

"I think we should do it together," Roni told him, not wanting to put everything on him alone. He had gone to Joshua and told him he was his father. She could at least be there for this conversation.

"No, your dad isn't here for me to ask for your hand in marriage, so Joshua is the man I need to ask." He smiled at the prospect. "What I am going to do if he says no?"

CHAPTER 15

He thought it couldn't be that hard talking to Joshua about them getting married. After all, in Joshua's mind he probably thought they already were. To him marriage was meaningless, but to the outside world, it was a legal declaration of love. Love, how can you determine what the heart felt?

Only five short years ago, he had been planning to marry someone his heart knew he didn't love. Ryan had learned from experience that you shouldn't bring someone into your life with that kind of commitment and not love that person. This time he was with the woman he loved and wanted the world to recognize it.

Roni called to let him know she was going to be late at the store and wanted them to have dinner without her. Ryan knew that would be a perfect time to speak with Joshua about their plans to get married. They could talk about things at his favorite pizzeria.

After ordering their large double cheese pizza, Ryan and Joshua sat at their favorite table near the TV. Joshua liked to sit there to watch the cartoons and explain them to his father. Ryan put a slice of pizza on Joshua's plate warning him it was hot.

"While we wait for the pizza to cool, let's talk for a minute." Ryan had hoped he wouldn't have to vie for Joshua's attention against a cartoon.

"About what?" Joshua looked up at him, very serious as if he knew it was something important and he needed to pay attention.

"You, your mommy, and me," he began before questioning, "Do you like us living together?"

"Yes," Joshua became frightened. "Why, are you leaving?"

"Oh, no, never." Ryan realized he might be confusing Joshua. "Well, see, your mommy and I love you," he paused as he chose his words wisely, "and we love each other."

"Then why are you leaving?" Joshua questioned.

"No, son, I am not leaving you. I promise."

"When Ty's daddy talked to him, he left the house and got another girlfriend." His eyes began to fill with tears. "Are you getting a new girlfriend?"

"No!" Seeing he was doing more harm than good, Ryan picked him up from his seat, placing him on his knee. "No, I love your mommy and I want to make us a family."

"We are a family!" Joshua said almost angrily at the suggestion that they weren't.

"I know we are, but I want to make it legal." Bearing in mind, Joshua was confused, he said, "When I say legal, I mean your mother and I would get married."

Joshua's brow wrinkled, trying to understand. "Does that mean you have to get divorced like Ty's mommy and daddy?"

"Well, we will get married like Ty's mommy and daddy, but we will be like them before the divorce," Ryan explained.

"Oh, you will make funny noises at night and wrestle without shirts?" Joshua seriously asked.

Ryan could see Joshua was taking him in a direction he was not ready for. "Ah, I think your pizza is cool enough to eat now." He placed Joshua back into his chair. Grabbing a bite of his pizza, he continued, "Joshua, I love your mommy and I want to marry her. Will that be okay with you?"

"If you get married, will you have to get divorced?" Joshua looked afraid of losing them as Ty did with his parents.

"No, I want us to be together forever," he smiled to reassure him. "I just want you to be okay with it if we get married."

"Nothing will change?"

"Nope, just a piece of paper at the courthouse to make it legal." Ryan grabbed another bite.

"What does legal mean?" Joshua inquired of his dad.

"Legal in this case means we are under a contract." He tried to think of how to make it simple. "By contract, I mean we sign a license that binds us legally. Then you and your mommy will have my last name and be Grants."

Joshua began to feel less frightened at losing his family and started to eat his pizza. "Daddy, can I come to the marriage?"

"Definitely; that's if your mommy says yes." He didn't want Joshua to know they had discussed it the night before.

"If she says no, can you still get married?"

"No," Ryan chuckled, "she would have to say yes before we can get married. If she says yes, I will buy her a ring and we will be engaged."

"So when do we ask her?"

"I will ask her and we will let you know what the answer is." Ryan felt he had explained everything to him.

"No, I want to ask her too!"

"You want to ask her, why?"

"You said I could be at the marriage."

"Yes, but that won't be the marriage, I will be asking her to marry me." He shook his head because he knew their conversation was getting lost. "Okay, you can be there when I ask her, but I have to buy a ring before I ask her and you can't tell her about the ring."

"When will we be asking her?"

"I have to find a ring and then we will ask her."

"When do we buy the ring?"

"If you eat all your pizza we will go tonight." Ryan realized this was a losing battle with Joshua, because he was an inquisitive child.

Both sat there eating and chatting. Joshua wanted to get his mother a blue ring, but Ryan explained that wouldn't be appropriate for the occasion. During their meal, Ryan called Abe to see if he would be at the store after they finished eating. Although they were closing, Abe agreed to wait for him and Joshua. Ryan didn't tell Abe why he was coming, but he would get his opinion on something nice for Roni when he got there.

Abe was waiting in the back when they rang the buzzer at the door. He came out, letting them in. Before Ryan could explain the reason for their late visit, Joshua blurted out they needed a marriage ring.

"You're coming to get what?" Abe asked, tickled at Joshua's enthusiasm.

Feeling a little embarrassed, Ryan said, "We are looking for an engagement ring for Roni." In the back of his mind he wondered how was he going to explain all of this to her.

Putting his hands over Joshua's ears as he squirmed, Abe said, "Finally, you got some balls."

He had to laugh at Abe's comment. "Yes, I guess so. You know her taste better than I do, so show me what you got."

Abe had learned the craft of jewelry making from his father and grandfather, having some very intricate pieces he had designed. His eye for detail was phenomenal; many of his pieces boasted an Egyptian design. Each piece was beautifully created with platinum and gold settings as the diamonds sparkled from the reflections of light. Ryan and Joshua admired the rings, mesmerized by their exquisiteness.

"What do you think, Abe?" Ryan asked because he wasn't good at these things and wanted it to be something Roni would like.

"I tell you what, because it's for Roni I will design it special." Abe gave him a smile. "I owe her anyway."

"That would be great, but I kind of wanted to give it to her soon. Joshua is supposed to be keeping it a secret and you see how well that's going." Both laughed at Joshua as he went from case to case looking at the jewelry. Remembering his last remark, Ryan asked, "What do you mean you owe her?"

Looking to make sure Joshua wasn't able to hear the conversation, Abe related, "When I came out that I am gay, my family disowned me. Well, actually, to them I am dead. I was so distraught," Abe pulled up his sleeves, "I tried to kill myself. Roni and her dad took me in and helped me get back on my feet." Looking around at the shop, he stated, "They helped me get this shop to start my life over. Ryan, they saved my life." Not caring how he looked to Ryan, he simply said, "They are my family now."

Ryan didn't know what to say but understood why Abe felt he owed her. "I understand why you feel that way and appreciate you doing this for her." He paused before asking, "Abe, how long have you known you are gay?" Ryan had wanted to ask since finding out about his sexual orientation.

"All my life I felt I was different. Back when we were in college, I came out; Ansari and Roni knew. Well, Ansari kind of stumbled upon it."

"He stumbled upon it? How do you just stumble upon that?" Ryan thought about ways Ansari could have found out. Ryan felt embarrassed at his question.

"No, he didn't catch me in the act," Abe laughed at the strange look on Ryan's face. "Remember back in college how Steve always harassed Ansari?"

"Yeah, he was just an asshole."

"Yes, he was, but he was more than that. He was still in the closet." Seeing the shock on Ryan's face, he instructed, "Oh, close your mouth." Abe checked to see if Joshua was still out of hearing range. "When we first got to school, Steve would always try to come on to me. I let him know I wasn't interested, but you know Steve, he didn't want to take that for an answer."

He paused because of the bitter memory. "One night when he got drunk he came into our room. Ansari was at the library or somewhere. I was lying on my bed and I heard someone come in; thinking it was Ansari I didn't get alarmed." The memory made it hard for him to talk. "Before I could move, Steve was on top of me and..."

"You don't have to tell me; I understand." Ryan felt anger and sympathy for what had been done to Abe.

"If Ansari hadn't come back when he did, Steve would have raped me," he said, appreciating his friend. "Steve knew we knew his secret so he taunted us to keep us quiet, which didn't work with Ansari."

"Why didn't you report it?"

"I am gay and most people can't accept that. If I had gone to campus security, I would have been blamed." Feeling angry, he pointed out, "I went there for an education, and that is what I got. Steve is still a jerk and will always be one, whether I told on him or not."

Ryan had always respected Abe but now his respect for him had grown. "How long will it take you to create something for her?"

"I just need a couple of days because I already have something in mind." Having told Ryan of the past, Abe began to feel the pain of old memories. "Thanks for listening, man, and not judging me."

"Hey, you are with family." Ryan understood how hard it was for Abe to tell him about the past. "We don't judge."

A few days later, Ryan worked through lunch in order to leave early, then got on the subway. Abe had called the night before informing him the ring was ready. Ryan was thankful because he was already in hot water with Roni over having to propose openly. She was right; he let a four-year-old con him so easily.

After telling Abe, Joshua had promised not to tell his mother, but that did not keep him from telling everyone else. Joshua informed them they couldn't tell his mommy but he and Ryan were marrying her. Ryan smiled at the thought of the little swindler being involved when he asked Roni to marry him; it was genius on Joshua's part.

When Ryan arrived at the shop, Abe was in the back and the sales associate had to go get him. It didn't take long for him to appear with a piece of black cloth, shining the ring. Ryan walked over to the glass counter as Abe gently laid the cloth on the counter with the ring for viewing. Ryan was almost afraid to pick it up. Finally, Abe encouraged, "You can touch it."

"I know, but that is just beautiful." Ryan watched how the light caught the diamonds. "This is breathtaking, Abe. You did this in two days?"

"Well, I have to admit I had an idea in mind when you asked."

The straight baguette black diamonds complimented the band with the two smaller chocolate diamonds, which were positioned on each side of a beautiful emerald-cut chocolate diamond in a flawless platinum setting with antique sculpting. It was so elegant, matching Roni's personality perfectly. "Wow, she is going to love this!"

"I hope so; it is a one of a kind and no one will ever have that design." Abe was very proud of his creation, looking at Ryan as he speechlessly turned it in the light. "So when are you going to give it to her?"

"Maybe I will propose tonight after dinner."

"After dinner tonight..." Abe gave a disappointed look. "You mean after all my hard work I don't get to see her when you give it to her?"

Oh, no, not someone else to add to the mix; Roni was going to kill him. "Abe, I want to propose to her soon."

"Well, you can do it after Sunday dinner during dessert."

"We don't have any plans for dinner Sunday." Ryan gave him a puzzled look.

"Yes, you do. Shondra is inviting us all to their place on Sunday. Luc is preparing a special meal to celebrate your engagement," Abe told him matter-of-factly.

"Wait, Shondra is involved now?" He thought to himself, *I am a dead man.*

"This is an important day for you both and we want to be there," Abe smirked a little. "Besides if we are there she won't shoot you down."

Putting the ring back on the counter, he tried to explain to Abe, "I just wanted something simple."

"Ryan, we love you both and want you to be happy," he sighed. "If you want to do it tonight I will understand."

"I appreciate your understanding." Looking down, he noticed that Abe had picked up the ring. "Hey!"

"I said you could propose tonight but you will have to wait till Sunday to give her the ring." Abe walked briskly to the back of the shop. "See you Sunday."

On the way home, he would have to figure out a way to tell Roni their friends also wanted to be there for the proposal. He could just come out and tell her, or he could say he hadn't gotten a ring yet, surprising her on Sunday. Yes, he would pretend he hadn't gotten a ring yet so she would be surprised.

Ryan wished he could have given her the ring after dinner; it was going to be hard keeping it a secret from Roni, but the ring was so beautiful he could understand why Abe wanted to be there to see her face when she saw it the first time. "Why is it getting so complicated?" he shouted, walking out the door of the store.

It was already Sunday and Ryan didn't know how to propose to Roni. Would he have it in his pocket and wait until the perfect moment to bring it out? Maybe he would get on one knee as they did in the movies. With all the excitement, how was he going to let Joshua know he was proposing during dessert? That should be easy. He would take him to the bathroom before dessert and let him in on the secret. Ryan formed a game plan in his mind.

Roni wore a coral sleeveless dress with a printed scarf. Her natural hair fell loosely to frame her face. She looked so beautiful coming down the stairs.

"You're pretty!" Joshua said watching her descend.

"You are gorgeous! Definitely worth the extra twenty minutes," Ryan teased her, kissing her on the cheek as they made their way down the hall.

Laurence was in the family room pacing on the phone with lady number whatever. Seeing her, he gave a thumb's up and mouthed, "It took you long enough." He loved his big sister and thought the world of her, but he played the role of a bratty baby brother daily. Walking by, she hip bumped him to show her love as they went out to the garage to drive to Shondra and Luc's for dinner.

Shondra opened the door, holding Hadiya in her arms. Roni reached for Hadiya. "Come to Auntie Roni." Holding her, she teased, "You are getting big, little lady."

"Come on in. Abe, Sam, and Thuy are already here." She winked her eye at Ryan then pulled him aside. "Luc has prepared a strawberry and chocolate dessert. Before he brings it out he will place the ring on top of Roni's dessert for you."

They had planned everything. "Who all knows about this?" he asked, trying to keep his voice down.

"Counting Joshua, everyone but Roni." Shondra started to walk away. "Come on, everyone is waiting."

Ryan came in with everyone already seated. Generally, they would sit with Joshua between them, but today he was sitting between Laurence and Roni. They had not started eating and his palms were already sweating.

The smiles on Abe and Sam's faces made it even harder for Ryan to calm down. A couple of times during the meal Abe leaned over to Sam and they would get a little chuckle over him being the butt of their little joke.

Sam, Abe's partner, was a classy older gentleman, stringent in dress. He always seemed to wear a tie even to informal dinners like this one. His salt and pepper hair gave him a distinguished look with his deep-set dark eyes and olive complexion. You could tell he worked out because he had a lean muscular body much like Ryan.

He and Abe had met about three years ago and were friends in the beginning, because Sam understood some of the things Abe had been going through, having gone through them himself. In the last year, their relationship had become closer, making them a couple.

As always, Luc's dinner was delicious; unfortunately Ryan couldn't remember what he ate. His stomach was starting to do a flip because he was so nervous. He didn't even notice Shondra reaching for his plate. It was time for dessert now and he hadn't told Joshua about the proposal.

Excusing himself, he asked Joshua if he needed to go to the bathroom. Joshua said no at first, then realized his dad was hinting that he wanted him to go. As they went into the bathroom, Ryan squatted down and began to whisper, "Now, I am going to propose to your mommy during dessert, okay?"

"You got the marriage ring?" Joshua asked.

"Yes, Luc is going to put it in her dessert."

"In dessert..." Ryan had to get him to lower his voice. "What if she eats it?"

"She won't eat it. Luc will put it where she can see it before she starts eating." At least Ryan hoped she didn't eat it.

"Come on you two, Luc is bringing dessert to the table." Hearing this, Ryan held his stomach, sick with nerves.

"Daddy, are you going to spit up?"

"I hope not." Feeling very nervous, he opened the door letting Joshua out first.

Shondra and Luc began placing dessert dishes on the table, each one getting closer to Roni. Ryan became more nervous with each dish placed. Everyone at the table was waiting for Roni to receive her dish and see her face when she found the ring. Joshua peeped around, smiling at his father, excited about the proposal to come.

Luc almost bumped his head while setting down Roni's dish filled with fresh cut strawberries glazed with chocolate, on top of a small chocolate Bundt cake; instead of the usual mint leaf for decoration was the engagement ring.

Roni was so busy talking it took her a moment to notice the shiny object in her dessert. Looking down, she saw the diamonds catching the light sparkling. At first, she was not sure of what she saw, but was shocked at the sight. "Oh my God!" she picked it up, looking at the ring and fanning herself with her hand. "Oh my God!" She turned to look at Ryan who was already on one knee. Holding the ring between her fingers, she put her hand over her mouth to suppress her scream.

"Roni," Ryan called her name to get her attention, but he still didn't know what to say. After looking into her eyes he knew why he loved her and the words began to flow from his lips. "Roni, I love you. Will you give me the honor of being my wife?"

Fighting back the tears, she nodded her head as she reached to hug Ryan. "Yes!"

Joshua jumped up and down, laughing as everyone at the table applauded. Ryan took the ring from Roni and placed it on her finger. She held it up, admiring it on her finger as Thuy and

Shondra came over to admire the ring. Both women pushed Ryan out of the way so they could see.

"Oh, Roni, that is beautiful," Shondra screamed.

"I love the design," Thuy chimed in.

"Abe designed it especially for you," Ryan told her.

"Oh, Abe, it is beautiful!" She took it off to look at the artistry of the ring. "It looks antique. Thank you so much." In the band she saw an inscription in Hebrew. "Abe, what does this mean?" she asked, showing it to Ryan.

"It is Hebrew and tells a little story," he began. "Ryan's name means little king, Veronica means victory in Hebrew, and Joshua means God's victory." Abe felt a special joy at telling them the story. "Once there was a little king that found his victory, and together they had God's victory."

CHAPTER 16

The flight was entertaining after Roni switched seats with Ryan so he and Joshua could look out the window. Even though she was working on her laptop during the flight, she occasionally caught some of their antics.

Although their trip to Virginia had been planned, she still had some of the daily business to finish up for the month. Usually Laurence helped her with the day-to-day grind, but after finishing his yearlong hiatus from college, he had started medical school. Roni knew he had a lot of studying to do so she didn't bother him with the store. Even with a great store manager, Roni still made the major decisions.

Maybe she shouldn't have come down this visit with so much going on at the store, was her thought, but she wasn't kidding anyone. Roni was just nervous about meeting Ryan's family for the first time. She had talked on the phone with both Pete and Pearl, but that wasn't the same as meeting them face to face. Once they met her, they might not like her. Most of the people she knew didn't judge people based on pigmentation, so she questioned if they would.

Rubbing her temple, Roni knew she was being silly because Joshua just adored Pearl and Pete. Every time they called, he couldn't wait to get on the phone and even wanted to call them. Roni finally put the numbers in speed dial so he could phone when he wanted to. That made Pearl very happy, because lately there had been a nightly call to his great-grandma to say goodnight.

Ryan saw the concern on Roni's face. Reaching for her hand, he kissed it to put her at ease. "Don't worry, it will be fine," he assured her. He knew his grandmother and father would be fine with Roni. Even Jake would like her, although he might frighten her with his size.

He laughed at that thought, because at first sight, most people would think Jake to be mean but he wasn't. Jake was just an oversized teddy bear with a bunch of tattoos, only eating small dogs, not children.

Joshua was excited about going back to Virginia. He loved going out in the woods with little Jake and Libby, but this time it was hunting season so they wouldn't get to go too far from Mama Pearl's house. Ryan saw he was disappointed learning that the hiking trips were not going to be as they were back in the summer, but his safety was more important.

During deer season, you had to be careful even if you were on your own land. Sometimes rogue hunters sneaked on to your property to hunt. That was dangerous enough, but the possibility of stray bullets or an arrow was an added danger.

Ryan wanted him to enjoy himself but didn't want him injured in the woods, so he planned to hunt some but also teach Joshua how to use a bow and arrow. Then there was the fishing, which Joshua had loved back in the summer when they went out on the lake.

He had taught Joshua how to swim in the lake just in case something happened and he wasn't around to protect him. Many things could happen around water and he wanted Joshua to be prepared for anything. Ryan had been proud to teach him the rules his dad, grandpa, and even Jake had taught him over the years.

Retrieving their overhead bags from the top compartment, they filed into the tiny aisle, walking like schoolchildren excitedly on their way to recess. Joshua had been there before, so he told his mother where to go. The only difference was that they weren't renting a car. Ryan had wanted to rent one but his dad insisted he didn't need to waste money. Between Pete and Mama Pearl, they had transportation.

Besides, if Pearl met Roni for the first time at her home, it would be a little uncomfortable. Pearl felt she might just talk with her on the ride back to the house, putting her at ease. Actually, Pearl wanted to get a good look at her without appearing to be staring. All the pictures she had seen showed Roni to be a strikingly beautiful woman. Although Roni didn't like taking photos, Ryan had convinced her to do a family portrait, which Pearl had displayed proudly on her mantle.

On the way to the airport, Pearl found out that Pete had the same idea about wanting to sneak a peek at her. They both laughed at their silly behavior, but were genuinely curious about Roni. Pete, like Pearl, often spoke with her on the phone and they liked her, but he was nervous about their first meeting. It would be an awkward situation for him, because Helen was still being difficult. Helen could act juvenile if she wanted to, but Pete was not going to lose his son because of her.

Walking through the corridor, Joshua left both his parents behind. He was walking briskly in almost a gallop trying to get to the luggage area. Roni started to call after him, but Ryan told her Joshua was fine because they could see him and the airport wasn't that big. She had to admit he was cute, acting as if he was in charge and knew where he was going. Both Ryan and Joshua had gone to get their haircut the day before and were very handsome.

Before Ryan took Joshua for his first professional haircut, he had never been inside of a black barbershop. When Roni asked him to take Joshua, he turned to Laurence for help. Laurence took him to the barbershop he and his father went to; it was a family tradition for them.

The eldest two barbers remained the same, although others had come and gone over the years. Sitting Joshua in the chair, he had been a little afraid of the buzzing noise. The owner, Modest, sat Ryan down in his chair. "Look, Joshua. Your daddy's getting his hair cut." He had then whispered to Ryan, "Sit still so he can see you aren't afraid." Ryan didn't know he was actually going to cut his hair, but had been pleasantly surprised at the skill and the price. He and Joshua went every two weeks now on schedule.

Turning the corner, Joshua saw Mama Pearl and his Grandpa Pete scanning the area looking for them. Joshua turned back, informing his parents he saw them and quickened his steps to get there faster. Ryan had to tell him to slow down because they weren't going to leave him. As he got closer to Mama Pearl, he tiptoed trying to sneak up on her, but he started to giggle, causing her to turn around.

"Come here, you little rascal," she exclaimed as she gave him a big hug and kiss. Then Joshua reached for his grandpa to get a hug. "They're walking too slow," Joshua laughed, talking about his parents.

Roni was beginning to get nervous about turning the corner and Ryan noticed she had slowed her pace. Grabbing her hand, he pulled her close to show she was with him for anyone that questioned it. "Take a deep breath. Trust me, they are not as frightening as your Nana Ann." Ryan remembered meeting her the first time and she was nowhere near as sweet as Pearl.

Well, she wasn't as sweet on first sight, because Ann was a very guarded woman, which made her intimidating. Ryan had almost hyperventilated when he'd first met her, but over time, she had begun to trust him with her only granddaughter. "They already like you and will love you once you meet," he tried to persuade her as he kissed her lightly on the lips. "Come on, you will be fine."

Turning the corner, Roni saw Joshua already sitting with his grandpa and Mama Pearl. He was just chatting away while they hung on his every word as he told them about their flight. Neither noticed Ryan nor Roni approaching, almost missing the chance to see her. If Pete hadn't glanced up, they both would have missed the opportunity.

Both Pete and Pearl stared because they couldn't help it. She was beautiful. Pete rose from his seat to greet her; he felt his words wanting to stutter before he could even speak. Pearl also got up, but the closer Roni got to them the more real she appeared. They could see the freckles on her nose as she smiled. Her smile made it clear where Joshua got his dimples. "Looking for us?" Ryan teased them as he pulled Roni in front of him to introduce her.

Before Ryan began an introduction, Pearl interjected, "No introductions needed, Ryan." Pearl held out her arms to hug her. "Hi, Roni, it is so nice to finally meet you," she said with her Virginian twang.

Receiving the hug, Roni replied, "Nice to finally meet you too, Mama Pearl."

Pete was still finding it hard to speak because women just made him nervous. "Hi, Roni, nice to meet you," he extended his hand.

"Nice to meet you too," she ignored his hand hugging him as she did Pearl. This made him smile as he hugged her back.

"How was your flight?" Pete asked.

Ryan answered before Roni could, "She wouldn't know, she worked the whole flight."

"Well, that stops right now," Pearl scolded her. "You are on vacation and here to enjoy yourself."

Making a little funny face, Roni conceded, "I will try."

"No trying, just doing," Pearl gave her a sweet lecture. "Let's get your bags and get out of here." With a high-pitched laugh, Pearl grabbed Roni by the arm as they headed for the baggage claim.

The ride back to Pearl's mostly involved teasing Roni about not being able to relax. Pete had to tell her twice to just point to the bag, he would get it; her nature was one of being independent. Ryan had gotten used to her always stepping in to help others, but she still found it hard to accept help from anyone. Gradually she was beginning to depend on him more.

"Roni, Ryan says you're a designer," Pete commented.

"Yes, I do mostly children's clothing and nursery ensembles," Roni proudly responded.

"And, she manufactures what she designs," Ryan chimed in so she wouldn't minimize her skills and accomplishments.

"Yeah, she has the baby store, the urban store, and is working on...What's that store called, mommy?" Joshua asked, very proud of his mother.

"Evening attire and bridal wear," she smiled. "Currently I am working on my wedding dresses," she told Pearl. Roni was hearing for the first time all of her accomplishments aloud. She never thought about what she did, she just did it.

"Have you decided where you are going to have the wedding?" Pearl inquired.

"Well, Ryan and I want it close enough that both families can be involved. I will probably go down to Rock Hill while we are here to look at locations. We are thinking about doing a garden wedding or a small intimate ceremony at a chapel."

"Either one will be beautiful. Have you picked your colors for your bridesmaids?"

"I am thinking about using lilac or lavender for them. It really depends on the date we select." Pearl and Roni continued their conversation as if the men weren't in the car.

"Jake called last night wanting to know what time we were getting in," Ryan told his father to interrupt their silence.

"That boy is happier than a frog in a pond full of mosquitoes," Pete joked about Jake. "What day ya'll going out?"

"I don't know yet, will have to check with him on your work load. Don't want to steal your help to go hunting."

"Not much going on at the shop right now. Did a motor rebuild last week and a transmission, but mostly general maintenance right now; people just trying to maintain what they got. Jake has gotten a lot of the bikers coming in now for work on their bikes, but I leave that up to him."

"He's hanging out with the bikers?"

"No, just does a little tattooing on the side at some of the shops. You know Jake, he makes friends so easily." Both laughed because they knew that wasn't true. If Jake liked you, he liked you, but if he didn't you couldn't change his mind.

Driving up to the log cabin, Roni saw why Ryan loved being there and Joshua couldn't stop talking about it. The winding drive up to the house was scenic and pristine, making Roni happy she had brought her digital camera. She was seeing ways to change Joshua's room, because she wanted to move him from the nursery to a larger room.

He was getting older and needed more space for himself. He would like a mural of the house and woods in his room, but the nursery had to remain the same with the mystical creatures. After all that was something her mother had painted and Roni couldn't bear to cover it.

They had barely gotten the door open before Joshua was already out and running around with excitement. Seeing his cousins Libby and little Jake on their bikes coming up the drive, he ran down to greet them. Little Jake picked him up, swinging him around while Libby, not far behind, got a hug. Roni enjoyed watching Joshua with his cousins. They seemed to love him as much as he loved them. It was supposed to be that way. Not seeing differences, but only loving each other.

Libby saw Roni at the car and walked over to her. "Hi, I'm Libby. You must be Roni?" She looked up at her with an innocent smile and light brown eyes. Her hair was much like her mother's, blonde, but wavy like her dad's or the little he had left.

"Hi, Libby, Joshua has told me many wonderful things about you and little Jake," she praised, giving her a little hug. "Thank you so much, I really appreciate you looking after him while he was here before."

"Oh, he was no trouble, just funny at times," she laughed still staring at Roni because she had never seen anyone so pretty. Well, only in magazines with the stars, but Roni was real and right in front of her.

Ryan asked little Jake to help bring in the bags and carry them upstairs to their rooms. Walking by Roni, he waved shyly as he briskly moved past her. Libby informed her little Jake was very shy around girls. Her momma said he was fourteen and his hormones were racing. Roni only got a quick glimpse, but could tell he was a handsome young man.

"Welcome to my abode." Mama Pearl was tickled at herself. "I always wanted to say that."

The cabin was beautiful. Roni couldn't help being in awe; she had never been inside a cabin, but loved the homey feel of it. Ryan enjoyed the expression on her face but also loved the way everyone was treating her. It gave him confidence that they loved him and would love her the same way.

At least most of them would; the jury was still out with his mother. He hadn't spoken to her much since he and Joshua had left back in the summer. They did fine with the usual pleasantries, but when it came to Roni and Joshua, the talk was negative. He loved his mother and would do anything for her, but the hatred she had for his family was taking its toll.

Sure, his dad had had concerns about him being in an interracial relationship, but he'd gotten past them and started seeing Roni as the woman he loved. Pete would call and talk to Roni longer than him, which made him proud of his dad.

Joshua came rushing in. "Mommy, can I go bike riding with Libby and little Jake?"

Ryan saw she didn't know what to say. "Don't worry, they just ride around in this area and it is all family."

"You don't have a bike. How are you going to ride?" she asked.

"Yes I do. Daddy bought me one when we were here last time," Joshua reminded his mother, "and they taught me to ride without the baby wheels."

His excitement tickled her. "Okay, but you have to change clothes first." This made Joshua a little disappointed. "It won't take long, just be patient."

"Come on, mommy, I will show you my room." Joshua grabbed her hand, pulling her up the stairs.

Mama Pearl gave a hearty laugh seeing that. "Ryan, you and Roni need to let him come down and spend some time during the summer," she suggested to him.

"Yes, Roni and I will talk about that." He knew she had concerns about Joshua being there without one of them. "Let's see how this trip goes first." He kissed her on the cheek as he passed by. "Thanks for everything."

Roni was enjoying their visit to Virginia; it had been better than she expected. They went to church on Sunday at Mama Pearl's request because she wanted to show them off. So Roni made sure they had something for conversation.

She wore her burnt orange A line dress that was tailored for her body with a cropped ¾ length sleeved jacket and a peter pan style collar. The one button closure only accentuated the dragonfly broach on the lapel. Walking into the church, she knew they would be looking and she wanted them to have a vision to remember.

Mama Pearl made sure Roni sat next to her during service. Ryan allowed Joshua to sit with his cousins provided he didn't talk during services. He only chatted a little and Ryan gave him a chastising look. Roni felt the stares in their direction, but was determined not to let them bother her.

After service a group of old hens, as Mama Pearl called them, gathered not far from the church doors and was whispering about Roni and Ryan. Mama Pearl just casually walked over while they were busy with their heads together. "Speak up, ladies, God can't hear you," she told them before joining her family. Neither Roni nor Ryan knew what she had said to them, but the smirk on her face didn't need words.

That evening, Mama Pearl had a family dinner at her house with Pete, Helen, Jake, and his family invited. Ryan was a little uneasy with Helen being there, but Roni assured him it would be fine.

Helen didn't talk much, just looked at Joshua strangely. Joshua thought she was spooky, but his mother told him to be nice and respect her. She didn't speak much to Roni after their initial introduction. There were tense moments but they handled them accordingly.

At Ryan's request, Roni made her famous blackberry cobbler and Jake tried to eat the whole thing. She promised to prepare one just for him before leaving, after he had his second helping.

There were many laughs and old stories about Ryan from Mama Pearl and Jake. Jake told the tree story much differently than Ryan and they jokingly argued over the details. They entertained the whole table; even Helen had to laugh.

On Monday morning, Jake and Ryan did some hunting and he killed a deer the first day. The two were home by nine A.M. and walked in while Roni was doing her yoga exercise. Ryan sneaked up on Jake as he watched her, teasing him that he was eyeing his woman; Jake was so embarrassed he left. Roni told Ryan to stop teasing Jake, but Ryan couldn't help it, it was fun. Besides, they were like brothers and Jake would be fine later.

Roni drove down to visit her mother's family in South Carolina and discuss wedding plans with her Aunt Betty. It was only a three-hour drive and she felt Ryan needed to spend some time with just his family. She and Joshua spent the night, giving her time to talk over the wedding plans with Betty and Bianca.

Bianca was probably more vocal about how she wanted *her* wedding to be, making Roni and Betty laugh at her details about what she wanted. Betty reminded her that weddings cost money and she didn't have a job yet. Bianca didn't care because she was in her own dream world with her plans.

Some of her ideas were interesting, like having the ceremony in the backyard. Roni thought it might be pretty with the pond and there was a flat area to arrange chairs. Her only concern was the weather. If it rained, what would be plan B?

She had originally thought about doing it in New York, but that would make it hard for some of their family to attend. Her grandparents on her mother's side refused to travel. Ryan's family might not want to come to New York for the nuptials, because the travel arrangements could be expensive. If they had it in South Carolina all could attend the ceremony.

Joshua was happy to be back when they returned to Virginia around midday on Thursday. With Justin in New York attending Julliard studying music and theater, he had no one to keep him busy. So he was glad to get back to little Jake.

Libby was different, more like Bianca talking about boys and polishing her nails. She didn't spend much time with Joshua, but was more interested in Roni. Although she was a tomboy, she was growing into a beautiful young woman.

"Girls, yuck!" Joshua would say when talking about Libby. Roni would remind him that *she* was a girl, but in his mind she wasn't, she was just his mommy.

Ryan and Jake had gone hunting again; both had killed a deer, but Ryan was going to give the meat of the second one to Jim at the Steelys' farm. He really liked Jim and they had become close, with them going up at least once a month to restock. Besides, he enjoyed being able to give them something special because they had been very kind to him.

Roni was tired from the drive and left Joshua in his dad's care, deciding to take a nap. Lulling between sleep and wakefulness, she could smell the fresh sheets on the bed. Smiling to herself, she knew Ryan had freshened up the bed as if he knew she would be tired.

The smells of baking cookies awakened Roni. Putting on her clothes, she went downstairs finding it to be after four o'clock. She hadn't planned to sleep so long, but welcomed the nap. The aroma of peanut butter cookies coming out of the oven was intoxicating. Smiling at her little munchkin baking cookies with his great-grandma, it was a delightful sight. Joshua, with his apron on, tried his best to stir the cookie dough.

"I smell cookies," Roni said as she came into the kitchen.

"Yep," Joshua informed her, "me and Mama Pearl are baking cookies."

"Oh, really now," she rubbed his back.

"He said peanut butter is your favorite," Mama Pearl let her know.

"Yes, they are." Roni smiled at the mature woman before her. "Thanks for making me feel at home."

"Oh, you're welcome, sweetie," Pearl said, putting another batch of cookies in the oven. "I'm really sorry for how Helen is acting."

"It's okay, I expected it."

"That still doesn't make it right." Pearl stopped, giving her a loving look. Roni could see Ryan in her eyes. "I'm proud of the way you are handling things, because I wouldn't be able to do it," she told Roni.

"Well, Mama Pearl, I do it for Ryan. She is his mother and I respect her." Roni smiled lovingly at Pearl.

"True, but if it was me, this house would look like we were in a wrestling match." They both laughed before Pearl continued, "I understand why, just know I couldn't be that strong."

Roni gave her a simple smile and said, "You would be surprised at what you can do for those you love."

As the two women continued with their conversation, they heard the door open. Ryan came into the house carrying wood for the fireplace. Putting it down in the hearth, he informed Pearl and Roni he was going to be outside chopping wood to restock the supply. Joshua wanted to help, but Ryan was afraid the axe might fly off the handle or something dangerous. So he asked Roni to take Joshua to the store a few miles down the road to get him away from the house.

Since their arrival, Libby had been a constant visitor. She wanted to know about growing up in New York and about Roni in general. Having just started high school, she was eager to hear about college, trying to make decisions for what she wanted to do when she grew up. Roni encouraged her to find something she liked to do and make a career out of it. Libby enjoyed talking to Roni because it made her feel like she had a big sister to look up to.

Libby was walking up the drive while Roni and Joshua were on their way to the store. Without hesitation, she jumped in the jeep to ride with them. "How was school today?" Roni asked.

"It was okay," she told Roni. "I can hardly wait for it to be over."

"Don't wish your life away," Roni advised her. "It will be over before you know it."

Joshua loved riding in the old jeep his daddy had from college. Ryan had sold it when he went to New York but Pete had bought it back from the man that had purchased it. He figured it would be something Ryan could use when he came home for visits, and besides, Pete felt Joshua would get a kick out of it.

They arrived at the little store with the old-fashioned candy counter. Since they had come to Virginia, the people in the store had come to know Joshua and Roni. The owners were an adorable old man and his wife who was legally blind.

Mr. Sims was a little round man who wore glasses low on his nose. His wife, Emma, was a sweet woman who made preserves and pickles to sell in the store. Roni was curious as to how she did so much having poor eyesight. Finally, she concluded if life put obstacles in your way, just go around them.

"Hey, Emma, here come our favorite customers," Mr. Sims greeted them. Libby informed Roni he called everyone that.

"Mrs. Emma, you have any of the candy pecans?" Joshua asked. He had developed a love for them since his Mama Pearl had baked them in his cookies.

"Sure do, how much do you want?" she asked him.

Roni requested, "Just a quarter pound will be enough. He hasn't had dinner yet."

"Mommy, can I have some crickets?" Joshua asked, after hearing them in a cage.

"What do you need crickets for?"

"Fishing. Daddy's going to take me before we go back to New York."

"He will come get some for you."

"No, they won't be open in the morning," Joshua pleaded his case.

"Okay, just a few." She knew they weren't for fishing; Joshua just liked looking at insects. Looking at Libby, she said, "I hope they don't chirp all the way home."

Libby laughed. "Sorry, they will, and the darker it gets the louder they get."

Roni picked up a few things, taking them the counter to be checked out, noticing an old truck pulling into the parking lot. She thought to herself they were probably coming in from hunting somewhere, and she was right. A couple of the men were riding in the truck bed and were climbing out as they started out the door.

After opening the jeep door, she helped Joshua into his seat. He of course had to hold his crickets, looking at them through the mesh held on top of the can with a rubber band. All Roni could think was how noisy the ride home was going to be. Libby smiled at the look on her face when looking at the crickets. Roni was so involved with getting Joshua in the jeep she didn't notice the man coming up behind her.

When Libby saw him coming in their direction, she called her name to warn her. "Roni!" She started to open the door but Roni instructed her to stay in the car.

"Well, looky here, fellas, she's driving a stick," he said, getting a silly laugh from his buddies behind him. "You sure you can handle all that?"

Pretending she didn't hear him, she proceeded to go to the driver's side of the jeep.

"I'm talking to you." His tone became sterner as if he were speaking to a child. "You that gal Ryan brought down." He recognized Roni from church.

Roni was wearing Ryan's jacket that he had left on the washer after coming in from hunting that morning. Knowing she was outnumbered with her son and Libby in the car, she tried to walk around him.

He grabbed her by the arm pushing her up against the jeep. "What's your problem, gal? Don't you hear me talking to you?"

Mr. Sims had been watching from inside and got his broom handle from behind the counter. He shouted back to Emma, "Call the sheriff! We got some idiots out here." He was walking as fast as he could with his bad leg. Barreling out the door, he shouted at the man, "Cal, leave them alone!"

"Go back in the store, old man!" Cal sneered, his friends chiming in to incite the situation. "Ain't nobody asked you to come out here."

"Cal, leave them alone!" he told him stronger this time. Mr. Sims could tell he had been out in the woods all day drinking and probably smoking that funny weed. "Now, do you want Emma to call the sheriff?"

Cal released his grip on Roni, expecting her to show fear, but instead she jerked away never losing eye contact. She knew she could not show him any fear because men like him thrived on that. Looking toward Mr. Sims, she gratefully said, "Thanks! We will be back tomorrow."

With an animated voice, Cal advised her, "I'll be waiting." He turned and began walking toward the store as the voices of his friends echoed his comments. "Why don't you mind your own business, old man!"

Driving out of the parking lot, Joshua was afraid. He kept turning to look back, making sure they weren't being followed. When he couldn't see them anymore, he started to cry uncontrollably. Roni tried to console him without success. Both he and Libby were terrified at what had just happened. "Don't worry, we are safe now," she tried to comfort her son. It was not an easy task, as she was just, if not more, frightened than both he and Libby.

While driving back to the house, Libby tried to comfort Joshua. The more they tried to comfort him, however, the louder he got. As Roni was getting him out of the car, he began to scream and cry hysterically to the point he had cried out his tears and was mainly making a dry heaving sound.

Ryan and Jake were in the backyard when they heard Joshua's screams, and both ran immediately to the front of the house. "What's going on?" they frantically asked.

Before Roni could answer, Libby was telling the whole story, beginning with them getting into the jeep and Cal accosting Roni, preventing them from leaving. Roni didn't want her to tell them every detail. She knew Ryan might get angry and do something without thinking.

Both Jake and Ryan were angry at Cal's bigoted antics. "Are you okay?" he asked Joshua as he held on to him, and then looked over at Roni. "You alright?"

"I'm fine. They were just being stupid," she tried to minimize the situation. "We are fine. Don't worry about it." She was hoping her downplaying the situation had convinced him when Libby interrupted again.

"Ryan, he pushed her up against the jeep." Libby grabbed his flannel shirt, showing him how Cal had pushed Roni.

"Wait a minute, he touched you?" Ryan asked Roni.

"He didn't hurt me, I am okay." Her heart was beating faster now.

Angered beyond reason, Ryan said, "Take him inside," as he gave Joshua to Roni.

"Ryan, no!" she screamed to him, bringing tears to her eyes. "Please, we are fine. It's over!" She let Mama Pearl take Joshua as she tried to stop Ryan. In her heart, she knew Ryan wanted to protect them. "It's not worth it!" she pleaded, afraid of him getting into danger.

He put his hands on her shoulders, pulling her close. Ryan hugged her then whispered in her ear, "You are worth it." Getting into the jeep with Jake riding shotgun, they bolted down the drive.

When they arrived at the community store, Cal and his friends were still hanging out. With a couple of cases of beer in the back of the truck, they were about to leave until Ryan pulled into the parking lot. The jeep tires screeched as he slammed on the breaks. Ryan didn't give the jeep time to come to a complete stop before he was out and in Cal's face. "You stay away from my family." His eyes were wild with anger as he clenched his fist.

"Oh, you the knight in shining armor?" Cal glanced back at his cohorts for support, which they eagerly gave. Popping the can on a beer, he taunted, "Nobody cares about your little concubine."

"Cal, I am not playing with you. Stay away from my family!" Ryan moved closer to him as Jake came up behind him to protect Ryan's back.

Drinking his beer, Cal could barely stand without swaying on his feet with his big belly sticking out over his pants. "Did she say I did something to her?" he asked in a defensive tone. "Who you going to believe, me or your little nigger whore?"

Before the words had completely parted from Cal's lips, Ryan hit him in the face, almost losing his balance. "You stay the hell away from my family!" Ryan looked down at the small little man with the bloody face.

Jake grabbed Ryan to keep him from hitting him again. "Come on, you proved your point." Looking down at Cal, he said, "I should've let him kick your ass."

Ryan walked back to the jeep fuming while Jake ran to catch up to him. As they got back in, Jake quickly turned the ignition, spinning the tires as he drove out of the parking lot. "I should have let you finish it, but those bastards don't fight fair. They had guns in that truck and would have used them if they felt they were losing."

"Yeah, but I wished you hadn't stopped me." Ryan was still angry, and anger was an emotion he didn't like to see in himself.

"He ain't nobody and never will be. You proved your point." Jake tried to calm Ryan down, but he had wanted to hit Cal, too. That was the unwritten law: you didn't mess with a man's family. If Roni had been white, it never would have happened. "How is your hand?" he asked Ryan, seeing he was favoring it.

"I guess it is okay." He felt the pain going up his arm. "I'm just glad it is my right hand," he forced a smile to mask the pain he was feeling. Unfortunately, the pain wasn't in just his hand, but also in his heart. He had thought he would be able to bring his family to Virginia and not worry. Now he wasn't so sure.

CHAPTER 17

Everyone was on edge waiting for Ryan and Jake to come back. Mama Pearl was trying to keep her head, but was worrying more with each minute they were away. Roni was sitting on the couch holding Joshua, as he whimpered out of fear that his daddy wasn't coming home. Looking to his mother for comfort, he asked, "Are they going to hurt daddy?"

Wanting to comfort him, she told him not to worry; his daddy would be okay. Seeing the worry in Pearl's eyes, she felt she was lying to her son and that his daddy might not be okay. Why hadn't he just listened to her and let it go? You couldn't reason with people like Cal. All she could see in her mind was them ganging up on Ryan and Jake, or worse, shooting them both. That thought made her hold onto her son tighter, trying to console herself.

Hearing the sound of the jeep coming up the drive, Joshua jumped from his mother's lap, running to the door. "It's daddy!" he screamed as he ran out the door with Libby behind him.

With her hands trembling, Roni wiped her face so Ryan wouldn't see her tears. Both she and Pearl went to the door, with Roni stopping to catch her breath. Pearl nudged her, "It's okay, he's back." Both were thankful they were safe.

Ryan was getting out the jeep, his hand swollen from hitting Cal, but he picked up his son holding him tightly as he cried. "I told you I would be back," he said, trying to console him. "Don't worry, daddy's fine."

Seeing Roni as she came out onto the porch he could tell she had been crying. He put Joshua down as he and Jake walked toward the house with Roni coming down the steps to meet them. The fear in her eyes became real as she moved closer to him. "Don't worry baby, I'm fine." Ryan held her to give some comfort.

"Come on in the house," Pearl told them as she rubbed her arms, "it's getting chilly out her."

"What happened to your hand?" Roni asked.

"Oh, it's nothing. I'm fine."

"Ryan, it's swollen," she pointed out as her nurturing nature took over.

"Baby, I am fine. Don't worry about it."

"I better get some ice." Roni went into the kitchen to get ice for his hand. Pearl saw her rush out of the room and motioned for Ryan to go after her.

Joshua started to follow his father only to be called back by Pearl. "Your daddy and mommy need to talk, sweetie."

Walking into the kitchen, Roni had her back to Ryan. "Baby, you okay?" he asked.

Turning around with tears streaming down her face, she pounded his chest. "Don't ever scare me like that again!"

Holding her in his arms, he told her, "Baby, I'm fine," while letting her lean on him. He tried to put her at ease. "Roni, if I hadn't confronted him, you and Joshua would never be able to come back here," he said, pulling her closer. "You and Joshua mean the world to me and no one will disrespect you. I love you and I would die for you," he explained his reason for hitting Cal.

Hearing those words, it became real to her that when he had left, he didn't know what would happen. Cal was someone he knew better than she did, but he had been willing to risk everything to protect her. She couldn't look at him, because she was too busy listening to the sound of his beating heart.

"Ryan, Charles is here to see you," Pearl told them. The tone of her voice was not very pleasant.

Roni looked up at Ryan. "Who is Charles?"

"The sheriff," he informed her, not wanting to alarm her. "It will be fine. He probably just needs to talk to me, because the Simses had called him." Kissing her, he playfully told her, "Stop worrying."

They both went out to the porch where Mama Pearl was arguing with the sheriff. "Now Charlie, I have wiped your snotty nose almost as much as Pete's," she remonstrated, becoming upset. "You know they were dead wrong and that Cal stays in trouble for one reason or another."

"I know, but Mama Pearl I still have to do my job," the sheriff tried to reason with her. Charles had grown up with Pete and knew the family well. "When I receive a report I have to check it out."

"Oh, bull," Pearl began to rant, as Ryan walked out on the porch to speak to him.

"Mama Pearl, let me handle this." Ryan wasn't sure if he was going to be arrested. "Roni, take Joshua into the house."

"No need, Ryan, I'm just following up. Mr. Sims told me what happened. About them assaulting your missus there." He looked up at Roni on the porch. "Cal wanted to press charges," he said, seeing the fear in Ryan's eyes. "But I reminded him that he drew first blood," Charles explained while leaning on his left leg, twirling his shades on the bottom step.

He was the usual small town sheriff, voted in more because he knew everyone. On his skinny frame, he wore a belt bigger than his arm that had an oversized radio and gun. Carrying those heavy items, Charles felt, announced he was sheriff to those that didn't know. "I'm just here to diffuse the situation," he told them, rising up and putting his hand on his pistol. "How much longer you staying here?" he asked Ryan.

"Just a couple more days, we are leaving Sunday afternoon," Ryan assured him.

"Okay, just stay away from them if you can. You know that crew is about as dim-witted as they come." Tipping his hat as he turned to go back to his patrol car, he said, "Ya'll have a good evening."

Jake looked at Libby. "Let's get home before your momma starts to worry."

Watching them walk away, Ryan told him, "Jake! Thanks for having my back."

"Always," he said, looking back at Ryan, "but I am getting too old for this." Both shared a laugh, trying to put it behind them.

"Let me get that ice for your hand." Roni went back inside to retrieve the ice pack.

Pearl started in behind her when she heard a car coming up the drive. Seeing it was Pete and Helen, she took a deep breath because the last thing they needed was a dumb remark. She opened the door for Joshua. "Go see if you can help your momma." She wanted to keep him from hearing Helen act like a fool. Making sure he was secure inside, she asked, "What're ya'll doing here?"

Pete walked up to the steps, looking at Ryan. "You alright son?" he asked, gazing at Ryan with great concern.

"Yeah, I'm fine. Just sprained my hand, nothing serious." He showed him his swollen hand.

"You sprained your hand?" Helen questioned.

"I think so; it doesn't feel like it's broken. I will be fine."

Pearl wondered how they knew about Ryan so quickly. "Who told you about this?"

Still looking at Ryan's hand, Pete said, "Charlie came by the house before coming up here." Seeing how swollen his hand was, his father asked, "You sure you're alright? You may need to have that looked at."

"Dad, I'm fine," Ryan tried to explain. "It was nothing. Cal grabbed Roni while she and Joshua were at the store. I went up to speak to him about it and one thing lead to another," he shrugged his shoulders, "and the rest is history."

"You should have never brought them down here," Helen admonished Ryan. "They just don't belong."

"Will you please shut up?" Pete shouted. "Do you ever listen to yourself?" He was very offended by her comments. "Our son could have been killed by a bunch of redneck bullies, and all you can do is blame Roni for Cal's stupidity." Disgusted by her lack of concern for Ryan, he roared, "My God, woman, he did what any man would do. He stood up for the people he loves." He looked at Helen angrily. "And that is more than I can say for you."

"Ya'll staying for supper? We're having chicken stew and deer hash," Pearl chimed in, getting great joy out of what had just transpired.

Pete and Helen didn't stay for dinner, but left shortly after making sure Ryan was fine. Pearl was tickled at the way Pete had finally stood up to Helen for his son. Helen was pushing her son away and couldn't see it. For Helen, it was too easy to worry about what others thought instead of looking into her own heart for answers.

Watching her around Joshua, you could see she wanted to be a part of his life, but kept her distance. She would sneak a peek at Joshua but turn away when someone saw her. There was no doubt in anyone's mind that Joshua was Ryan's son. He even laughed like him with that little silly grin.

After Pearl and Roni finished putting away the dishes, they sat down in the den with a cup of tea. Pearl felt it was time for her and Roni to have one of those woman-to-woman talks. She didn't know how to begin the conversation, but she needed to help Roni understand why Ryan had stood up for her earlier, even if it had cost him his life. Pearl figured the best way to start a conversation was to just jump into it. "Roni, are you still nervous about what happened today?" she asked.

"Yes, Ryan could have been killed." Roni felt the fear returning to her heart.

"Well, sweetie, he had to do that." She paused to take a sip of tea. "If he hadn't, he wouldn't have been the man he was raised to be."

"I know, but it was so frightening. I have never seen Ryan that angry." She wasn't sure how to continue. "I could never forgive myself if something had happened to him or Jake."

"And he wouldn't be able to forgive himself if something had happened to you or Joshua. That's why he had to protect his family."

"I hear you, but it wouldn't have been worth him being killed."

Stopping Roni before she could continue, Peal said, "Don't minimize yourself to him, Roni. He is willing to stand up to anyone for your honor. He has stood up to anyone that has made an unkind remark about you." She turned to face her. "He even puts his mother in her place when it comes to you. Deep down inside he knows that Helen accepts Joshua, but he lets her know that you, Joshua, and him are a family. If she wants him in her life she has to accept you."

"Mama Pearl, I really don't care if Helen accepts me. I just want Ryan to have a relationship with his family."

"That's just it, Roni, you are his family. He has chosen to be with you because he loves you." Feeling she needed to explain further, she said, "I need to tell you a little something about me." She thought about how she would begin the story of her life. "I am sure Ryan knows about this, although he has never mentioned to me that he does.

"You see, when I was young, I was stupid." She smiled at her youthful foolhardiness. "I was just out of high school, wet behind the ears, and too dumb to know it. Finding work wasn't easy back then unless you wanted to work in the factories, but I found a job working in a small diner over on the interstate. Being from the country, I wasn't used to men paying me attention, but I was a hot little number. In more ways than one." Both women shared a chuckle over Peal's comment.

"There was this trucker that would come through a couple of times a week and always sat in my section of the diner. Roni, he was gorgeous. He was tall with a lean build and a smile that would curl your toes when you looked at him." Pearl smiled about the man from her past. "He was always telling me how pretty I was and would always ask me out when he came in.

"Well, at first, I tried to pretend I wasn't interested, but I definitely was interested in him. After about two months of him asking, I finally gave in and decided to go out on a date. He treated me nice, too; we went and saw a movie and had dessert afterwards, he was the perfect gentleman. I thought I had died and gone to heaven with this man. He was everything I had dreamed of as a girl. All I saw was marrying him, moving out of that one horse town, and having a bunch of babies."

Pearl stopped to reflect on the story. "Well, I thought that, until I found out I was pregnant with Pete." Seeing the look in Roni's eyes, Pearl confirmed, "No, my husband wasn't Ryan's grandfather by blood," she told her hoping she would understand. "When I told the trucker about the baby, he acted like he would be there for us. Oh, if I had let him tell it, it was going to be a beautiful love story. I was so excited thinking we would get married and raise our child together. Needless to say, that was the last time I saw the bastard."

Roni listened to her and felt her pain, because she knew what it was like being alone going through a pregnancy. Although Roni had chosen it, the pain was still there. She hadn't told Ryan because she'd been afraid he would reject her; Mama Pearl had told her child's father and she *had* been rejected. In many ways, they were from different generations, different worlds, and different races, but with all their differences, they still felt the same pain from heartbreak.

Regaining her composure, Pearl continued, "During this time, Pete was also a regular at the diner and he would sit at the counter. He wasn't a trucker but was always on the road, going to different places, picking up parts for the garage he was working at. Unlike my son's father he wasn't flirty or anything. We would talk when he got his meal and sometimes if there was a game on the radio, we made small bets on them.

"If we lost the game we would always say double or nothing." Pearl smiled at the thoughts of her dead husband. "One day he came into the diner; it was about a month or so since I had seen the trucker, and I was feeling real low. He tried to tease me as usual and I just burst into tears. Thank God, no one was there because it was before the lunch hour. I told him what had happened and that I had let myself get pregnant.

"He could see my fear, because back then women just didn't have children and not be married. He just looked at me telling me not to worry, to just take it one day at a time. Big Pete was special. He was older than I was and was widowed, losing his wife and only child in a car accident about two years prior to our meeting. In some ways I think he blamed himself for their deaths because he had been driving, but it was a rainy night and a deer ran out in front of him."

Pearl walked into the kitchen as Roni followed her. "He was banged up badly himself in that accident, but survived." She got back to her story. "He came by every other day before lunchtime and we would talk. As I told you before I was young and stupid, not knowing which end to hold onto. All that time I had been talking to the trucker, Pete had had a crush of his own on me. With our age difference, he was a little shy talking to me, so he would just make general conversation.

"Right before I was starting to show, he asked me to marry him. I was shocked. He told me that he knew I didn't love him and would not want me to be a wife to him until I was ready, but that my baby needed a home and he could provide us with one." Pearl felt a warm glow at the thought of how wonderful Pete had been to her, because he hadn't had to take that kind of responsibility for her or her child.

"At first I said no; I liked Pete but I didn't want him to marry me out of pity. He told me to think about it a few days and he would ask again. I took the next couple of days to think about it and wasn't sure I could be a wife to him. I told this to Pete and he said, 'Let's just give this baby a home first and take the rest one day at a time.' That was his favorite saying.

"When the baby was born and I saw it was a boy, I named him Peter to honor the man who took care of us. It was years later that I found out that Pete had spent a night in jail for kicking the shit out of the trucker that knocked me up." She laughed thinking about how Ryan had done the same for Roni. "I found out the trucker wasn't much of a man. His wife lived about an hour's drive away and he already had three children with her."

"Did Pete ever meet any of his siblings?" Roni asked.

"No, my husband and I never told Pete he wasn't his father. After the accident, Pete couldn't have children so we both got a second chance." Remembering back, Pearl said, "My sister-in-law took it upon herself to tell the truth to clear her conscience. I don't know whose conscience she was clearing because she didn't have one." Both women laughed.

"My husband didn't speak to her for a long time after finding that out. Ryan's dad never told Pete he knew about him not being his biological father. He didn't change anything about their relationship, just went on like before he was told. I asked him after we buried Pete why he never said anything. Looking at me without cracking a smile, he said, 'Say what? As far as I'm concerned I buried my daddy today,' and with that we never spoke of it again."

Roni could tell he had made Pearl feel special because of the way she talked about him. Hearing Pearl's story made Roni understand why she treated her like family without question. She had been the woman on the outside herself.

"The one thing Pete taught Ryan and his father was nobody threatens your family, and you're not a man if you don't protect your woman." She hugged Roni. "Good night," she said, then turning back added, "No matter what you think, Roni, it was his job to protect you." Pearl left Roni in the kitchen, giving her time to absorb what she had learned about her new family.

Roni was beginning to understand the man she loved. Even though she knew he loved her, until now, she hadn't known how much. For a man to feel like one, he has to be able to protect and provide for those he loved. If she took that away from him, she would lose the man and she didn't want to lose Ryan. In their case, her strength might be her weakness. She needed to control her strengths to give Ryan the opportunity to be the man he had demonstrated he was.

Turning off the lights, she heard Joshua's laughter as he and Ryan made up their own bedtime stories. A smile filled her heart as she walked up the stairs to be with her family.

CHAPTER 18

The weather was getting colder in New York with the winter air blowing in. Ryan's hand had healed well after they had come home. Roni had taken him to the ER later that night back in Virginia when the swelling had worsened. After doing X-rays they had found out it wasn't broken which was a good thing, but he'd had a terrible sprain. The doctor had given Ryan a prescription for a painkiller and he'd slept most of the next day when he wasn't milking sympathy out of Roni.

During the winter months, not many new constructions were going on so things were slow for the firm. With Roni being in the area, they planned to have lunch together. Ryan was getting his coat when he passed Miguel in the hallway.

"Going out for lunch?" Miguel asked.

"Yeah, meeting my fiancée downstairs." Ryan loved calling her that, but couldn't wait to call her his wife.

"When do we get to meet this woman that has you smiling all the time?" Miguel asked as they talked waiting for the elevator.

"Well, if she's in the lobby when we get downstairs I will introduce you."

As they got off the elevator crowded with lunch goers, he saw Roni sitting in the lobby watching the people go by. "There she is," he smiled as they walked in her direction.

"Roni is your fiancée?" Miguel asked. "I didn't know that?"

"You know Roni?" It was a question Ryan found he frequently had to ask when it came to her.

"Since she was a little girl. Her father hired me to work at this company. Larry was a great man and gave me a chance before I even finished my education." Miguel laughed softly. "I was going to night school and working during the day for him doing construction jobs. Back then there was only three of us doing small jobs, but over the years he and Bernice built this company into what you see today."

Ryan was shocked. Roni had never told him she knew his boss. Why did she keep secrets from him? Just when he felt everything was going well, something new emerged. He didn't want Miguel to know he was upset about her not telling him about her history with the firm, so he suggested Miguel say hello to Roni before he left. The two men walked toward her. "Roni," Ryan called her name as they approached.

She turned at the sound of his voice and saw Miguel with Ryan. "Miguel!" She hugged him. "How are you?"

"Doing well; you didn't tell me you were engaged to Ryan," Miguel playfully scolded.

"Yes." She showed him her ring.

"That is beautiful." Looking at Ryan, he teased, "We pay you too much." They laughed together, but Ryan still had a strange look on his face. Roni didn't like that look, because it was the look of hurt. "You guys have a great lunch." As Miguel walked away, he turned back to Roni. "Give me a call later; I've got something to run by you and Laurence."

"Roni, what is he talking about?" Ryan wanted to know.

"Let's get to the restaurant so we can talk about it." She grabbed his arm as they walked out of the lobby. "I will explain everything."

At the restaurant, Roni explained to Ryan that she and Laurence were owners of the firm. They had inherited it when her father passed. Pegasus was her parents' empire. She told him how Larry and Bernice had built the company from nothing into one of the top ten firms in Harlem.

Larry had done the architectural designs while Bernice had been in charge of interior design and creation. Together they had been a great team, each not afraid to be honest if they felt something was wrong with the other's plans.

"Why didn't you tell me about this before?" Ryan asked.

"I don't know. It just never seemed important." Roni saw he was angry. "I'm sorry, but we were getting along so well. I just didn't know how to bring it up." She struggled with an answer.

"Did you get me the job with the firm?" Ryan needed to know the truth about being hired.

"No, I would never do that without asking you!" she exclaimed.

"Why should I believe you? You're always keeping secrets, Roni."

"Really, I just didn't think it mattered about the firm."

"Didn't matter? Roni, we will finish this conversation later. I need to get back to work." Sarcastically he said, "My boss may not like me being late."

Roni felt terrible that she had hurt Ryan again. Feeling defeated, she went back to work, dreading the conversation to come later that evening.

Work was not easy for Ryan and he was glad he didn't see Miguel. He was very upset with Roni and not sure he could hide it. All the way home, he just became angrier because she had gotten him hired at Pegasus. Landing a position with one of the top firms in New York had been his greatest accomplishment and the thrill of that had just been taken away.

Walking up to the brownstone, Ryan slowed his pace, not wanting to face Roni. How could she just not tell him things and think it wouldn't affect their relationship? He loved her but it was getting difficult not knowing her. Stalling until he couldn't do it anymore, he put his key into the door, turning the lock. Looking up, he saw Joshua coming down the hallway as per his usual routine.

"Hey, what are you up to?" He began to tickle him. Roni stood in the doorway of the kitchen with a solemn look on her face. Ryan felt he should speak to her but was unable to hide his anger.

Miffed at his behavior, Roni went back into the kitchen without saying a word. She was getting more upset as each minute passed. It showed as she was preparing dinner. Ryan could hear her in the kitchen slamming things around. He knew they needed to talk and asked Joshua to go to his room and play before dinner. Joshua obeyed, but felt the tension in the house. After he went upstairs, Ryan walked into the kitchen to confront Roni about what he had learned earlier.

"Why must you continuously do this to me?" he asked with irritation in his voice.

"Don't chastise me, Ryan! I am not a child," she retorted. "Besides what difference does it make who owns the firm?"

"The difference is that it is you!" he snapped back at her. "Why do you keep secrets from me? I have been totally honest with you and you still keep things from me." Ryan paced in the kitchen. "You could have told me you got me hired instead of acting like you didn't know."

"I didn't know, not until you told me!" she replied, angry that he insinuated differently.

"Oh, please, Roni, be honest. You pretended to not know I had landed the job at the airport. Just playing me like a fool."

"I told you I didn't help you with getting hired and I didn't."

"Stop lying to me!" As soon as the words parted from his lips, he knew he was wrong.

"You are acting like an ass right now," she coldly told him, masking the hurt she felt.

"So I'm the ass." Feeling very heated, Ryan started out of the kitchen but turned back. "Why don't you just be honest with me?"

"Ryan, go to hell!" Roni was so livid she could scream.

Grabbing his coat from the banister, Ryan picked up his keys and left the house, not seeing Joshua at the top of the stairs. Although he didn't know where he was going, Ryan walked down the street, trying to calm down. He had forgiven Roni so much in the past that he was just tired of being the one having to forgive. Why couldn't she just admit she was wrong and apologize?

He walked about three blocks and saw Danny's was coming up at the next corner. Walking in, he sat on a stool at the bar, ordering a beer. Sitting there nursing his beer, he tried to calm himself, but right now, he was just too angry.

"Give me one of those, just charge it to him."

Hearing Laurence's voice, Ryan asked, "What are you doing here?"

Laurence looked at Ryan seriously. "Looking for you."

"Laurence, I am not in a good mood right now."

"Have you eaten?" Laurence asked without acknowledging what Ryan had said. "Give us two cheeseburgers all the way with an order of fries."

"Laurence!"

"Don't worry, I won't tell Roni you had a cheeseburger and she won't smell the onions on your breath, because you ain't kissing nobody tonight." Seeing an empty booth, he told the bartender, "Have them bring it over there, please."

Knowing he didn't have a chance arguing with Laurence, Ryan sighed and grabbed his beer to take to the table. "Why are you here, Laurence?"

"I saw you storming out of the house while I was walking up. Went inside, spoke to Roni, and she told me you'd had an argument." Their waitress came to the table with their food and Laurence never missed an opportunity to flirt. "Thanks," he said, flashing his signature smile, which made the waitress act giddy.

"Yes, and it was a bad one," he told Laurence. "Why does she keep secrets from me? I just don't understand why she is so difficult."

"Get used to her being difficult, but she hasn't kept any secrets from you other than Joshua."

"The two of you own Pegasus and she didn't share that tidbit of information with me."

"We own the company but we are not part of the daily business. Besides, you are not married yet and it wasn't your business."

"True, but she let me think I got the job on my own merit, making me look like a fool in front of my colleagues."

"Are you finished acting like a spoiled little boy?" Laurence took charge of the conversation. "Damn, you two can be so childish. She didn't get you the job with the firm, dumbass," Laurence told him. "I did!"

"What?" Ryan asked in disbelief.

"Roni didn't get you the job, I did."

"Why?"

He looked at him seriously. "When I saw you in the lobby I knew you were Joshua's father. I called up and spoke to Miguel, asking him to give you a serious look. He wasn't told to hire you, just give you an interview. The rest was up to you." Taking a bite of his cheeseburger, Laurence said, "Look, I didn't do it for you, I did it for Joshua."

"What do you mean you did it for Joshua?"

"There are a lot of things I can be to Joshua. I can be his uncle, his friend..." The waitress returned with two more beers and Laurence flirted on instinct. "Even his advisor on the opposite sex, but the one thing I can't be or want to be is his father." Laurence paused for a moment. "Have you ever wondered why we never asked Roni who Joshua's father was?"

"The thought has crossed my mind," Ryan admitted.

"After Joshua was born my dad wouldn't ask, because if he knew who you were, he would have found you and told you about Joshua. He always said when Joshua got older, he wouldn't care if Roni was mad, he would demand that you be informed and allowed to make the choice if you wanted to be in Joshua's life."

Ryan was confused, not knowing how to respond to the information he had just been given.

"It is time you two grow up and stop thinking it is all about you. Joshua didn't ask to be part of your shit, but he's stuck with it." Laurence gave Ryan a long stare. "Roni has a real hard time trusting people, and to her, our owning the firm wasn't a secret. She just didn't want it to be a wedge between the two of you."

"You sure you are not going to tell her about the cheeseburger?" Ryan tried to change the subject to lighten the mood.

"Don't worry," Laurence laughed, "I will save that information for when it works to my advantage."

He didn't know how, but Ryan knew he had to apologize to Roni for his behavior earlier. It wasn't going to be easy, but their relationship had always been complicated.

During their walk back home, Laurence and Ryan joked about how he would have to grovel at Roni's feet. Laurence assured him if she kicked him out, he could sleep on the couch in the family room.

As they arrived at the bottom of the steps, Ryan looked up as if there were a hundred of them. Seeing Joshua sitting on the bottom step of the stairs through the door, he knew he couldn't stall any longer so he and Laurence went in.

Seeing his daddy coming in the door thrilled Joshua, but he wasn't sure if he was going to stay or leave like Ty's daddy. "Where you go?" he asked.

Before Ryan could answer, Laurence interjected, "Out with me. Come on, let's go upstairs," he encouraged, getting Joshua out of the room so Ryan could talk to Roni.

Hearing the voices, Roni stood in the doorway still angry by Ryan's accusations.

Seeing her, Ryan ushered her back into the kitchen so they could talk. "Roni, I'm sorry." Not getting a response, he confessed,

"I was wrong for accusing you of keeping things from me." He pulled her close, squatting down to look her in the eyes. "Please forgive me for being stupid."

Even though she tried hard not to, she had to laugh at him being silly. "Being cute isn't going to work," she told him. "You didn't accuse me of keeping things from you; you accused me of lying." She moved around the counter to finish putting up the dishes. "I have never lied to you," she stated, turning back to face him, "and I don't like being called a liar."

"You're right; I shouldn't have called you a liar."

"No, you shouldn't have, but you made it perfectly clear how you felt even without saying it."

"Well, I didn't feel you were being honest with me." Ryan started around the counter where Roni was standing. "You don't know how small I felt finding out from someone other than you about Pegasus. It was like I didn't matter to you."

"So if you had known that Laurence and I owned Pegasus, you wouldn't have taken the job?"

"No, I am not saying that."

"You never even asked why I was in the building when you were there for your interview. Why?"

"I don't know. At the time, it wasn't important. All I wanted to do was be with you."

"Right, it wasn't. When I saw you that day all I thought about was you and Joshua having a life together. I wasn't sure about us or if there would be an us again. I admit I should have told before now, but we were so happy. I didn't want to lose that again."

"Roni, you are going to be my wife, but you don't let me into your life fully. It's like you feel you have to hide a part of who you are away from me so I can't hurt you."

She looked away because Ryan had spoken the truth she tried to hide. "I wasn't trying to keep anything from you. Our relationship has been so crazy, that..." she tried to explain, but couldn't.

"Please understand it's not about the firm or you owning it. Sometimes I just feel like I am the only one in the room that doesn't know the punch line to the joke." The look of pain showed on his face as he started out of the kitchen. "And it's not funny anymore."

"Ryan, my not telling was never meant to go this long. I wanted to find the best way and time to tell you, it just never came up." Moving closer to him, she said, "Seeing the joy on your face every day when you left for work was something I didn't want to take from you."

"Well, you did. I just wish you would have told me after I got the job that you were my boss."

"Is that the problem, you feel I am your boss?" Roni was getting a little irritated. "Laurence and I are not involved with day to day business. We are on the board for major decisions." Feeling a need to explain further, she stated, "Look, you are a damn good architect and if we weren't together you would still be at the firm. That is business and this is our relationship; they shouldn't have anything to do with each other."

Wanting him to understand that the two were separated, she tried to explain, "Baby, I am not your boss and never will be. We should be a team, there for each other; if you can't understand that I am sorry." She passed him to go upstairs. "It seems like when it comes to us I can't do anything right."

"Don't say that." He walked toward her, pulling her close. "Since the first day I met you, we have had a complex relationship. I wish I didn't feel hurt by this, but I do," he said, choosing his words wisely. "You are providing everything in this relationship. This is your house, you own your own business, and the one thing I thought was my contribution turns out be yours, too. It's like you don't need me. I feel like I am just leeching off you."

Finally, she began to understand where the hurt was coming from. It wasn't about the firm, but more about her taking away his manhood. Maybe that was why she hadn't come out and told him. She didn't want to make him feel less than a man, but she had without trying. "Ryan, you bring so much to me and Joshua. Without you, we are not complete." Caressing his cheek, she simply stated, "You complete me. I can't imagine life without you in it anymore."

Ryan kissed her hand. "Roni, there are some things about me you don't understand." Leaning back on the door jam, he explained, "Being able to provide for you and Joshua means the world to me. It just seems that has been taken from me now. I know you didn't have anything to do with me being hired, and Laurence only got me an interview. I know the rest was up to me, but now I feel no matter how well I do at Pegasus it will be because I am your husband."

"Are you going to resign?" she asked.

"I don't know. Right now I am too confused."

"Miguel loves working with you. He always refers to you as that Southern kid." Both laughed as Roni continued, "My dad would have loved you, too; you have the same passion he did for Pegasus." She kissed him lightly on the lips. "He would have wanted you to stay, and so do I." Walking up the stairs, she began to understand the man she loved.

CHAPTER 19

With all the drama of Ryan finding out about the firm, Joshua was confused. Laurence tried to explain to him that adults disagree sometimes and that his parents had their share of arguments, too.

Joshua reminded him about Ty's mommy and daddy; how they ended up living in separate places. Hearing Joshua talk, Laurence knew his wisdom was no match for a four-year-old that was living the experience. In time, Laurence knew Joshua would see them disagree and learn that didn't mean they were splitting up. At the same time, he couldn't help but feel for Ty, he was just a kid. Marriage was not easy, but children shouldn't have to deal with adult stupidity and selfishness. Thinking to himself, Laurence vowed never to have children.

After they settled their disagreement, Ryan and Roni explained to Joshua that they weren't splitting up, but he was going to have to understand they wouldn't always agree. When they didn't, they had to discuss it. Sometimes it would be simple; other times it wouldn't be. They would work through it as a family, growing closer in the process. Over time, they knew he would eventually understand.

Pegasus had started doing more contracts outside of New York. With the new contracts from New Hampshire and Boston for subdivisions and remodeling projects, Ryan sometimes was out of town overnight. Joshua had become accustomed to him not being there every night and knew he wasn't leaving them.

Before knowing about his engagement to Roni, Miguel had wanted to talk to Roni and Laurence about expanding their contracts. He had also wanted to promote Ryan to that position. Getting the promotion meant a lot to Ryan, especially after finding out it was based on his skill and the respect of his colleagues. Miguel felt Ryan worked even harder than before it had been revealed Roni was part owner in the company. He was right; Ryan had to prove to everyone nothing was being given to him.

Saturday morning was warming up as Ryan drove to the airport to pick up his family. Mama Pearl, Libby, and his parents were on their way for a visit from Virginia. Uncle Walt, Aunt Betty, and Bianca had arrived the night before for the meeting of their families.

While Roni was making her wedding plans, she decided to have the women there for their dress fittings because their wedding day was fast approaching. It would also give Ryan's family a chance to see where they lived and worked.

Joshua was doubly excited because he was now old enough to play tee ball. With Ryan being his coach, Joshua felt like he was a pro. They had a game that afternoon and Mama Pearl would get to see his team play for the first time.

Ryan bragged that Joshua was a natural. Roni would laugh because she knew he was just a little biased on that assessment. After all, his teammates were only five and ended up running into each other more than catching anything. She did have to admit they were cute with their batting helmets sliding on their heads when they ran the bases. Joshua, of course, was the handsomest, but again she was a little biased, too.

Driving to the airport was a pain Ryan dreaded. The traffic was always congested and parking was non-existent. He had asked his family to pick up their luggage in baggage claim and he would pick them up out front. It would be easier to find them if they had finished the tedious task of getting their luggage. Ryan almost laughed aloud when he saw them. Mama Pearl and Helen were disagreeing as usual, Libby didn't know what to think, and Pete was just ignoring them all.

Pulling up to the curb, Ryan let the window down. "Need a ride?" he asked. The look on Mama Pearl's face was priceless. She undoubtedly had been fed up telling cabbies no.

"About time you showed up," she playfully scolded him. "I thought I was going to have to cuss out another taxi." Hugging him as he came to greet them, she asked, "Where is Joshua?"

"Oh, he's at home waiting for you. We have a tee ball game today."

"Tee ball?" Pete asked. "Getting him started early," he laughed at the thought. Pete was so excited to be visiting Ryan and Roni. All he and Jake had talked about at the garage was his impending trip. His only fear was Helen saying something callous to embarrass him in front of Roni's family. Jake had suggested Pete buy her a ticket for Timbuktu instead of New York as they both laughed at the suggestion.

"Hi, Mom," he hugged Helen. "Libby, you're trying to grow up on me," he teased, hugging her as well. "You and Bianca are about the same age so you won't be alone this trip," he assured her.

"Who is Bianca?" Libby asked.

"Roni's little cousin from SC. I think she is about fourteen," he told Libby. "Don't worry, you will like her," he said, seeing apprehension in her eyes.

On the drive home, Mama Pearl and Libby were so excited seeing the big city. It was as if they were watching one of their favorite TV shows. Pete was looking but like always never giving too much of himself away. Pearl and Libby were all giddy, looking at the tall buildings, but the dirty streets and homeless people were all Helen saw. She always had a way of only seeing the negative in a situation instead of looking at the whole picture.

Ryan could feel her staring at his head, which made him feel uncomfortable. "You are letting your hair grow out, I see," Helen commented.

"No, I just haven't had the chance to get to the barbershop. Joshua needs to go too," he told her.

"You haven't had time to shave, either."

"I've had time, but I like the beard." Since coming back from Virginia, Ryan had started sporting a detailed curtain beard under his chin. After spraining his hand, he hadn't been able to shave as well as he'd have liked to, so Modest suggested he grow a little facial hair. "Might make you look older than fifteen," he'd teased Ryan.

Hearing the conversation, Pearl pulled up to look at his beard. "I like it!" Looking back at Libby for her input, the girl gladly agreed.

Pete looked over. "I hadn't noticed it." He inspected Ryan's face. "It gives your face character."

"Well, I don't like it," Helen retorted. "Makes you look like one of those thug guys."

Libby almost bit her lip off trying to keep from laughing, because she knew Helen didn't know what thug meant. Besides, Pearl was giving Helen a "you are so stupid" look that made Libby red in the face.

This was what Ryan had been hoping wouldn't happen during their visit. Roni's family was meeting his for the first time and he wanted it to go well. Her family wouldn't be as understanding as Roni. Even she was beginning to tire of the off-colored sarcasm. He knew Roni's grandma Ann would not cut his mom any slack, but maybe that was what she needed.

Ryan just pretended not to hear his mother's comments, looking instead to his dad. "Uncle Walt is at the house."

"Walt, the one with the 1972 Monte Carlo?" The thought of talking cars excited Pete.

"Yeah, you will like him. He's a mechanical engineer." Ryan heard his mom huffing at the comments. "Mom, what is your problem?"

"I just think you are making a mistake marrying that girl." She paused because of the remarks being made by everyone in the car. "Ryan, you can do better and that is all I am going to say."

"Please let that be it, Helen," Pearl interjected. "Get it all out of your system before we get there."

"I just want what is best for Ryan," Helen tried defending herself.

"Oh, like that little whore Amy is better for him?" Pearl reminded her that Amy was now getting a divorce because her husband had found out the baby was not his. Remembering Libby was in the car, she apologized, "Sorry, sweetie."

"It would be different if she had married Ryan," Helen tried to convince herself.

"Yeah, because I would kick her butt if she did that to him," Pearl said.

"Mama Pearl, just let that go," Ryan pleaded as they drove onto their street. "We are here." Pulling up in front of the brownstone, Libby was in awe. Ryan smiled at her because she reminded him of himself when he had first come here.

"Which one is yours?" Libby asked.

He pointed to the one with the beautiful bay windows. "Right there," he said as he continued getting the luggage from the car.

"Wow! Which floor do ya'll live on?"

"That whole building belongs to Roni and Laurence. We stay on the top three floors, and Laurence stays in the basement apartment when he is home."

"Cool!" Libby was so excited at being in New York she had to remind herself to breathe.

"Libby, go on in. They are expecting you." He knew how shy she could be. "Just ring the bell," he told her as she climbed the steps.

Ryan began taking the bags up the steps, not seeing his father stepping in front of his mother before she went in. "Helen, you will respect our son and Roni in their home. No more comments, no more looks. Do I make myself clear?"

"Well, I..."

"Do I make myself clear?" Pete reiterated.

"Hey, I'm Walt," a strong baritone voice came from behind them.

"Pete, nice to meet you; I heard about that Monte Carlo." They both laughed.

Walt could see Helen needed an exit from the discussion so he extended his hand to her. "Nice to meet you, you must be Helen?"

She smiled only because it was the proper thing to do. "Nice to meet you."

"The ladies are in the house," he said, looking at Pete, "so I try to stay as far away as possible," and gave a broad grin before he picked up the bags.

Pearl and Libby had already gone inside, getting hugs from Roni and Joshua. Roni introduced the families and made a special note of her little cousin Bianca sitting in the corner acting bored. "Bianca is fifteen now and moody," Roni told Libby. Bianca had been warned to be on her best behavior and find common ground. This was going to be Libby's first visit to the city and Roni wanted her to have a good time.

"Roni, you aren't dressed yet?" Ryan asked, concerned for time.

"Just about to go up," she told him, while still in conversation with the women. They were all sitting around the dining room table with fabric swatches and sketches for the wedding dresses. Roni was explaining her vision for their special day. "The bridesmaids will be in dresses with different shades of lilac with a low-cut back."

Ryan went upstairs to change his clothes. When he came back downstairs he saw Roni hadn't moved. "Roni!" he reminded her.

"Okay, okay, I'm going." She picked up her stuff. "Ryan isn't allowed to see them," she laughed.

"Roni!" he scolded again. "Please get dressed."

"I'm going." Climbing the stairs, she hollered back to him, "Put the coolers in the cars. We'll need to get some ice on the way."

Pearl was tickled watching them, only noticing Joshua when he climbed into her lap. "What are you up to?" she asked.

"You come to see me play today?" Joshua asked her.

"Yes, I wouldn't miss it." She gave him a big hug. "You going to get me a homerun?"

"I will try!" Joshua excitedly exclaimed.

"Big baby," Betty teased Joshua, but he didn't care, he was with his Mama Pearl.

Bianca and Libby were becoming friends, finding they had music in common, each liking one of those teen boy groups. This made Ryan happy about their visit. Mama Pearl and Betty were chatting as if they had always known each other. His father was discussing cars with Walt, talking about the first ones they'd owned.

The only person not talking was his mother. She was sitting, sulking at the table. Ryan wished that she would at least try to get to know Roni's family, but he couldn't make her. He saw Roni coming down the stairs, so he asked everyone to get in the cars.

Their drive was only a few blocks away at the community park. Joshua was so excited he forgot his glove, but Roni saw it on the stairs and brought it to him. Making fun of him, she said, "You would lose your head if it wasn't for me." Joshua didn't care as he ran across the field to meet his friends. Ryan was close behind him with the team's gear as Roni and the rest of the family found seating in the bleachers.

Roni sat next to Helen so she wouldn't feel left out, but it didn't help with her sad look. Helen feeling and acting sad didn't seem to faze Pete, as he was waiting to see his grandson play ball.

"Who is that?" Libby asked, seeing Justin and Laurence coming toward them.

"Where?" Bianca asked, looking up from her phone. "Oh, that's Laurence and my brother, Justin."

"He is gorgeous!" Libby gushed.

"Yes, Laurence is fine," Bianca agreed.

"I like the dreads on him."

"Dreads, you are talking about Justin?" Bianca asked. "Girl, you need to get your eyes checked."

"Yeah, he is fine." Libby's eyes were fixated on Justin as they approached them. Libby was right; Justin had grown up very well. He was not a scrawny kid anymore, but a handsome young man like his father, Walt.

"Hello, my people." Laurence walked up to the bleachers with Justin.

Roni did the introductions and Laurence took over, flirting with the women as usual. Both were instantly mesmerized as he told Mama Pearl she was much too young to be Ryan's grandmother and referred to Libby as being as cute as a button.

Although he was older, Justin was still very shy around women. He sat near Bianca and Libby, which gave Libby an opportunity to talk to him. Seeing them chatting, Roni told Mama Pearl Jake would kill them both if he knew his daughter was flirting. Mama Pearl informed her if she were just a little younger, she would give her some real competition.

Joshua's game didn't last very long, and they didn't keep score for these events because it was about learning sportsmanship and having fun. Although Ryan wouldn't tell Joshua, he'd kept a mental score and they killed them. Since the women were going by the store for fittings after the game, Ryan took the team out for pizza.

Roni had the women try on the dresses so the seamstress could measure them for proper fit and hemming. Thuy and Shondra met them for their fittings while Pearl and Helen looked around the store. The two were able to go from the children's store to the urban wear over to the formal clothing. Roni had told them if they saw something they liked to let her know. While they were there, it could be fitted for them.

After trying them on, Libby and Bianca loved their dresses. They were very sophisticated with an hourglass waist, making them both feel older than their early teen years. Betty and Roni were discussing the low cut in the back. At first, they were concerned it would make them look too mature, but decided it wasn't too mature, being right below the shoulder blades. The two smiled at each other, feeling they had won their argument.

Pearl was very impressed with the accomplishments Roni had achieved. Helen was too, but she was still being silly not admitting it. As long as she didn't say something stupid, Pearl was happy. "Helen, look at the little children's clothes. They are so cute."

Glancing in Pearl's direction, she replied, "I guess so. They are too urban looking for children."

Pearl felt as if she should have just kept her thoughts to herself. "Just forget it, Helen. You would mess up a wet dream."

The first night of the family gathering went better than either Roni or Ryan had hoped. Even Helen was beginning to try to be part of the festivities. As long as she was at least trying, Ryan felt better. It gave him hope she would eventually be a part of their lives.

Dinner was catered by Gino's, their favorite little Italian restaurant. They had the lasagna with salad and fresh baked bread. Roni poured some olive oil in bread dishes with crushed pepper and balsamic vinegar. Pearl had never seen this before and had an inquisitive look on her face. Seeing it, Roni explained that in Italy they didn't use butter on their bread, instead using the olive oil mixture. At first Pearl was a little apprehensive, but after tasting it, she couldn't keep her bread out of the dish.

After Joshua went to bed, the teens went upstairs to the third floor apartment to hang out in the guest room. The women sat around talking in the family room, while the men retired to the parlor talking cars, football, baseball, or any sport that was physical. They were all up late getting to know each other, with only Joshua getting a good night's sleep.

Betty was up before Roni, preparing breakfast, and was soon joined by Pearl who wanted to help. The two ladies decided to make a big Southern breakfast with country ham, thick sliced peppered bacon, homemade sausage, grits, biscuits, with both sausage and red eye gravy. They even prepared scrambled eggs with cheese for Joshua, and cut up fruit.

The aromas of the cooking breakfast awakened Roni so she decided to get her shower, leaving Joshua and Ryan in the bed. She looked back at them, smiling that Joshua had his head on his father's chest.

Getting in the shower, she welcomed the warm water as it ran down her body. In her heart, Roni knew she was a lucky woman: she had the love of a good man, and they had a beautiful son together. With everything going her way, why was her heart still heavy?

She wouldn't let Ryan know about her feeling down, because he was happy that their families were getting along, with the exception of Helen. It hurt Roni to know Helen didn't like her when all she had done was try to be nice and respect her as Ryan's mother. No matter what Helen said, the reason for her not wanting Ryan to marry her was the color of her skin.

"Okay, you two, time to get up!" she said, hearing the moans in the background as both Joshua and Ryan squirmed in the bed. "Get up!" she told them again as she pulled the covers off them. "Come on, Aunt Betty is cooking breakfast and I don't want to miss the hot biscuits," she laughed leaving them to get dressed.

Roni heard Betty and Pearl's voices in the kitchen as she came down. Both women were talking about cooking cornbread and other comfort foods of the South, and hearing them together encouraged Roni. "Do you need any help?" she asked.

"No, honey, you have done enough. What are you doing up?" Pearl asked surprised at seeing her.

"Smelled breakfast cooking and it was calling me," she told them as they all laughed.

Betty agreed with Pearl. "You have done enough this weekend. We can handle this. You sit down somewhere," she scolded Roni.

She was right. Roni had been busy trying to make everyone feel at home, which wasn't hard for her side of the family. They had visited many times in the past, but with her new family, it was different. Betty had told her, "Just treat them like you treat us," and for the most part that was working. Only Helen was still proving hard to get to know. If she wasn't Ryan's mother, she wouldn't care; but she was, so Roni had to make the effort.

The house was filled with laughter as they all sat around chatting about their lives after breakfast. Bianca, Joshua, and Libby walked to the park and to the ice cream parlor later that day. Ryan and the men sat outside in the backyard, relaxing before going to Shondra's later for the engagement party.

Roni had told Luc and Shondra they didn't have to throw a party, but they wouldn't hear of it. This was the first time they would have both families together to celebrate the impending marriage.

Around four P.M., they started taking turns getting ready with showers and makeup. Laurence had gone to pick up his Grandmother Ann, who was joining them for the party. This worried Roni a little, because she knew her grandmother was a no-nonsense woman that spoke her mind and didn't care if you liked what she had to say or not.

Ann had worked on Broadway in her youth as a dancer and costume designer. Using her skills as a seamstress, she'd obtained many jobs on plays doing wardrobes. Being involved in the industry allowed Ann many opportunities to dance in chorus lines for shows. After she married Roni's grandfather, she quit performing to be a wife and mother. Although performing was still in her blood, she only took small jobs, doing wardrobe and teaching dance to children in her small studio.

"Hello everyone!" came the brassy voice of Ann as she walked into the hallway. "Where is my favorite grandson?"

"Here I am!" Joshua ran to give her a hug.

Laurence whispered to her, "I thought I was your favorite?"

"Oh, be quiet," she told Laurence as she received a big hug from Joshua. "I think you are growing up on me, young man."

"Hi, Nana." Roni came into the hall to greet her grandmother. "Let me introduce you."

Ann walked into the family room where everyone was waiting. Although she was in her seventies, she was still a very beautiful, sophisticated woman. Still sporting her dancer frame, she wore a tailored suit of turquoise with matching accessories. Her features were strong like her personality. Walking into a room, she demanded respect and always received it. Keeping her hair neatly cropped, she wore natural makeup to show her deep, dark eyes with thick eyelashes. Removing her shades, she asked, "How is everyone?" as she posed to get the full effect of all in the room.

"Hi, Nana." Ryan came in behind her, kissing her on the cheek.

"Hello there," she greeted him with her eccentric personality.

"Okay, everybody let's load up," Ryan instructed as he held out his arm for Ann to grab, and then escorted her to the car.

Shondra and Luc had closed down the restaurant that evening for their party giving them privacy. The dining room was set up with a large round table big enough to accommodate the family. There were smaller tables set up for their friends. People from the firm, Thuy, her date, Abe and Sam, as well as the Steelys had come down to the city for the event. Justin and some of his friends from school were there, keeping Libby and Bianca giggling. They were performing later after dinner.

Everyone was talking and enjoying their selves, all except Helen. She was just staring at Ryan and Roni who seemed to be in their own little world. They only acknowledged anyone if they were asked a question or someone teased them about ignoring everyone. The cynical look on Helen's face showed her disdain for Roni. Helen would try to give a phony smile, but her true feelings were obvious.

Luc's dessert was Roni's favorite: chocolate cake with strawberries topped with chocolate syrup. Ryan quickly devoured his, but kept stealing bites of Roni's when she wasn't looking. Their little antics only sickened Helen, not because they were so close, but because they didn't care what she thought.

Shondra approached the stage to introduce Justin and his friends for their performance. This was the first time he would perform for his parents with the band. They shyly took their places on the stage, with Justin smiling broadly as he looked out at his parents. With the help of the band, they sang the love song by Bryan McKnight "Do I Ever Cross Your Mind." The sound of the harmony of those young men's voices was heavenly. After they finished their first song, they received a standing ovation. Betty and Walt were beaming with pride at their son for following his dream.

While the band was taking a break, Justin put on some dance music. This made Roni want to dance. Grabbing Pete's hand, Roni escorted him to the dance floor with Shondra joining them. Ryan cheered his father on as he did something that resembled a seizure, making Pearl laugh aloud. "Ryan, go help your daddy, he's in trouble."

Watching them dance encouraged others to join in and soon everyone was on the dance floor, except for Helen and Pearl. Helen wasn't trying to hide her feelings about Ryan and Roni dancing together. "Why are you encouraging him?" she asked Pearl.

"It's called having a good time, Helen, but you wouldn't know anything about that," Pearl retorted.

"I just don't understand why you are so willing to accept them. We still don't know if that is Ryan's son. What does she have to offer him? He can do so much better."

Before Pearl could speak, Ann contributed to the conversation, "She's right." Neither Pearl nor Helen had noticed her still sitting at the table.

"Ann!" Pearl gasped, shocked at her comments.

"She is right, Pearl. After all, Roni is a college graduate who speaks three languages fluently and is accomplished in Egyptian hieroglyphics." Ann looked at the two women sitting a couple of chairs away from her. "With her building a manufacturing business from the ground up, giving her recognition in the designing world, why would Roni want your son? He is just some simple country boy with absolutely nothing to offer her."

Ann looked back to the dance floor where everyone was laughing, doing a line dance. "Look at him. All he has to offer her is good looks. If he hadn't knocked her up, he would have been the last thing on her mind. She brings the social graces of many generations of influential people; all he brings is a grease monkey and a school teacher." Turning back, she gave Helen a sinister look.

Both Helen and Pearl were shaken by Ann's words. Neither knew how to respond or if they should.

"Evil words aren't they? No matter who speaks them," she continued to stare at the women. "Personally, I like Ryan in spite of his mother. I have to admit I would much rather Roni married a black man, but that isn't my choice." Ann felt a need to express herself more. "Helen, we both know the only reason you don't like my granddaughter is the pigmentation of her skin, because she damn sure has more to offer Ryan than he has to offer her.

"Why don't you just be honest with yourself? You can dress it up any way you want, it is still bigotry." Getting up from the table, Ann smoothed her skirt. "I think I will join my family now. I can no longer stand the stench at this table." Remembering a small fact, she said, "Oh, I almost forgot." With her hands on her hips, she looked at Helen. "Pegasus, the firm where Ryan works, was built from nothing by my son and Roni's mother. The two of them built it into a multimillion dollar architectural firm while being black." She walked away, leaving the two women speechless.

"Helen, what size shoe do you wear?" Pearl asked.

"What has that got to do with anything, Pearl?"

"I just don't want you to choke on it when you have to eat it."
Pearl was feeling much better now that someone had finally put
Helen in her place with such style. "Wait up, Ann, the smell is
getting to me, too."

CHAPTER 20

Everyone was ready to go to bed after returning home. Joshua was already asleep, so Ryan undressed him then put him to bed. He couldn't stop watching Joshua sleep, wishing he could slow down his growing up. It had only been a little over a year since he had come into his life and so much had happened since that night they'd first met. They had gone from strangers, to friends, to being father and son.

Caressing Joshua's little cheek, he leaned over kissing him on his forehead. Smiling as Joshua squirmed in the bed, Ryan laughed quietly. Leaving the lamp on, he went back downstairs to see if he could help Roni before going to bed.

"What are you still doing up?" Roni asked.

"I thought I would help you finish up down here."

"No, you have to work tomorrow. I can get a nap in during the day."

"You are bringing my dad down to the firm tomorrow?" Ryan asked.

"Yeah, I will call you when we leave the spa. Do you mind a late lunch?"

Pulling her close, he said, "That will be fine," then pushed her hair out of her face. "I love you."

"Love you more," she told him as their lips met for a tender kiss. "Hey!' she shouted after Ryan pinched her on the butt.

"Don't be down here too late. You need your rest too," he warned her as he went up to bed.

Roni checked the doors after finishing in the kitchen. While checking them she was frightened to find Helen sitting in the family room in the dark. "You startled me, Helen. I thought you had gone up to bed."

"I came back down." Knowing she needed to say more, she finally asked, "You really love my son, don't you?"

"Yes," Roni smiled. "He brings my life to full circle." She was tickled at how that must have sounded. "Cheesy, huh?"

"Just a little." They both shared a laugh. "I can tell, but I tried not to see it," she smiled. "Sometimes as a parent you have to let your child grow up. I know he isn't like Joshua in size, but he is still my baby." Playing with a piece of tissue, she spoke to Roni without looking at her. "When I first found out about Joshua, I was so angry, because Ryan had messed up his life or at least I thought he had. Then I found out you were black," she said, feeling embarrassed by her actions, "and that made me even angrier."

Helen knew she needed to explain her position. "I was raised that we should stay with our own kind. Well, stay with our own race. Ryan had never shown any interest in black women before so I guess I was shocked." She thought how silly that sounded, because no black people lived in their area.

"I really don't know how to apologize for how mean spirited I have been toward you. You have been very understanding, but I know it is wearing thin. If you can find it in your heart, let me try to start over with you." She looked at Roni as if she was a small child caught doing something wrong. "I can't promise to be like Pearl or Pete, but I do want to be a part of your lives." Not getting a response, Helen began to weep.

Seeing her pain, Roni sat beside her on the couch. "It's alright, Helen. Stop before you make yourself sick." She got her more tissue. "One thing you need to understand about me, Helen, is that whatever I do is for Ryan. I have never cared if you liked me. As long as you didn't do anything to harm my son, you didn't even have to speak to me," she said, looking at Helen in the darkness.

"But you are Ryan's mother and he needs to have a relationship with you. For him and only him I will erase the past and start our relationship at this point. Now the rest is up to you." Roni gave her a smile. "You need to get some sleep; we will be leaving early in the morning."

"Thanks, Roni." Helen started to leave but turned back to face Roni. "Watching you two tonight I got so angry seeing you show your love for each other. I tried to convince myself that you weren't right for my son, but in reality, it isn't my choice. He loves you, Roni, and you bring his life to full circle. Good night!" She walked up the stairs to her sleeping quarters on the third floor.

Having to process their conversation, Roni sat in the family room for a few minutes looking out into the backyard. She looked at the moonlight shining in through the window. Feeling the weight of the day coming down on her, she checked the doors for the last time, turned on the alarm, then went up to bed.

The following morning, the ladies scrambled around the house getting ready for their day at the spa. Joshua would stay with Uncle Walt and Papa Pete doing men things, which would be napping until the ladies returned. Roni didn't realize how hard it was getting women ready to go somewhere. She didn't want to be late, because after the spa they would be meeting the others at Pegasus so Ryan's family could see where he worked.

Helen was trying to be more talkative and was actually getting into the conversation with Betty and Pearl. Although Betty felt she was a bigot because of how she had treated Roni, she didn't hold it against her. She knew from experience that sometimes you had to be the bigger person in these situations. In this case, she was doing it for Roni and Ryan, not Helen.

Lady Godiva Holistic Retreat was heavenly. They had set aside an area for them at Roni's request so they could be together. Their massages were done first to relax them, which Roni needed more than anyone, followed by deep cleansing facials. While their masks were setting, they received their pedicures, with Libby and Bianca getting some funky color polishes on their toes. They couldn't decide which ones they wanted so they got all ten toes a different color. Roni asked them about their fingernails, which neither had an answer for, but they still loved their toes. Even after the soothing massage, Roni was on edge because she didn't want to be too late for Ryan to eat lunch.

They arrived at the firm around one thirty P.M. just a little later than she wanted. Ryan was standing near the reception desk as they got off the elevator. "There they are now," Ryan told the young temp working in the office as Joshua ran toward him. Scooping him up, he asked, "Are you being good for your mommy?" then laughed, giving Joshua a sneaky smile.

He kissed Roni. "Did you have fun at the spa this morning?"

"Yes, hated to leave." Seeing the young woman, Roni spoke to her. "Hello."

"Oh, Roni, this is Cindy our new temp. Cindy this is my fiancée, Roni."

"Nice to meet you," Roni smiled. "Baby, I need to speak with Miguel." Looking at Joshua, she teased Ryan, "Don't let him get into trouble."

"Roni, how did you find that restaurant for the party last night?" Diane asked. "Troy and I want to go back for our anniversary. It would be nice to have a little gathering like that one." Diane had been with the firm from the beginning when Larry and Bernice had first started building their clientele. She had been just out of business school and still wet behind the ears. Bernice took her under her wing, teaching her the things she needed to know to be effective as a receptionist. Roni had even been a flower girl at her wedding when she and Troy were married.

"Let me know when you want to plan it and I will get Shondra to contact you," Roni told her.

"Shondra is Mawuli's daughter, right?" Diane asked, remembering he worked there as the director of construction.

"Yes, he and Sabra weren't able to come last night, but they are very proud of her and Luc." Remembering what she had come to her desk for, she questioned, "Oh, Diane, is Miguel busy?"

Looking down at the switchboard, she said, "His line is clear," and picked up the phone. "Miguel, Roni is here." She waited for his response. "He says come on back."

Ryan was so caught up with talking to Roni and Joshua, he almost forgot about his family being there and walked over to talk to them. "Hi, did you ladies have fun this morning?" They all had big grins on their faces. "Let me show you around. Most of the staff is out to lunch so you won't get to meet some of them personally." Putting Joshua down so he could walk, he began his tour for his family.

"That's his fiancée?" Cindy asked Diane. "Why does she need to speak to Miguel?"

"Because she owns the company," Diane informed Cindy. "I suggest you get back to work and stop trying to flirt with that man." Seeing the fear in Cindy's eyes gave Diane joy as she scurried away.

Pete was fascinated and extremely proud of his son as he showed him one of the buildings he had remodeled. With the building's historical past, Ryan explained he'd had to do a lot of research to get the detailing correct. Seeing the before and after pictures no one would've believed they of were the same building. "You recreated this?" Pete asked.

"Yeah, I took an old photo from when the bar was originally opened and built around it. The new owners wanted to keep the historic feel, but modernize it some. We were lucky much of the original fixtures were still there and we only had to do minor repairs to them."

"You always said you wanted to build things." Pete patted Ryan on the back. "I'm real proud of ya son!"

Although he had never acted as if it made a difference, hearing his father tell him he was proud meant the world to Ryan. He knew his dad had been disappointed that he didn't want to be a mechanic like him but he'd never tried to stop him from following his dream.

After the tour, they left Pegasus for lunch. It was late but that was probably a good thing. The little Greek restaurant was almost empty except for a few patrons. This allowed the servers to push together a couple of tables so they could all sit together. Bianca and Libby were being teenage girls as usual.

Betty and Roni were tickled by their behavior, remembering how they were at that age. Roni thought to herself that it wasn't so long ago that she was like them, looking at every young man she saw, whispering with Shondra and Thuy. She hoped Libby and Bianca would forge a friendship that would keep them in touch for years to come.

CHAPTER 21

If Roni had known doing a wedding would require so much work, she and Ryan would have eloped. No matter how much she completed, more things needed to be done. Aunt Betty finally had to sit her down, making her take a break before dinner. With the rehearsal party tomorrow night, she was anxious trying to make everything perfect.

Trying to relax, Roni took a bubble bath before slipping under the covers to get a nap. She knew Ryan would be arriving soon with his dad and Jake. Libby and Sara had come early with Pearl and Helen to help Roni with the preparations. Although Roni was very hands-on, Sara, along with Betty, took some of the responsibility.

Sara made sure the caterers would be on time for the rehearsal dinner while Betty made sure the music for the wedding and reception was taken care of. Justin and his friends would be singing at the reception, but they would need a DJ for their breaks.

Helen was trying hard to show she was a changed person, all while trying to stay out of Ann's way. Pearl, on the other hand, was having fun keeping Joshua out of everyone's hair. He had come down with Roni earlier and was bored because he didn't have anyone to play with. Really, he was missing his father and couldn't wait for him to arrive.

Roni didn't know how tired she was, because she never felt Ryan slipping into the bed to watch her sleep. If he hadn't caressed her cheek, she wouldn't have awakened. "Hey, when did you get in?" she asked still groggy from her nap.

"About twenty minutes ago," he said, smiling at her sleeping so hard. "I was just enjoying watching you sleep," he told her.

Pulling him closer, Roni kissed him tenderly. "I missed you."

"Missed you more," he laughed, glad their separation was over.

There was a knock on the door. "What ya'll doing in there?" Aunt Betty playfully asked. "You will have plenty of time for that after the wedding," she teased them. "Dinner is ready."

"Do I have to get up?" Roni whined.

"Yeah, next she will be sending Uncle Walt to check on us."

"I heard that!" the voice on the other side of the door said, making them all laugh.

They both knew they needed to get up, because lying there looking at each other was becoming too tempting. Ryan was up first, pulling Roni to her feet and into his arms to hold her. She felt so good next to him he didn't want to let her go.

Uncle Walt had prepared dinner on the grill because he loved to barbeque. Aunt Betty had prepared her famous potato salad and marinated cold slaw. She had also made a peach cobbler for dessert. Everyone was at the table but Roni and Ryan, so all eyes were on them when they sat down, making them both laugh at their families.

Although the women had been there all week with Roni, now the men had arrived and were getting acquainted. Jake had made himself at home with the dinner table and would soon be Betty's favorite with his large appetite. Little Jake was being very quiet because he didn't have anyone there his age other than Libby and Bianca.

They were so busy giggling about Justin and his band they didn't notice he was feeling ignored. Once Roni saw he was feeling left out, she started talking to him, making him blush. When he smiled, you could see a lot of his father in him. Obviously, his shyness came from his mother.

"Uncle Walt!" a familiar voice shouted.

"Roni, tell me you didn't invite him?" Walt teased.

Recognizing the voice, Ryan quickly rose from his seat as they ran to meet each other. "Ansari!" Ryan shouted as both men laughed hysterically as they hugged. "It is great to see you. How have you been?"

"Doing well and I see you are, too." He smiled, seeing Roni on her way to greet them. "I am so happy for you and Roni."

Seeing Effie, Ryan hugged her. "Now I was totally shocked to find out about you two."

"Don't feel bad, so were we," Effie told him as they all laughed together.

"They lie," Felipe teased. "They sneaked around behind my back!" he told them as he hugged Roni. "How are you?" he asked, then seeing Ryan, "You are one lucky man, I am happy for you."

"Yes, I am; meeting you guys was the best thing that ever happened to me."

"No, being dumb about African American studies was the best thing to happen to you," Abe chimed in as they all laughed together as friends and felt nostalgic for their college days.

"Oh, guess who I saw?" Ansari asked. "Steve," he told them.

"Steve!" they all said in unison.

"Where were you?" Abe asked.

"I was at the dealer's getting the oil changed in my car." They all smiled, remembering Ansari's prediction of Steve's career path. "No, no, he wasn't selling used cars. He was selling cars, just not used ones."

Abe was curious about the encounter. "Did you speak to him?"

"Well, actually, he saw me first and came over to speak." With a seriousness in his voice Ansari told them, "He apologized for how he treated us in college. I know you are shocked to hear that, but not as shocked as I was. He has matured and seems to be trying to get his life together."

"I guess time will change you," Abe added.

"No, actually it was a drug overdose and a divorce. He married that girl that was after every man on campus."

"Oh, no!" they all exclaimed knowing who he was talking about.

"Yeah, I know, I couldn't believe it either. The marriage didn't last and fortunately, no children were brought into it. I told him about you two getting married. He sends his best for you and is sorry for the way he acted toward all of us."

"Wow, if you see him again tell him thanks," Ryan said to break the strange silence.

"Hello, everybody!" Shondra exclaimed as she, Thuy, and Luc came into the backyard.

"Oh, these are my best friends since I was little: Thuy, Shondra, and her husband Luc from New York." Looking at her college friends, she introduced, "These are my college buddies, Effie, Ansari, and Felipe."

Seeing Thuy and that she wasn't attached, Felipe went into flirt mode. Roni stood behind him along with Effie, making dog sounds as they all laughed.

"Come on, ladies, I have matured since college."

"I hope so, because I don't want to have to give you a beat down," Roni jokingly warned.

Thuy had to admit Felipe was a very handsome man. Since college, he had grown out his hair, wearing dreads and a neatly trimmed beard. Thuy saw he took care of his body with the ripples of muscles showing through his T-shirt. Although she tried, her eyes were fixated on him, unable to look away.

Ryan saw there might be a spark in Felipe. He remembered looking that way at Roni when they first met. "Thuy is an attorney with the public defender's office," he told Felipe to get a conversation moving between them, because if it hadn't been for Felipe, he wouldn't be marrying Roni.

"An attorney, so if I get into trouble in New York I can call you," Felipe smiled with his island charm.

"Don't wait until you get into trouble to call," Thuy flirted back, making the women turn their heads immediately in her direction and shocking Shondra and Roni, because Thuy had always been very shy with men. This was a side of Thuy they hadn't seen before, but they liked it.

Ryan looked around at his friends and family, feeling a special joy seeing them all together. Never would he have imagined meeting Roni would bring so many people together.

With so much to do before the rehearsal, Roni was very tired. She had to talk with the caterer, then confirm the appointments for hair and nails tomorrow. Then she had to make sure the chapel was going to be available for the rehearsal that night. There never seemed to be enough hours in the day lately for her.

Ryan saw she was still tired and begged her to slow down, but being Roni, she refused. Finally, Luc stepped in, taking charge with the caterer while Shondra took over the appointments for the bridal party before the wedding.

"Roni, have you decided how you are going to do your hair tomorrow?" Shondra asked, because in making appointments she needed to know the time allotment for each member of the bridal party.

Her hair was something Roni hadn't considered. "I don't know. What do you think?" she asked Shondra.

"Do you want it straightened?"

Before thinking Ryan interjected, "No, why would you want to straighten it?"

"Just something different," Roni tried to reassure him.

"Why do you want to be different?"

Roni hadn't really thought much about a different hairstyle. "Well, it does have to match my dress," she informed Ryan, not understanding his objections had nothing to do with her hair, but were brought on by a bitter memory of a time when he thought he had lost her.

"I guess it doesn't matter," he said, kissing the top of her head. "I just like it natural, but it's your day. You do what makes you happy."

Although he had never made a comment on her hair, it felt good knowing he didn't want her to change. "Trust me, you will like it." She knew whatever she chose would be fine because he loved her just the way she was.

Shondra finished with the appointments, then helped Roni and Thuy get the dresses packed in the car to take to the hotel. Since it was the night before the wedding, she and Ryan couldn't see each other before she walked down the aisle. Therefore, the bridal party had a couple of suites for the women to get ready, leaving the men on their own at the house with Uncle Walt.

"Roni, are you okay?" Thuy asked seeing her waver a little on her feet.

"I'm just tired and the humidity here is so heavy."

"True, but you are a little flushed. Are you sure you feel okay?" Shondra inquired of her.

"I'm fine. Come on, let's get these dresses to the hotel. We will need to hang them so the wrinkles can fall out."

Both Thuy and Shondra looked at each other, concerned that it wasn't just fatigue and humidity. Even before they had left New York, they had noticed her being tired a lot, giving them cause to question her health.

Roni saw the distressed looks on their faces. "Please don't say anything to Ryan or Laurence. I don't want them to worry."

"Is there cause to worry?" Shondra questioned her.

"No, I am fine and will be able to rest after tonight." Roni saw they didn't believe her. "I promise."

"Roni, if you are not better..." Shondra didn't want to think about her being ill. "When we get to the hotel you will take a nap before rehearsal tonight," she told Roni.

"I will, after..."

"After we get to the hotel, you will lie down and get some rest," Shondra scolded her, "or I'll tell Aunt Betty." Having to laugh at her being a snitch, she hugged Roni, trying not to show her worry. "Come on, let's go." They got into the car and drove away, leaving the men with Uncle Walt.

Joshua, meanwhile, kept busy playing with his cousins from Spartanburg while Ryan and the others laughed and talked about old times. Ansari extended an invitation to Atlanta for them to visit after Effie had the baby. All were shocked to find out she was expecting again.

"Cutting it close there, aren't you brother?" Felipe teased, giving the group a laugh.

"So true, but this was by accident. We had planned to allow AJ to get a little older before we gave him a sibling." Thinking about his son just fifteen months old, he said, "I guess he will have a playmate sooner than we thought."

Ryan looked out into the yard, seeing Joshua playing with his cousins. He and Roni had never discussed having more children. He knew he wanted Joshua to have a brother or sister, because he had neither. It was hard being the only child. Although he had Jake who was like an older brother, it wasn't the same as having a blood sibling.

Looking over at Jake, Ryan was grateful he was there, but at the same time he remembered Joshua didn't have anyone that close to him. While they were in Italy, he and Roni needed to talk about extending their family.

"When are you and Roni going to have another?" Ansari asked Ryan.

"To be honest we haven't even discussed having any more."

Jake was shocked. "What do you mean you haven't discussed it? You don't want any more?"

"So much has happened in such a short length of time we just haven't discussed extending the family." Ryan looked back out at Joshua. "But we will have plenty of time on the honeymoon."

"Well, you will at least get some practice in," Felipe teased him, "and you know practice makes perfect," Felipe and Ansari said together laughing.

Ryan reached over and pretended to choke him, all the while hoping Roni would want more children. He had not been able to share the experience with her during her pregnancy with Joshua. Even listening to Ansari talk about the morning sickness, feet swelling, and mood swings, the more he desired to be there to experience them.

"I remember one morning around three o'clock, she awakened me asking why I hadn't put the cap back on the toothpaste." Everyone laughed at Ansari as he did his fake Jamaican accent mimicking Effie.

"I told you she was a devil woman," Felipe told him in jest.

"So true, but I wouldn't trade her hell for nothing." Ansari danced in his chair raising his eyebrows, making them laugh.

The time came quickly for the wedding rehearsal. As always the men walked around as if they were in a locker room in different stages of dress.

"Daddy," Joshua walked down the hall, "where is my shirt?"

"On the bed," Ryan told him.

"Which bed?"

"The one we slept in." Getting into the shower, Ryan welcomed the warm water as it flowed over his body. In a matter of hours he and Roni would be married, something he had wanted since the night they had first made love. Ryan smiled thinking of the future Mrs. Veronica Somers-Grant.

The rehearsal went well; even Joshua didn't complain about the length of time it took to practice. Ryan was apprehensive about using the chapel instead of the garden, but had to admit it would be a beautiful setting tomorrow.

Shondra scolded Roni about tiring herself out. Although she had taken a nap earlier, her skin was still a little flushed. That was beginning to worry Shondra, prompting her to mention it to Laurence. He, like Shondra, had noticed Roni didn't appear well, but he didn't want to alarm Ryan. They both tried to convince themselves that she was just putting too much on herself.

Shondra remembered how Roni's mother, Bernice, had been fatigued before she became ill. Now she was seeing the same pattern in Roni.

Laurence had noticed in the last month she seemed to be less active. Most evenings she would be upstairs before ten and that was just unusual. Ryan normally had to force her to go to bed. He wondered if Ryan had noticed her exhaustion.

"Roni, let Luc handle the serving staff," Ryan advised her.

"I know, but I am just so hands-on," she reminded him.

"You keep interfering with me, I will put you across my knee, little girl," Luc teased.

Grinning at that thought, Roni told him, "Okay, it is all yours, Luc."

It was hard for her to sit still. Again, Roni tried to take the lead in handling things until she saw Luc giving her a warning. She just laughed as she took her seat at the table, making Luc smile at her behavior.

Ryan leaned over kissing her on the cheek. "Honey, just let Luc handle things from here, because you don't want to be tired tomorrow." Like Laurence and Shondra, her fatigue was beginning to worry him. True, she had been very busy this week but her energy level was lower than normal. Most times a wedding would be a simple task; unfortunately, this one was taking a frightening toll.

"That's what you get for marrying a perfectionist," Roni teased but knew she needed to slow down. She wanted to be beautiful for her wedding.

"You have to keep your strength up for tomorrow night." Ansari flashed a devilish grin.

"Oh, leave them alone," Effie told him. "They will find the strength for that," she predicted, getting a roaring laugh from all at the table.

It was like being back in college with their friends, teasing each other. They were so happy to be together and hoped to always be there for each other.

Looking at Thuy and Felipe talking, she nudged Ryan. "I think we might have a Betty and Walt thing going on over there."

"Yeah, I think he needs a fiery woman to keep him in check." Both smiled at Felipe and Thuy flirting.

During dinner, Roni was yawning, prompting Ryan to ask if she was tired. As usual, she said no but was hiding her fatigue to keep him from worrying. Besides, she wanted to mingle with their guests.

Ryan didn't believe her, staying close to keep an eye on her. He didn't want to keep questioning her health, but it seemed to be deteriorating before his eyes. Even though she was very beautiful, her skin seemed to be pale. "Roni, are you all right?" he asked her as she began to stumble.

"Yes, I'm fine, just felt a little dizzy."

"That's it; you are going upstairs right now!"

"But..."

"No buts this time." He looked at Laurence who was on his way toward them. "Tell everyone Roni is going up to bed. I will stay with her until Shondra and the others come up." Ryan refrained from carrying her because he didn't want the others to know she was sick. After they entered the suite, Ryan chastised her, "Roni, you can't keep running yourself down like this. I know you want things to be perfect, but as long as we get married, it will be fine. The festivities don't matter."

"You are right. I promise to get some rest tonight, so I will have more energy tomorrow." Pinching his butt, she shimmied her shoulders at him. "I hope you can keep up with me!" she challenged, making Ryan laugh at her clowning around.

Ryan stayed while she took her shower, then laid down next to her until she fell asleep.

The sound of women coming into the suite awakened Ryan. Betty knocked on the door to check on Roni and let Ryan know they were there. Hugging Betty, he said, "If you need me tonight just call me."

"Don't worry; you will be the first to know." She kissed him on the cheek.

Getting back to the house, the men were tired and had prepared for bed. Sleep didn't come easy to Ryan, because he couldn't stop thinking about Roni and her being so tired. Joshua sleeping like a wild child wasn't helping either. Walking down the hall to the kitchen, he saw the front door was open. As Ryan went to close it, he saw Laurence sitting on the porch. "You can't sleep, either?" he asked

"No, just worried about Roni." He turned to look at Ryan. "You know that is how our mother started before she found out she was sick," Laurence said, not wanting to show emotion. "Ryan, if something happens to her, I don't know what I will do."

Sitting beside Laurence, he felt his pain. "Laurence, she says she is fine. We both know she overworks herself with the small details." Trying to encourage him and not show his own concerns, he said, "Let's just get through tomorrow and see how she feels."

"I know, but Roni is my strength. Watching her..."

"Laurence, don't talk like that. She will be fine." Ryan was beginning to fear the worst just like Laurence.

Seeing he was frightening Ryan, Laurence agreed, "You're right, she is just over extending herself as usual," and got up from his chair. "You better get some sleep too, or you both will be too tired for your honeymoon," Laurence forced a laugh before going inside.

Trying not to think negatively, Ryan went back to bed and worried about Roni.

CHAPTER 22

The women were up early getting their hair and nails done. Roni was well rested, but Mama Pearl encouraged her to relax. Pearl was tired just watching Roni go from one room to the other making sure the hair was perfect, neglecting herself in the process. One of Roni's greatest faults was always putting everything and everyone before herself.

"Hello?" Roni answered her phone.

"Just wanted to check on you this morning," Ryan told her.

"I'm fine. Well rested and ready to go," she excitedly responded.

"Good, but try and rest before the wedding," he scolded her.

"I will, I promise. Love you; see you in a couple of hours."

"Love you more and I can't wait."

Speaking with Roni didn't change his fears. Although she was sounding better, he couldn't shake Laurence's words. He knew Laurence meant well and was deeply concerned about Roni after losing both their parents to illness: their mother to cancer and their father to a heart attack. Both he and Roni couldn't afford to lose each other, because in their minds they were all they had.

Getting the men dressed was more complicated than the women with their hair and makeup. Ryan dressed Joshua before getting into his tuxedo, instructing him not to get dirty. Joshua sat on the bed watching his father dress, smiling.

"Daddy, can I go with you on the moon thing?"

"The honeymoon, and no, you will stay with Mama Pearl until we get back."

"Not fair!" Joshua pouted.

"So you don't want to go fishing in the lake and hike in the woods?" he asked Joshua.

After giving it consideration, he said, "Well, I guess I don't have to go on the moon," and laughed with his father as Ryan finished his tie.

"How do I look?" Ryan asked Joshua for his approval.

"Pretty," Joshua smiled.

"Pretty? Okay, if you say so. Let's get the others so we won't be late." Ryan scooted Joshua out the door.

Ryan and Joshua were in the car with Laurence, Uncle Walt, and his dad, Pete. "I spoke to Roni this morning. She's feeling more rested today," he informed them.

"Good, but keep a watch on her during the honeymoon," Laurence requested.

This was a side of Laurence Ryan had never seen before. Ryan knew he loved his sister, but not until now did he know how much. Even though he was trying to appear happy, the worry showed through in his eyes. "Don't worry, I will take good care of her."

"You better, because I know where you live." Laurence gave Ryan a sinister look before laughing.

As they pulled into the parking lot of the chapel, they saw Luc and Sara. Sara was making sure the flower arrangements were done properly, while Luc showed the men to their places as ushers. Ryan was thankful to both of them for stepping in and taking charge so Roni wouldn't feel the need to.

Ryan and Jake were in a room that looked more like a closet than an actual room. Jake smiled at Ryan for being so nervous. "No matter how bad you want it, you'll still be a ball of nerves on this day."

"Why? I want to be married to Roni."

"Your heart does, the rest of you is still nervous," he teased Ryan. "Don't worry, once you see her walk down that aisle you will forget how nervous you are."

Ryan gave him a smile at the thought of her walking down the aisle. Although she hadn't allowed him to see her wedding gown, he knew it would be beautiful. The thought of her wanting to share her life with him only broadened his smile.

The knock on the door brought Ryan back to reality, along with the nervous jitters. He opened the door. "You gentlemen can take your places," the Chaplin informed them.

Like Ryan, Roni was feeling a little queasy about the impending nuptials. Her stomach was in knots as she laughed, telling the others Ryan had tried to get her to elope last night. Shondra let it be known she had lost ten pounds to fit in that dress, so he had better not try to sneak Roni away before she could wear it.

"Five minutes, ladies," Sara informed them.

Everyone looked for their bouquet, then took a last minute look at themselves in the mirror. All were scrambling around, but Roni seemed to be moving in slow motion. No matter how hard she tried, her feet seemed to be encased in cement, prompting Shondra to ask if she was okay. She firmly assured her that she was fine.

The bridesmaids lined up for their pending march into the chapel, passing Laurence as he came in to escort Roni.

"You ready, big head?" Laurence had to torment Roni before escorting her down the aisle. "I wish mom and dad could be here. You are so beautiful," he said, smirking a little before adding, "with your ugly self."

She gently shoved him. "Thanks for being there for me. I don't know what I would have done without you." Kissing him on the cheek, they walked out the door.

"You okay?" Jake asked Ryan.

"Yeah, just nervous," he told him.

"Just don't pass out like I did," he said, making Ryan laugh at the memory as they went to take their places at the altar. Jake was honored that Ryan had chosen him to be his best man; although they were cousins, their relationship was that of brothers.

"You got the ring?" Ryan asked.

Patting his jacket pocket, he assured him, "Right here."

Ryan's nervousness intensified as he walked to the altar, seeing their family and friends waiting to share his and Roni's moment in time. Although Bernice and Larry weren't present, there was a small table at the first pew where they would be sitting. On it was their wedding picture with a candle to represent them. Seeing the memory candles saddened Ryan because he would never have the chance to meet them and let them know how much he loved their daughter.

The bridesmaids made their way down the aisle, looking beautiful in their dresses. Bianca and Libby were more excited to be wearing heels and makeup than being in the wedding. Ryan gave them a sarcastic smile as they giggled at him while taking their places.

Everyone in the chapel softly laughed at Joshua as he practically ran to the altar with his pillow as the ring bearer. He didn't care; he was ready get up there where his dad was winking his eye at him before looking at Teresa the flower girl as she came down the aisle.

Looking back to the entrance of the chapel, Ryan tried to see Roni but only saw Laurence. He was obviously telling Roni about Joshua running down the aisle. Laurence looked up and saw Ryan looking in their direction, leaning over to inform Roni.

"I am so nervous," Roni said. "My stomach feels like I have butterflies."

"Roni, promise me you will take care of yourself on this honeymoon. I know you want to have fun, but you still need to rest. This wedding has taken its toll on you," he told her, but he felt her fatigue had an underlying issue.

"Laurence," she whined.

"Promise me."

"I promise after the reception I will go straight to bed."

"I know you will go to bed, but you need to go to sleep," he admonished, giving her his sneaky smile.

"We will go to sleep after we finish," she shyly told him.

Hearing the music of the wedding march, he told her, "We're on."

She walked into the doorway, filling Ryan with awe as he looked at her. He appreciated Roni not showing him her dress before, because she was so beautiful. The dress had a V neckline with an hourglass cut to accent her small waist. Roni looked like a 1940's Hollywood starlet in her couture dress with the low cut back. The sweeping train was accentuated by the love knot at the small of her back.

Ryan was grateful she wasn't wearing a veil but had chosen a headpiece to emphasize her natural curls as they fell around her face. Today her beauty surpassed all other times he had seen her as she looked up at him awaiting her arrival.

Standing at the altar, Ryan took his place beside her, unable to remove his eyes from her. "Who gives this woman to this man?" the Chaplin began the ceremony.

"I do!" shouted Joshua, getting laughter from the crowd and all in the wedding party.

"That's my line," whispered Laurence as he smiled at Joshua. "We do," he announced to include Joshua who was still grinning with excitement. Leaning over, Laurence kissed his big sister on the cheek before giving her hand to Ryan. Even though the gesture was only symbolic, he felt as if he were truly giving her to a man who loved her.

The ceremony moved quickly, and the beautiful soprano voice of Betty singing Ave Maria during the prayer brought tears to Helen's eyes. In the past, she had been so afraid of what others thought, but she had come to love Roni as she would her own daughter. Her biggest fear was not of Ryan marrying a black woman, but of losing him completely. Once she had allowed herself to accept Roni, she had gained a daughter and a grandson.

"You may kiss the bride," was what Ryan had been waiting to hear since he saw Roni coming down the aisle. Kissing her tenderly as if she were a fragile china doll, he whispered, "Love you."

"Love you more," she responded before they turned to leave the chapel.

All eyes were on them with smiles and applause as they walked into the reception hall. Ryan was happy the wedding part was over, but now the shock of reality began to set in. His concern about Roni being so tired came back into play. During the ride in the limo, she had been yawning, making him question her again. "I'm fine. Stop worrying," she'd told him. Although he tried to be happy, Laurence's words haunted him of how their mother felt before her diagnosis.

"Will the bride and groom come to the dance floor?" Shondra requested. "Roni, Ryan made a special request for you." Grabbing the microphone, she began to sing "How Do I Live Without You" with Justin in a duet. Hearing the harmony of their voices brought Roni to tears as she and Ryan danced together as husband and wife.

Looking into her eyes as they glided across the dance floor, he told her, "That is something I really don't want to think about."

"What?"

"Living without you," he said as he forced himself to smile trying not to show his fear.

Everyone was enjoying themselves during the reception. While talking with Felipe and Ansari, Ryan lost sight of Roni. Looking around the ballroom, he saw Thuy coming to join them. "Where is Roni?" he asked her, trying not to sound panicked.

"Oh, she is changing her dress. It is the first door on the left down the hall," she informed Ryan.

He was not sure how long she had been gone, but didn't want her to be alone for any length of time. Getting to the door, he knocked softly. When Roni opened the door, he was relieved to see her. "I was wondering where you got off to."

"Come in, I'm just changing into my reception dress. That wedding gown is a headache, trying not to step on the train." She turned around for him to zip up her dress that was much like her wedding gown in cocktail length. "Thanks! Oh, I almost forgot..." She went to her bag with her wedding gown, retrieving a small box. "This is just a little something for you." She gave Ryan a gift.

"Roni, what is this? You didn't have to..."

"Just shut up and open it," she teased while looking on excitedly.

Seeing the thrill in her eyes, he decided he could wait a few minutes before discussing his concerns about her health. Untying the purple bow on the small box, he lifted the lid. Pulling back the paper, he saw an object that looked like a digital thermometer. Turning it over, he saw the word "positive." Looking up at Roni smiling with her big dimples, Ryan asked her, "How long have you known?"

"I found out before coming down here."

"Who else knows?"

"Counting the doctor, only you. This time I wanted to make sure you knew before anyone else. Between you, Laurence, and Shondra, it's hard trying to keep a secret."

Ryan was frozen in thought, looking at the pregnancy test too happy for words.

* * * *

"Is that when grandpa found out about Auntie Tov?"

"Yes, that is when he found out about Auntie Tovah," Joshua told his little girl. "Now it's time to go to sleep." He pulled the cover up, kissing her on the forehead. "Love you, sweetie."

"Love you too, daddy," she said as she blew him a kiss.

Looking back into her room with the Pegasus mural behind her bed and the star nightlights on the ceiling, Joshua remembered Ryan telling him stories.

"Hello?" he answered the phone. "Hey dad, you just get in?" Hearing Roni in the background, he said, "Tell mom hi."

About the Author:

As a young girl, Melody Porter dreamed of becoming a writer someday. In her preteen and teenage years, she wrote small plays for her own enjoyment. Unfortunately, being from a small town in South Carolina her dreams were put on hold, with marriage, motherhood and caring for her mother who wanted her to stay close. After her divorce, she raised her daughter alone, which required most of her time. Once her daughter became an adult, the characters again began to take on life in her head.

In December 2008, she along with a friend was listening to a radio personality, Michael Baisden. Mr. Baisden was doing a segment on living your dream. The two friends began discussing their dreams. Her friend Diane mentioned she wanted to own a bed and breakfast. Melody told her how she always wanted to be a writer and she had actually written a short story to submit to a romance magazine while in college.

Diane inquired about the story and once hearing the synopsis, she wanted to hear more asking Melody to re-write the short story. Once Melody began the writing, the story took on a life of its own. Unable to rest until the story was told she spent many nights putting the visions she was seeing into words. It was as if the hunger in her soul was finally allowed to feed becoming a small novel ***Joshua's Closet***.

You can reach Melody via emailing her at *joshuascloset@hotmail.com*.